W9-CFG-763

THE BOY, THE WOLF, AND THE STARS

SHIVAUN PLOZZA

THE BOY,
THE WOLF,
AND THE
STARS

HOUGHTON MIFFLIN HARCOURT
BOSTON   NEW YORK

hmhbooks.com

The text was set in Minion Pro.
Cover design by Mary Claire Cruz
Interior design by Mary Claire Cruz
Paper texture © Houghton Mifflin Harcourt

Library of Congress Cataloging-in-Publication Data
Names: Plozza, Shivaun, author.
Title: The boy, the wolf, and the stars / Shivaun Plozza.
Description: Boston : Houghton Mifflin Harcourt, [2020] | Audience: Ages 10 to 12. | Audience: Grades 4–6. | Summary: Abandoned as a baby in a forest to be eaten by Shadow Creatures, twelve-year-old Bo and his pet fox embark on a quest to return the wish-granting Stars to the Ulvian sky before the Shadow Witch can steal the star magic.
Identifiers: LCCN 2019044236 (print) | LCCN 2019044237 (ebook) | ISBN 9780358243892 (hardcover) | ISBN 9780358387701 (ebook)
Subjects: CYAC: Fantasy. | Stars — Fiction. | Wishes — Fiction. | Magic — Fiction. | Abandoned children — Fiction. | Adventure and adventurers — Fiction.
Classification: LCC PZ7.1.P626 Bo 2020 (print) | LCC PZ7.1.P626 (ebook) | DDC [Fic] — dc23
LC record available at https://lccn.loc.gov/2019044236
LC ebook record available at https://lccn.loc.gov/2019044237

Manufactured in the United States of America
DOC 10 9 8 7 6 5 4 3 2 1
4500806314

For Fenchurch, the Nix to my Bo

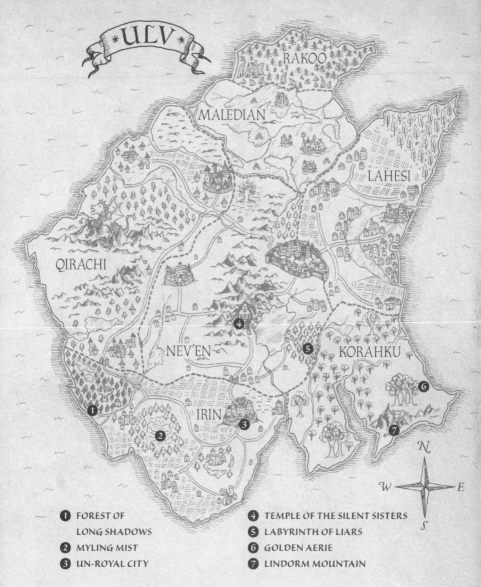

·ULV·

RAKOO

MALEDIAN

LAHESI

QIRACHI

NEV'EN

KORAHKU

IRIN

1	FOREST OF LONG SHADOWS		**4**	TEMPLE OF THE SILENT SISTERS
2	MYLING MIST		**5**	LABYRINTH OF LIARS
3	UN-ROYAL CITY		**6**	GOLDEN AERIE
			7	LINDORM MOUNTAIN

THIS MAP will help you safely explore the illustrious land of Ulv.
Should you happen to lose your way, prepare to come face-to-face with
many a dangerous beast. The forests are nice (though many of them will
eat you) and the inland seas are lovely (though most will drown you) and
remember to lock yourself inside at night before it gets Dark . . .

So the greedy wolf swallowed every single Star, while the Moon hid herself forever, afraid of being eaten next. Without the Moon and the Stars, it became Dark. And out of the Darkness crept Shadow Creatures, hungry beasts made entirely of shadow and evil.

Of course these days, people believe Stars are just a myth, a story to be told at bedtime when Shadow Creatures are clawing at the locked doors and frightened children need hope, need a Light to quell the unending Darkness.

—Excerpt from *The True Histories of Ulv*, Vol. III,
"The Origin of the Dark"

CHAPTER ONE

HIDDEN IN THE SHADOWS of the forest, Bo peeked under the low-hanging branches of a tree and watched the village children play a game. Spinning and dancing, they gathered in a circle, facing the center with their arms stretched wide and twinkling their fingers. "We're the Stars in the night sky," they chorused, as one child — a boy — crept into the middle of their circle, a blanket flapping around his shoulders, gray and coarse like a wolf's pelt.

Bo longed to play with the village children, but the last time he tried to join in, they had pointed at him, chanting: "Devil-child! Shadow Creature!"

Bo was lucky an old woodcutter had found him when he was a few days old, abandoned in the forest. But he was unlucky the villagers knew he had survived a full night alone in a place infested with Shadow Creatures before Mads, the woodcutter, had rescued him. "The child must be a Shadow Creature too," the villagers said. "How else could he survive the Dark? Or perhaps he struck a deal, a promise to lure innocent villagers into the forest for Shadow Creatures to devour in exchange for his own life."

So Bo could only watch from the forest edge as the Star-children spun in their circle and sang: *"Wolf so hungry, wolf so bold, don't hurt us, do as you're told."*

The wolf-child howled: *Ah-wooooo! Ah-wooooo!* A shudder ran the length of Bo's spine at the sound. *Ah-wooooo!* Baring his teeth, the wolf-child roared: *"Little Star, little Star, the hungry wolf knows where you are. He'll chase you round, up and down, he'll never stop until you're found."* The wolf-child covered his eyes with his little wolf paws and counted, "One, two, three . . ." as the Star-children danced clockwise around him.

Bo edged forward, gripping the tree beside him, the prickly, crinkly bark rough against his fingertips. He felt a pinch at his waist and looked down. A spiky vine had caught hold of him, just above the little pouch clipped to his belt. He pulled and twisted the vine, hearing it tear his shirt as it finally ripped clean off.

"Curse this forest," muttered Bo. He'd need to stitch the tear tonight before Mads saw it — the old man hated when Bo ruined his clothes.

Bo's head whipped up as the wolf-child shouted, "Ten!" and

charged, scattering Star-children, who screamed and laughed and twinkled their little fingers.

"You can't catch me," they each cried.

But the wolf-child caught them all. One by one he gobbled up every last Star-child.

Bo crept forward, eager to see more, but a small growl from behind made his shoulders slump and his chest heave with an almighty sigh. "Well, I wonder," said Bo. "Who could that be?"

He turned and saw a fox padding toward him, his tail a fiery plume flecked with white and eyes as golden as the Light in the Burning Season.

"You never listen, Nix," said Bo, hands on hips. "I told you to stay put, didn't I?"

Nix sat.

"Not now. Back there." Bo flung a hand toward the heart of the forest. "When I told you to stay by the sled. Remember?"

The fox cocked his head, snapping his mouth shut. He whimpered, low in the back of his throat.

"Don't argue." Bo turned around to watch the running, screaming, laughing children. "I know I'm not allowed to be here but it's just this once, okay? Besides, you need to listen to everything I say 'cause I'm the boss. Mads said so."

At the very edge of the green, Bo spied a little girl sucking on her thumb, resting her chin on her mother's lap. The mother wore her fair hair braided around and around her head, and Bo wondered if that was how his mother wore her hair. Every night in bed, Bo would close his eyes and picture the mother he had never met. Every night she wore a different face.

Bo crept forward, careful to stay hidden behind the low-hanging branches but close enough to read the unease on the woman's face as she watched the lengthening shadows stretch closer and closer to the playing children. The little girl curled the fabric of her mother's skirt through her stubby fingers and stared wide-eyed as the wolf-child stood triumphant in the center of the green.

"The hungry wolf has fed, now all the Stars are dead." The wolf-child puffed out his chest, beating it with a roar. *"The Dark will come, you'd better run, now all the Stars are dead."*

The little girl gripped her mother's skirt tightly. "Bad wolf," she said, frowning. "Why bad wolf eat Stars?"

The mother stroked her child's hair; Bo's scalp tingled as if the touch belonged to him.

"Because . . ." said the mother. Her lips stayed parted as if to speak further but no words came to her. Bo sometimes felt that way: as if all his words had scattered like Star-children hiding from a hungry wolf. The mother shook her head and sighed. "All I know is if we don't get you and your brother home this second, there will be no Stars to protect us from the Dark." She swept her child into her arms and called for her son. "Come inside now, Peter."

"Do I have to?" The blanket slipped from the wolf-child's shoulders. He pouted.

The Star-child at his feet giggled. "You can't catch me," she said.

"I already did," said Peter, snapping his teeth.

"Inside," said his mother. "Now." She frowned at the Darkening sky above.

Bo looked down and found Nix sitting quietly beside him. He could see the animal's right eye was weeping. A pink scar ran from the corner of the little fox's eye and along the bridge of his nose — curled and thin like a beckoning finger, a witch's finger. When the Dark was near, the scar wept.

Bo shivered.

It was true.

The Dark was coming.

The little fox barked.

"Fine," said Bo, bending to pick up the pile of kindling at his feet. "Let's go."

Bo hurried to his sled, passing shadows that rippled as though alive. He knew they weren't. Not yet. But he kept his distance anyway, hugging the kindling in the crook of his arm; Nix nudged his calves with a low bark.

"I'm coming, I'm coming," said Bo. "No need to be so bossy."

Nix trotted ahead, tongue flopped out the side of his mouth, his teeth as sharp as the broken animal bones scattered among the fallen leaves.

The sled was overflowing because all day Bo had been scouring the forest for kindling. He would have finished ages ago if it weren't for the village children and their games. And if it so happened that he'd accidentally napped half the day by the river's edge, then no one had to know.

"Stars!" said Bo with a snort. He grinned at Nix. "I think some of those kids still believe in them, don't you? Even *I* know Stars aren't real. Mums and dads made them up so we wouldn't be so afraid of the Dark." Bo glanced up: through the canopy of leaves, he saw the Darkening sky. Now it was a deep, pink-tinged blue but soon it would turn a solid, unending black. At least that was what Mads said. No one knew what the Dark looked like, and if they did see it, well, they didn't live to tell the tale. Not with the Shadow Creatures.

Bo dumped his armful on top of the sled but jumped back as the whole stack came crashing down.

"Skugs fud!"

Nix nipped Bo's ankle and barked.

"I know," said Bo. "But Mads isn't here, is he? The old man can't tell me off if he doesn't hear me."

Bo restacked the kindling, then looped the rope over his

shoulder and hauled the sled through the forest. Nix trotted by his side, sniffing the ground for signs of food.

"By the Light, Nix! Are you ever not hungry?" Bo laughed, a snort that danced from his mouth before disappearing into the lengthening shadows. They sure were getting long. A shiver tiptoed up and down his spine. He knew the Dark was coming, but there was still one last job to do before he could go home, a job he was already late for.

Every seventh day, it was Bo's responsibility to sprinkle a deep gold-red dust around the base of the oldest tree in the forest, a gnarled and twisted beast of a tree that haunted Bo's sleep. He was meant to do it exactly as the Light hit the third quadrant. "Don't ask, just do," Mads always said when Bo complained about this dull task. "Without that tree, there is no forest. No anything." That was what life with Mads was like — don't ask questions; just follow orders. Bo's head was so full of unasked questions he wondered how they all fit in there.

By now the Light was deep into the fourth quadrant, fading ever closer to the horizon. He hadn't meant to be so late. The Light had been warm and the grass soft and he hadn't meant to fall asleep, and then the village children had distracted him with their games. Time had slipped away from him. Bo had never once tended to the tree late, but he wasn't worried.

"All I'm doing is sprinkling a bunch of dust round an old tree," he said to Nix. "What does it matter when I do it?"

Bo pulled the sled farther into the forest, grumbling about dust and trees and Mads the whole way. When they broke into a clearing, Bo's heart quaked at the familiar sight before him.

Like a hunchbacked old man, the tree slumped in the center of the clearing, nothing within ten feet of it. "Smart of those other trees to keep their distance," murmured Bo as he left the sled at the edge of the clearing and hurried toward the ancient tree.

From beside the sled, Nix barked but did not follow.

"Coward," said Bo.

Nix growled but did not move.

Bo approached the tree carefully. Truly, it was a horrible thing. A trunk like a knotted mass of gray snakes. It wasn't tall but it was thick and wide and ugly as sin. Deep in the center at the base of the trunk was a hole, like a pit of unending Darkness.

"Let's get this over with, hey?" Bo unclipped the little pouch on his belt and untied the drawstring. The pouch felt surprisingly light. "What on Ulv?" Bo peered inside. It was empty. "But that's not possible! I filled it this morning. Mads even watched me do it, like always. He'd never let me leave the hut without making sure I had —"

Bo drew in a sharp breath as he noticed the hole in the bottom of the pouch. When had *that* happened?

He remembered the sharp pinch at his waist when he was

watching the village children and the rip as he tore the vine clean off. He'd thought it was his shirt that had torn, but perhaps it had been the pouch and perhaps the dust had seeped out and . . .

"Skugs fud!" said Bo.

Nix barked.

"I know, I know, but Mads will *kill* me."

Bo worried his bottom lip with his teeth as he frowned at the tree. If he missed tending to the ugly old thing just once, it wouldn't matter, would it?

"I'll sneak some more of that dust tomorrow and come back then," said Bo. "Mads doesn't have to know." Surely it wasn't *that* important. Mads would have told Bo *exactly* why he should never miss tending to the tree if it was terribly important. Wouldn't he?

Nix barked again but Bo ignored him. There was nothing he could do about it now. It was getting Dark; he couldn't stay any longer.

A gentle *hoot hoot* let Bo know he wasn't alone — a tawny owl blinked at him from the branches of a tree, holding his gaze for a long, long moment before flapping its wings and fluttering away.

Lucky it's only an owl and not someone who can tell on me, he thought.

Bo pocketed the ruined pouch and turned his back on the

tree. But as he walked away Bo could have sworn he heard a long, low, sighing hum emanating from the Dark hole in the center of the trunk. He looked over his shoulder — was the hole bigger? No, it was just his eyes and ears playing tricks on him.

Bo shivered and closed his eyes a moment. *Please don't let me dream about that horrible tree tonight,* he wished.

THE TRUE HISTORIES OF ULV, VOL. VI

On Wishes and the Dangerous Art of Wish-Catching

———◆———

The first recorded wish took place when a lonesome farmer looked up at the night sky and said, "I wish the girl from the butcher's would fall in love with me." When Celia Poplin awoke the next morning feeling decidedly more favorable toward a certain farmer, the villagers were abuzz — what witchcraft was this? How did it happen? And how can it happen to me?

It was, of course, pure luck that the farmer happened to look up at the exact Star whose job was to grant wishes — Mathias the Gift-Giver. Once this was discovered and every villager and their dog began demanding this and that and the other, Mathias got rather in a huff and decided to make things harder. The ritual for having your wish granted became thus: Hop on one foot to the highest ground, carrying three jellied pig's trotters, a wheel of cheese (stinkmonk preferred), and a mug of lindberry beer. Leave the offering on the ground and — still hopping — spin clockwise seven times while singing the Ulvian national anthem backwards. State your wish loudly, swap feet and hop counterclockwise in a circle seven more times, bow, repeat your wish, and — staying bowed — hop backwards all the way home.

Luckily, the Ulvians soon discovered there was another method for making a wish that involved far less hopping.

You see, a wish could also be made on a falling Star so long as you caught it *before* it hit the ground. Unfortunately, Stars almost always fell in the Valley of One Thousand Deaths (which, as you may guess from the name, is not a pleasant place). Once the Star was caught, the wish-magic could be extracted from inside. This was a tricky process and more often than not claimed one or two fingers. Children were considered the best at extracting wishes because of their small and nimble hands — such children led miserable, short lives and were useful only with all fingers intact.

All this occurred when Stars were plentiful (for more on the disappearance of the Stars, see *The True Histories of Ulv*, Vol. VI, "Stars and Other Celestial Objects Your Parents Told You Were Myths but Are, in Fact, Real"), and the wish-mining trade grew until it was the most profitable business in the land. Until the Stars vanished, of course.

Rumors persist that a small number of wishes remain, stored in glass jars and sold to the very, *very* rich, but this is likely — dare I say it — wishful thinking.

CHAPTER TWO

B O WOKE WHEN HE FELT a boot digging into his stomach.

"Get up, you lazy lump," grumbled Mads, the owner of the boot. "It's market day. Wood's not going to sell itself."

Bo rubbed the sleep from his eyes. He'd shivered half the night to the sounds of Shadow Creatures prowling outside, louder and closer than usual. Of course, Mads burned a candle throughout the night — without it, the hut would become Dark and the Shadow Creatures could find a way in. But it didn't stop Bo's fears: What if the Light blew out? What if the Shadow Creatures found a way in regardless?

When Bo had finally fallen asleep just before dawn he had dreamed of the tree, of the trunk bursting open and a horde of Shadow Creatures pouring out to eat him alive.

Bo sat up and looked blearily at the small, dank space around him: four wooden walls, an open fire, a cot where Mads slept, and a bucket for the kind of business it's not polite to talk about. Bo slept on the floor.

A lick of morning Light teased the corner of Bo's blanket. He wondered how early it was, if he had time to run to the center of the forest and tend to that beastly old tree before market. He glanced at Mads's cot in the corner of the hut, where, underneath, there was a box containing the gold-red powder he needed. But how was he to get hold of it without Mads knowing?

"Up, up, up," growled Mads as he plonked onto the edge of the cot to tie his boots.

Bo tried to stand but there was a dead weight on his feet where Nix slept. "Get up, you lazy lump," he said. The fox opened one eye but did not move.

Mads stood, tossing a knob of bread and cheese into Bo's lap. "Eat. Be quick about it."

Mads was a tall man, tall and thick and knobby and gray. And grumpy. But Bo was thankful the woodcutter had taken him in when his mother had dumped him. He'd been a scrawny, bawling, stinking little mite in soiled sheets with a note pinned to his shift.

"What did the note say?" he'd asked Mads once.

"That your father's dead and your mother never wanted you. Now don't go asking more questions or it'll be slop duty for a month," the old man had replied.

As long as Bo completed his chores, Mads fed him and gave him shelter.

Bo wriggled out from under Nix. The fox stretched, shaking

out his fur. Bo rolled his thin mattress tightly and stowed it away, then he halved his bread and cheese, sharing them with Nix. He chewed loudly, eyeing the shadowy space beneath the cot. He had nothing to fear from the shadows during the Light, when they were harmless once more. But if Bo couldn't get his hands on the box hidden there, and Mads found out he didn't take care of the tree yesterday . . .

Bo flinched as the old man snapped, "We're late." Mads shrugged on his coat and hid his wild tufts of silvery hair beneath a felt cap. It was morning and already the stench of lindberry beer clung to him. "No time for staring into space, you useless boy."

Bo swallowed the last of his breakfast and followed Mads to the door.

The tree would have to wait.

∽

The village of Squall's End was a coil of pearly white huts nestled in the Valley of Stropp in the province of Irin. A narrow road led from a forest in the northwest, where Bo lived, down into the village.

Mads hauled a cart stacked high with wood along the gravel road. Bo hurried along behind, stumbling on the hem of his hooded cloak, three sizes too big.

The Light was pale as it peeked above the first quadrant. Bo yawned.

"Keep up," said Mads.

Bo looked back at Nix, trotting behind him. "He means you."

Nix barked.

"Does too."

The road grew narrower as it entered the village. White-washed huts huddled in curved rows, crowding the edge of the road. Villagers were up and about, unlocking the heavy doors and window shutters that protected them against Shadow Creatures.

"How dare you step foot in this village," sneered a hunched old lady. She was bashing a rolling pin against a rug slung over a washing line, the dust mushrooming into the air around her. Bo coughed, tugging at the edge of his hood, pulling it farther over his face. *Maybe she isn't talking to me,* he thought. But the old lady spat at Bo's feet as he passed, leaving him in no doubt. "The Shadow Creatures were in a state last night, thanks to you," she said. "Howling and scratching and screeching. My best rose-bushes wilted and died. It's all your fault, Devil-child." *Bash, bash, bash.* "*You* lead them into the village, don't you? Looking for innocents to devour!"

A flush of bitter heat rushed through him. He turned away before the old lady could see the wetness in his eyes, but her words burrowed under his skin and pricked him all over like a thousand stikenbee stings.

"Pay her no mind," said Mads, the wheels of the cart croaking and groaning as he ambled on. "Superstitious claptrap."

Bo hurried to catch up, leaving the sneering woman and her cloud of dust behind. "It was bad last night, though, wasn't it?" said Bo.

Mads sniffed.

"The Shadow Creatures, I mean," continued Bo. "They were making a racket. I could hardly sleep. I thought they were going to break the walls down. It's never been like that before."

Mads looked skyward. "Some nights are worse than others," he said before shaking his head and speeding up. "Come now," he called over his shoulder. "We're late."

The road spiraled inward until it reached the village square, which wasn't a square at all but a large paved circle in the center of town. Most stalls were already set up, laden with fruits, vegetables, meats, cheeses, breads, and sweets. Only Mads sold wood; no other villager dared set foot *near* the haunted forest, let alone *inside* it. That was why they were so terrified of him; that, and his hulking size and ready fists. Bo hoped to one day be as tall as Mads — perhaps then the villagers would leave him alone too.

"Here comes the Devil-man and his Devil-child," muttered the baker as Bo passed, and a small child leaning against his mother's legs looked up at Bo with wide eyes.

"It's the Devil-child," the young boy whispered to his

mother. "He's come to eat me!" The child's bottom lip trembled as he gripped his mother's skirt. Bo pressed his lips together, tugging the hood over his face as the mother hurried her child away. But the cloak felt as if it had shrunk, leaving Bo vulnerable to every jeer, every stare, every hiss. He did not think there was a cloak big enough to hide him from the villagers and their hate.

Bo dragged his feet after Mads, who had set the cart in their usual spot on the very edge of the market square.

Mads pulled out his sign — WOOD FOR SALE — and leaned it against the wheel of the cart. He pulled down a large stump for a seat, threw his hat on the ground to collect the money, and sat, arms folded, glowering at the villagers, as if daring them to come close.

It was a busy day. Mads unscrewed the cap of his flask and took a swig. Bo leaned against the cart and tried to ignore the stares and whispers. Nix sat beside him, growling at every passerby.

But no one wanted to buy wood. The bad night had everyone spooked; they hurried by Mads's stall with their eyes averted, their heads lowered. Hours passed. No one came near them.

Eventually, Mads leaned over and pulled a handful of coins from his pocket. "Here." He tossed the coins to Bo. "Buy yourself some of that apple crackling you like." He took another swig of his flask.

Bo stared at the coins in his palm. Apple crackling was his

favorite: thin slices of tangy apple dipped in honey, deep fried, and then lightly salted. It made his stomach rumble just thinking about it, but it made him ache, too, because Bo understood why he was being sent away and why Mads wouldn't look him in the eye.

"Come on," said Bo to Nix, and they took off through the market crowded with locals and traders from all corners of the province, and even a handful of Irin soldiers in their green uniforms and brass buttons and swords sheathed at their waists.

"Real Korahku feathers!" cried a seller as Bo passed her stall. "Get your genuine Korahku feathers here!" Bo peered closely at the long, reddish-brown, metal-tipped feathers the seller held high above her head. "Plucked fresh today! Will slice a grown man's head clean off with a single swipe!" Playfully, the stall-holder made to swipe at Bo but stopped when she saw who was peeking out from under the hood. She drew back, fear contorting her face. "Get away from me, Devil-child. You'll curse my stall!"

Nix barked at her until Bo pulled him away. "Forget it," he said. "It's not worth it."

They continued through the bustling market, slowly this time. Bo kept his hood low and his hands in his pockets. Luckily, he knew the way to the apple crackling stall by heart. Left, right, straight, around, sharp left —

"A spot of rabbit for your little creature, young master?" asked a man on Bo's right.

Bo ducked his head low, hunching his shoulders. "Keep walking, Nix," he whispered, but Nix couldn't resist an offer of food. The little fox trotted toward the man, his tongue flapping out the side of his mouth.

"Traitor," mumbled Bo. He tugged at the hem of his hood, hovering meters from the stall.

"Here you go, little one." The strange man offered a strip of dried rabbit meat to the fox.

"Wait, Nix, we haven't paid for that," protested Bo, but Nix had already snapped up the meat and was sitting back, waiting for more. *There goes my apple crackling*, thought Bo. He opened his palm to count his money. "How much?" he said to the man, careful not to meet his eyes.

"No cost, no cost," said the man. His voice was smooth and gilt-edged. "My name is Galvin. And you?"

Bo pushed his hood back enough to sneak a glance at the stranger. He was middle-aged and rounded, all curves and lumps and mounds, with a pinkish, grayish pallor to his wrinkly skin. He was short — even for an Irin — and his restless eyes never settled in one place.

"I'm Bo."

"I like your fancy cloak, young Bo," said Galvin with a smile.

His teeth were made of solid gold, blackened around the edges. "Very courtly."

Bo dipped his gaze, his cheeks burning hot — no one had ever complimented him before. His eyes flicked nervously over the man's stall: it was full of *things*. Boxes and rings and plates and knives and carvings and things Bo did not have names for: rusted things and shiny things and sharp things and oddly shaped things. Bo shifted closer.

"See anything you like?" said Galvin. "All good prices for a fine young gentleman such as yourself."

Bo's fingers trembled as they hovered over each strange item. He wanted *everything*. He wanted it because it was new and strange, and suddenly Bo felt how small his life was, how little he knew of the world.

"Maledian merwolf hair?" suggested Galvin, waving his hand over a clear pouch bulging with coarse blue hair. "Or a necklace of troll's teeth, perhaps? Perfect for warding off tree sprites. Nasty little critters." He handed Nix another strip of rabbit.

Bo nudged the fox with his boot. "Don't be greedy," he whispered.

Nix barked.

"Are so."

Bo raised his head to ask Galvin what on Ulv tree sprites were when he noticed the shelf behind him. On it sat a hodgepodge of steaming potions in small glass vials and sparkly rocks and globs of gooey green sludge and brightly colored insects trapped in glass cubes. In the center of the shelf was a jar, and in it was a tiny spark of Light just bobbing in the air; when Bo looked directly at it, a sharp fizzle ran up and down his spine and he had to look away because it hurt his eyes. Bo's heart hammered in his chest.

"What is *that?*"

"What good taste you have," crooned Galvin with a golden smile. He hadn't even turned to look at what Bo was pointing at. He leaned in close, lowering his voice. "But it's the only one of its kind and too expensive for you, I'm afraid."

"I've got money," protested Bo.

Galvin laughed; his gold teeth glistened. "Do you?" he said. He sucked on his lips thoughtfully, then nodded. "Very well. Tell me, what do you know about wishes?"

Bo frowned. "When you want something, you say it to yourself and you hope it comes true. That's a wish, isn't it?" Bo often wished his mother hadn't abandoned him and his father hadn't died, but no matter how many times he wished for such a thing, it never came true. So he didn't think wishes were real.

Galvin motioned for Bo to lean in. He did and the Irin lowered his voice even more. "That's part of it, yes," said Galvin, "but if you want your wish to come true, you need a Star."

"A Star? No such thing. Everyone knows that."

Galvin slid his stubby fingers around Bo's wrist and pulled him in closer. "Not true, young Bo. Not true at all. Long ago, children not much younger than you were sold to ruthless wish-traders, just to extract the wishes from inside fallen Stars. Very dangerous job," he said. "And now that all the Stars are gone, no more wishes. Except this one." He jutted his chin at the silvery glass jar behind him.

Bo didn't believe a word of it and yet . . . how his heart raced when he looked at the little speck of Light in that jar! How it made him think of his mother, why she left him in the forest, where she was now, and if perhaps — *perhaps* — she missed him. Bo was so intoxicated by these thoughts that he stopped worrying about whether or not Stars were real or if wishes could be trapped in small glass jars. All he could think about was: What if he could wish to meet his mother and what if such a wish could come true? Surely she would tell him it had all been a mistake. How much she regretted leaving him! How happy she was to be reunited with her boy!

Bo licked his dry lips. "How much?" he asked.

Galvin jerked back, releasing his grip on Bo. "How much? *How much?* You could wish for anything — fame, fortune, love . . . What price would you place on such things?"

"I've got . . ." Bo counted. ". . . five Raha."

Galvin threw back his head and roared with laughter. "Five Raha? For the last wish in the land?" He patted Bo's hand. "Oh, my lad, you've had a treat for your pet. I took pity on you because of the way the villagers stare and whisper and spit at you. But I don't pity you enough to sell you the last wish in the land for five Raha. On you go." He waved Bo away. "Shoo! Be off with you and your five Raha."

Bo licked his lips again, his eyes on the glass jar. "How much do you need?" he asked. "I can get more."

Galvin's eyes danced. "Come back when you have a hundred times that amount."

Bo tried to hide his gasp—a *hundred* times? How would he get hold of so much money?

"I'll be here tomorrow," said Galvin, but he was already waving Bo on again, trying to clear a path for paying customers to approach. "Come back then. I'll just take two . . . no, *three* Raha now as compensation for the rabbit your fox ate." He snapped several coins out of Bo's hand before Bo could protest.

Bo shook his head as he walked away. "It's a trick," he said to Nix. "Has to be. No way that's a real wish. Stars are made up."

But still, as he headed back to Mads, looking over his shoulder at the strange Irin and his stall of glittering oddments, Bo couldn't help but wonder.

CHAPTER THREE

L ATER THAT DAY, once they had returned from market and the Light was hanging low in the sky, Bo hurried to the center of the forest, a mended pouch of stolen powder beating against his thigh as he ran.

"Hurry, Nix," panted Bo. "We've got to get this done before Mads returns from collecting water at the river."

As he ran, Bo couldn't stop thinking about the man from the market. On the way home, he'd asked Mads about the Stars. "If they're real, then where have they vanished to?" he'd said. "Wasn't really a magic wolf, was it? That's just a game and I'm too big to play it and I'm *definitely* too big to believe it's true. Right?" His questions had earned him a clip around the ear. "Don't be asking nonsense," the old man had snapped. "You're on slop duty for a month."

Bo broke through the line of trees and into the clearing, then stopped dead in his tracks and gasped.

No, thought Bo, *it couldn't happen* that *quickly.*

With a hammering heart, Bo inched forward, his wide eyes following the path of crinkled and blackened leaves slowly raining down from the beastly old tree's branches. The branches themselves were a sickly pale gray, and where once they had spread wide, they now drooped. But the worse part was the black hole in the center of the trunk. Overnight it had grown twice its size.

There was no denying it: the tree was dying.

Bo looked from the pouch grasped in his trembling hand to the tree in the center of the clearing.

He had failed. The most important job Mads had given him and he'd failed. His stomach lurched as he thought of telling Mads what had happened, the sting of the old man's boot as he would kick Bo out of the hut, telling him never to come back.

And Bo would be alone.

Alone.

Bo paused when he heard a strange whispering, swishing sound coming from inside the Dark hole. "I could throw the powder from here?" he said, a quiver in his voice. "That will fix it, right?"

From the edge of the clearing, Nix whimpered.

"I'll do it quick," said Bo. He untied the pouch and dug his hand in, grabbing a fistful. "Please be okay," he said as he flung the dust toward the base of the tree.

Nothing happened.

Bo frowned at the gaping hole in the center of the tree's trunk. "I'll come tomorrow and it will be back to normal," he said. Despite his confident words, his stomach was twisted in knots, just like the tree trunk.

Again, Nix whimpered.

Bo retied the pouch and hurried back to Nix.

It was close to the half-Light, the dull gray hour between Light and Dark. The Shadow Creatures would begin to awaken soon. "We'd better get back," said Bo.

He glanced over his shoulder one more time; the tree whispered and swooshed, the dead leaves falling. He couldn't help but think he had done something terribly, terribly wrong.

He ground his teeth together to stop his chin from trembling. Mads kept a roof over his head and food in his belly and all Bo had to do to earn his place was complete his chores; he had nothing else to offer, no other skill or use to prevent Mads from tossing him aside like curdled milk. What would happen now? Where would he go?

It would be okay. It *had* to be okay.

"Let's get back," he said to Nix.

But as he turned to leave, an unexpected noise stopped him in his tracks: *Ah-wooooo! Ah-wooooo!*

A wolf's howl. A *real* wolf's howl.

He gasped and spun around, fear pulsing through his veins. Where was it? Was it close? Mads always said, "Run if ever you hear a wolf. Hurry home and don't look back." But wolves never wandered into the forest. Not this forest. It was just Peter and his blanket and the game and —

Ah-wooooo!

The bottom fell out of Bo's stomach: It was real. And it was close.

He broke into a sprint, Nix right behind him.

"Hurry!" he shouted. "Hurry, Nix!"

They hurtled through the dense forest, tree branches clawing at them, Light fading fast, the wolf's howl echoing again and again. Bo ran until he tripped, landing face-first in the mulch.

He sat up with a groan, feeling Nix's cold nose sniffing his face.

"I'm all right," said Bo. He felt his head for bumps and looked up.

He froze.

He was on the edge of the small clearing that surrounded their hut, and in the center of the clearing was a giant wolf.

The blood drained from Bo's face: the creature was two times — no, *three* times — as tall as Bo, scraggy and lean, his white fur burnt in patches, the skin etched with scars.

Bo dared not move. He dared not breathe.

Had the wolf seen him? Heard him?

"Long time sleeping," rumbled the wolf, creeping toward what looked like a felled tree, a lump of knotted wood on the opposite side of the clearing. "Long time. In Dark. But. Suddenly I wake. And find you. At last." The wolf's voice was rough, as if the words had been dashed against rocks.

The fallen tree let out a loud, croaking groan as it began to ... to rise? Bo gasped: it wasn't a tree—it was Mads! And *oh* ... Bo's throat constricted as his guardian struggled to his knees, blood dripping from a gash in his shoulder, trickling down his arm to his fingertips. *Drip, drip, drip* onto the fallen leaves.

"It's impossible, Ranik," wheezed Mads. "You were gone. Burned by the Light. You fell."

The wolf crept closer. "I woke. In Darkness. Now. I come back. To find. Brother. Whispers across land. You have answers. I need. Tell me."

Next to the giant wolf, Mads looked like the smallest piquee bird. He winced as he tried to stand. "You're too late. The Shadow Witch killed your brother. She wanted to destroy the Stars and all good magic with them."

Mads always said there were no such things as witches. Even when Ma Yulg had been strung up by her ankles for a week after Lucky Karl said she'd cast a spell on his best pig, Mads had said it was all nonsense—there was no such thing as magic. He'd been the one to cut her down and threaten anyone who tried to tie her up again. So why was he talking about a Shadow Witch? And Stars?

"Liar," growled Ranik. "*You* know. Where to find. Keys. To cage. Brother still alive. Locked away. But alive. The owls talk. And I listen. Because they know. Everything."

Mads laughed. "You're wrong. He's long dead."

The wolf snapped his jaws: a cold, metallic *clink!* "Let me. Remind you. With my teeth." The giant wolf bore down on Mads, lips twisted and quivering in a snarl.

In a rush of reckless courage, Bo sprang from his haunches to his feet and shouted, "Leave Mads alone!" He blindly grabbed a fallen branch and thrust it forward like a weapon.

The wolf snapped his head toward Bo, jaws curling into a wide grin, his milky white eyes shining. "Who. Is this?"

Mads groaned but didn't have the strength to stand or reach out. "No one. It's no one."

Ranik laughed. "It's *some*one." The wolf turned from Mads, creeping slowly toward Bo. "If old man," he said. "Won't give keys. I take boy. Fair trade. Boy for keys."

Beside Bo, Nix growled.

"I didn't think this far ahead," whispered Bo.

The branch trembled in his grip as the wolf inched closer. "Stay back!" said Bo, but it was he who stumbled backwards.

The wolf snarled. "Dinnertime."

With a loud cry, Mads lunged for his fallen axe and swung it toward the wolf. The blade cut deep into Ranik's hind leg. The wolf howled in pain.

"Run!" Mads shouted to Bo.

Ranik turned and pounced on Mads with a roar, and the pair struggled — twisting, heaving, gritting their teeth, thundering with pain and effort. "Tell me. The truth!" cried Ranik. "Tell me. Or I eat out. Your heart. And find. The answer there."

Bo could feel the night settling in, the Darkness approaching fast. Soon, the shadows would grow claws and teeth and become Shadow Creatures. No one survived the Shadow Creatures.

Bo looked at the branch in his hand, so thin and easily broken. He needed to get Mads into the hut. He needed to chase away the wolf before Dark. He had failed Mads with the ancient tree but he could save him now. He could earn his place. But how?

All at once there was a flash of blinding Light. The shadows cringed and Bo flung an arm across his eyes, gritting his teeth. When the Light faded, Bo lowered his arm and blinked rapidly until his vision returned. Mads was in the center of the clearing with a ball of pure white Light anchored to the palm of his hand. The ball was spinning, spitting colorful sparks in all directions.

A sudden coldness seized Bo's core. He turned to where the wolf lay on the ground, unmoving. A swarm of questions buzzed inside him, threatening to burst from his open mouth.

It was . . . impossible.

Mads crumbled to his knees with a cry of pain.

Bo ran to him and skidded to the ground. He grabbed Mads by his shirt, soaked with blood. "Are you okay?"

"Go. To the hut," wheezed Mads. Blood trickled from the corner of his mouth.

Bo looked to the wolf. The beast's chest heaved, legs twitching—he was waking up. Around the wolf, shadows lengthened, their edges growing sharp and clawlike. Bo's heart hammered in his chest.

He was tall for an Irin his age but he was thin and gangly. Still, Bo gripped Mads under his armpits and dragged the old man toward the hut with every ounce of strength he had.

So close. Almost there.

Leaves rustled—was it the wolf climbing to his feet? The Shadow Creatures waking? Bo dared not look.

"Hurry, Nix," he said. Nix was by his feet, scampering and whimpering—the scar on his snout wept. "To the hut."

Bo crashed back-first into the front door as the sound of the wolf running toward them drummed in his ears: *thump-ta-thump, thump-ta-thump.*

He rattled the doorknob, heaving against the heavy wooden door that wouldn't budge.

Thump-ta-thump.

He pushed harder, twisting the knob left and right. "Come on! Come *on!*"

Thump-ta-thump. THUMP-TA-THUMP!

"Open! Please open!"

Finally, the door swung open and all three — Bo, Mads, and Nix — tumbled inside.

Bo slammed the door shut, bracing his shoulder against the thick wood as he turned the lock. His whole body shook as — *thump!* — the wolf crashed into the other side.

There was silence.

Bo breathed heavily.

Nix whimpered.

And then . . .

A howl.

Long and mournful. *Ah-woooo!*

A howl of bitter disappointment.

Bo quickly lit a candle to chase away the growing Dark and then crawled to Mads's side and gripped the old man's hands.

"Mads? What do I do?" he whispered. "Tell me. How do I fix you?"

Mads lifted a hand to Bo's cheek — two fingers brushed away Bo's tears. The rough drag of the old man's callused skin across his cheek was unfamiliar to Bo, and a tiny, locked corner of Bo's heart ached at the unexpected intimacy. "So many wrongs. No time to fix them all," said Mads. His sigh was long: the sound of the wind through bare trees in the Sorrow Season. He looked down at his palm — the orb of Light was gone but his pale, grayish skin was still glowing. "Shouldn't have been able to do that," he said. A troubled crease lined his brow. "Unless . . ."

Outside, the wolf howled.

"In the morning," said Bo, "I'll go to the village. I'll get help. Just hold on. Please?"

"No!" Mads grabbed hold of Bo's hands so tightly it hurt. "Not the village. You must leave. Find the Stars so *she* can't get hold of them."

"I don't—"

"The Stars!" urged Mads, wheezing. "Don't let the Shadow Witch find them. She will wake too—there is nothing to hold her back now."

"But Stars aren't real! You said so."

Mads's grip slipped, his hands landing on the pouch half-filled with gold-red dust. Bo watched Mads's face crumble with the realization that if Bo had the pouch *now*, then that meant yesterday, when he was supposed to sprinkle the dust on the tree's roots . . . Bo looked away, ashamed. "Oh, Bo," said Mads, and laughed, but it was a sad, rueful kind of laugh. "What have you done?"

"Hold on, Mads," said Bo. "I'll get help in the morning. Please just wait."

Mads shook his head, loosening the top few buttons of his shirt, slipping the crystal pendant that always hung around his neck over his head. He held it out for Bo. "You must release the Stars. Set them free. Three keys. Riddles lead you to each one. The Scribe can help . . ." He forced the pendant into Bo's hands. "The first riddle is . . ."

"Mads?" Bo squeezed his guardian's hand and called his name again and again.

But it was too late.

The old man was gone.

THE TRUE HISTORIES OF ULV, VOL. II

WHY YOU SHOULD NEVER WISH TO MEET A WOLF

---

here are more things to fear in this world than there are boils on a troll's bum. But few are more deserving of your blubbering, jelly-legged terror than wolves.

Wolves are carnivorous, cold-blooded beasts powerful enough to fight off Shadow Creatures — their one weakness is that they can walk only in the half-Light, that eerie hour or two before the Dark descends. Light burns their skin, you see: a horrible curse bestowed upon them many years ago as punishment (for more, see *The True Histories of Ulv*, Vol. I, "Why You Should Never Attempt to Eat the Sun"). For this reason, wolves rarely leave the northern ice forests of Rakoo, where days are a constant half-Light.

Aha! you might think. Why fear them? They live so far from me!

Oh, but listen: a most interesting fact about wolves (and

by "interesting" I mean "bloodcurdling") is that once they get a whiff of your scent they can track you for days and will, in fact, never give up chasing you. One wolf was known to have spent seventeen years tracking its prey!

Again, you might think, *But this changes nothing! I will never meet a wolf!*

Well.

The most astute of my readers will have noticed my use of a very important word in an earlier paragraph: "rarely." (Go on, go back and reread if you must. I'll wait.)

For *rarely* does not mean *never.* Because on occasion, wolves do *indeed* leave the northern ice forests. If they have reason to . . .

CHAPTER FOUR

THE NEXT DAY, Bo buried Mads under the boughs of a flowering blossom tree. It felt as though his heart had been clawed by Ranik, shredded to pieces he would never be able to fit back together. He was scared and confused and alone.

When he had woken at first Light, Bo had thought it all a cruel dream. But when he'd spied Mads, cold and still on the floor, he had remembered. With tears, he had remembered.

Mads was dead.

Bo was alone.

Mads had not always been the kindest father figure — mostly he was a mean old drunk with a sharp tongue — but he was all Bo knew. He was the only one who'd taken Bo in when no one else had wanted him.

Eventually, Bo had summoned the courage to check outside the hut, but the wolf had long gone, forced to hide from full Light like all wolves. But Bo knew Ranik would be back in the half-Light. He knew this because the night before, the wolf had pressed close to the door and whispered, "You cannot. Escape me."

Bo had clutched his stomach and gulped down the sour taste in his mouth when he'd heard it. He would have to leave. But where would he go? Where *could* he go?

"Goodbye," Bo said to Mads's grave, the mound of earth already lightly scattered with fallen blossoms from the tree above it. Nix pressed against Bo's calves, whimpering quietly. In his hand, Bo held Mads's leather necklace with the small crystal pendant. It was an odd shape — all points and jagged angles — and the thick leather strap was carved with peculiar little squiggles and marks, but Mads had worn it every day of his life, so Bo wanted to keep it.

Bo tied the leather strap around his neck, dropping the pendant beneath his shirt. He patted his chest, feeling the cold lump through the thin material. It was small comfort, however. Bo's head was filled with strange ideas about wolves and Stars and keys and witches, ideas that danced and darted and refused to come together to make sense. He didn't have any answers; he felt useless and afraid.

But there *was* something he could do. If he bought the wish from the man at the market, then perhaps he could save Mads. Bo wasn't sure if he believed in wishes but it didn't matter. If there was a glimmer of hope, the smallest chance that Bo could wish for everything to be the way it was before, he would take it. His life with Mads hadn't been perfect but what else could he wish for? Sometimes Mads had even been kind to him: swimming in the river, shadow puppets on the walls, little foxes carved out of wood for Bo to play with. Not always, but sometimes.

Didn't he owe it to the old man to try? Bo could prove his worth, once and for all.

Inside the hut, Bo grabbed everything that might be worth trading. How many Raha had the man asked for? Five *hundred?* Bo didn't have anywhere near that amount, not even after he found a tin of money hidden beneath the hearth. But perhaps he could sell some belongings. He searched high and low but they didn't have anything much of value.

Nix tied himself up in knots around Bo's legs. "I'm not leaving you behind, you silly thing," said Bo. "We're doing this together."

When he spied the box of gold-red dust under Mads's cot, a coldness gripped Bo's heart. He knew that, before he went to find Galvin, he should walk to the center of the forest and check on the old tree. For Mads.

Bo heaved his rucksack full of items to barter onto his back, and he and Nix set out, quiet in their grief. But when they arrived at the clearing, Bo's heart — which was already shattered to a million pieces — found a way to shatter some more.

The leaves and limbs were blackened and shriveled, and the hole in the center of the trunk was so large Bo could have walked into it without bending over. The mournful howling he thought he'd imagined coming from inside the tree trunk the day before was now so loud it made Bo's teeth rattle.

The tree was dead.

Worse still, whatever had killed the beastly old thing had spread to the trees circling the clearing, their branches bare of leaves, their bark peeling in long, jagged strips, their trunks splitting and toppling over. There was no breeze, no birdsong, no sign of life, save for the same tawny owl as last time. But with a gentle *hoot* and a flapping of wings, the owl left too and then there was silence.

A Dark funk settled over Bo, his insides crawling as though filled with Shadow Creatures.

How far would this . . . this *disease* spread?

Bo didn't bother throwing the powder on the base of the tree. He tossed the pouch on the ground where he stood, then ran, feeling so much shame that here, again, was another way he had let Mads down. *I can't get anything right,* thought Bo. *No wonder I was left in the forest to die.*

"What have you done?" Mads had asked when he saw the pouch, right before he'd died. These words whirled through Bo's head as he ran.

What have you done? What have you done? What have you done?

❧

As Bo neared the edge of the forest, he heard noises.

"Steady up!" rasped an old man's voice, just through the break of trees. Bo crept forward until he could see beyond the forest and to the narrow road.

A scattering of people marched along the road, headed away from the village. On their backs they carried bulging rucksacks and baskets filled with food and clothing; a young woman pulled a cart overflowing with furniture and bedding. "Mind you don't tip the thing," the old man said to her. "You're going too fast. I'd like to reach the Un-Royal City in one piece, thank you very much."

Flyaway strands of brown hair framed the woman's face; her cheeks were red with effort. "I need to go fast," she snapped. "The sooner we get away from this cursed place, the better."

Bo watched several more families pass, all carrying their worldly possessions, all looking over their shoulders at the village behind them, worry etched in their features. Bo even recognized some of the traders from yesterday's market, the ones who had come from far-flung corners of Irin and who usually stayed in the village for weeks, peddling their wares.

"Strange," said Bo to Nix. "Why do you think they're leaving?"

The little fox growled.

"You're right. The Shadow Creatures *were* bad last night. Louder than ever but you don't think—"

And then Bo saw him.

The man with the gold teeth and the lumps and bumps and the dancing eyes: Galvin. The man who owned the last wish in the land.

Bo burst out from behind the trees and onto the side of the road. An old woman gasped at his sudden appearance, tugging back the small child trotting along the gravel beside her. "Get away with you!" she cried.

But Bo was too preoccupied to worry. He weaved through the villagers, leaving the cries and whispers behind him, as he headed straight for the wish-seller at the back of the exodus.

Galvin pushed a wheelbarrow in front of him, a large knotted bundle inside it.

"Oh, it's you, is it?" he said. He didn't stop when Bo reached him, forcing Bo to jog alongside.

"I need to buy your wish," Bo said, already puffing. Nix was sniffing around the seller's wheelbarrow, no doubt searching for rabbit.

"Can't," Galvin said. Sweat was beading on his forehead. It wasn't a hot day, but the effort of pushing the wheelbarrow at such speed was clearly affecting him.

"Slow down," said Bo. "I need to explain."

Galvin laughed meanly. He had no gold-toothed smiles for Bo today. "Slow down? *Slow down?* I was told not to come to this village, did you know? Full of Shadow Creatures, they told me. The people are primitive and mean-spirited, they said." He laughed again, cold and rueful. "But did I listen?"

Bo stumbled as his foot caught the edge of the barrow's wheel. "Please slow down," he said, panting. "I don't have five hundred Raha but I've got twelve and I've got lots of things I can trade with you. Like rabbit-skin boots and three jars of pickled eel and . . ."

"Save your breath," said the man. With a sigh he stopped wheeling and turned to face Bo, his eyes slits of black as he squinted against the Light. He took forever to speak, content to stare at Bo, at every inch of him. Bo squirmed under the penetrating gaze before the man finally spoke.

"You should leave," he said. "It's dangerous here. Shadow Creatures are increasing in number and straying into the half-Light."

"That's impossible," said Bo.

The man snorted. "Says you, who knows *nothing*. A child was taken. Saw it with my own two eyes. Yesterday evening. Strayed too close to the shadows at half-Light and was snatched. All they've found were his shoes."

Though Bo had a hard time believing such claims, even the *idea* of Shadow Creatures in the half-Light was enough to fill him with fear, anxious thoughts burrowing like tree roots in his mind.

Galvin leaned in close, his golden teeth glinting in the Light.

"There are whispers an evil force is rallying the Shadow Creatures for an attack, to kill us all and take over the land. Some say it's the Korahku but that's just bad blood talking. I'd wager all my Raha it's the Shadow Witch come back for her revenge. Never did believe she was dead. She's too crafty for that." He roughly poked a stubby finger against Bo's shoulder, enough for Bo to wobble. Bo scowled as he swatted the Irin's hand away. Galvin chuckled, low and Dark. "This isn't a coincidence, child." He bent closer, his wrinkled, weather-beaten face right in front of Bo's. When he spoke, a wave of sour breath tickled Bo's skin. "You mark my words, young Irin. Someone is controlling those beasts. And just think, if they can stray into the half-Light now, who's telling what they'll be able to do next?"

Bo shuddered at such a thought but some part of him — a small, guilty part — was relieved. Ever since he discovered the decaying trees, his mind had been abuzz with horrible thoughts: What if he had set off a curse when he didn't tend to the tree in time? What if all of it — the wolf and the trees and the rise in Shadow Creatures — was his fault?

What have you done? What have you done? What have you done?

But what Galvin said eased the knot of guilt in Bo's chest. If it was the Shadow Witch, then it had nothing to do with him — it was just a coincidence it all started when he let the old tree die. And Mads had talked about the Shadow Witch too, so it *must* be true.

But did that mean his last words about finding the Stars were true too?

"Is that why everyone is leaving?" Bo asked. He glanced back toward the village. There was no one on the road behind them yet but he guessed there would be soon enough.

"Not all of them. But many. And when the rest of them see sense they'll leave as well. This place is too dangerous now." Galvin shook his head as he grabbed the handles of the wheelbarrow again. "You best be going yourself," he said, and took off, hunched over his bundle of goods.

Bo gave chase. "But I need the wish first."

Galvin shook his head again. "Sold it. This morning. On my way out of town. Some traveler who paid me double the price. Ha!"

Bo stopped dead in his tracks, his heart in his throat. "Sold it?"

Galvin paused. His shoulders rose and fell heavily with a sigh. "Listen. Best I can do is sell you a spirit charm."

Bo was hardly listening. The wish had been sold! All Bo's hopes — however small and fluttering they had been — floated away on the wind like ash. If there was no wish, there was no saving Mads, no going back to the way things were before.

"Only cost you eight ... eh, *nine* Raha," said Galvin. "It'll keep you safe from all manner of lesser spirits: fairies, pixies, water sprites, and the like."

Bo shook his head. "Fairies? Pixies? *Water sprites?* Am I likely to run into any of them?"

"Oh yes," said Galvin. He dug through his sack until he pulled out a small vial of blue liquid. "All the time if you're not careful. Nasty things. Not likely to kill you but will happily bite off a finger or two when you're not looking."

"But I really needed that wish," said Bo, voice cracking.

Galvin held out the vial. "This is much better for a young fellow such as yourself. Far more useful. Take it, take it. Only cost you nine, eh, *ten* Raha."

Bo dug into his pockets and pulled out a handful of coins. He started to count before Galvin swiped his palm clean. "That'll do," he said, shoving the vial into Bo's empty hand.

Before Bo could protest, Galvin had grabbed hold of the wheelbarrow and was pushing away from him. "If you come across a particularly nasty creature," he called over his shoulder, "throw the vial at its feet and chant, 'Be gone! Be gone! Be gone!' and you'll be safe."

Bo stood rooted to the spot, eyes on the little vial in his palm. *Safe?* he thought. Without the wish, without Mads, Bo didn't know if safe was possible.

CHAPTER FIVE

B O STOOD ON THE OUTSKIRTS OF THE VILLAGE watching smoke pour from the nearest chimney; it looked like a dragon clawing at the sky.

"Come on, Nix," said Bo. The fox growled, sniffing the air. Bo sighed. "I know but we don't have a choice. Can't stay in the forest because the wolf knows to find us there."

Having briefly returned to the hut to dump his items for bartering and fill his rucksack with candles, matches, food, and water, Bo hitched the bag over his shoulder and started walking, Nix chasing his feet. As they trudged the path into the village, Light warmed Bo's skin but a sharpness in the air whispered of the approaching Sorrow Season, when the sky would do nothing but weep for weeks and weeks. Bo's stomach churned as he thought of the home he was leaving behind.

"Don't worry," Bo said to Nix, trying to keep his voice cheerful for his friend. "We'll find somewhere in the village to stay and everything will be all right. Nothing to worry about."

Nix barked.

"I know Mads said not to go to the village but what choice do we have? We need somewhere to stay before it gets Dark." Finding shelter was the only thing Bo was certain of. He would find somewhere safe from vengeful wolves and Shadow Creatures and then . . . and then . . . and then he'd work out what to do next later.

As the first hut loomed before them, Bo tugged at his hood —without Mads by his side he felt thankful for the oversized cloak and the protection it afforded him. The village was silent, window shutters and doors locked tight; only the wind played in the street.

A low growl of unease rumbled from Nix.

"I know," said Bo. He lifted his chin to the Light, high in the center of the sky. "Should be bursting with people by now. Maybe more have left than Galvin said . . ."

It wasn't until they had passed several rows of houses that Bo began to notice the scratches. Every wall and every door had been clawed by Shadow Creatures. It hadn't been like that yesterday. No wonder the villagers were leaving. Bo tried not to let Nix see him trembling.

"Stay clear of the shadows," said Bo just in case.

The first sign of life was the Innkeeper's dog, a raw-boned beast with russet fur, tied to a post outside the inn. Nix bristled.

"Easy," said Bo.

The dog jerked his head at the sound of Bo's voice. He was an ugly beast; half his left ear had been torn clean off, and his fangs stuck out even when his mouth was closed.

Bo edged back — "Nice dog, good dog" — but the dog charged, spitting saliva as he barked. Bo tripped over his own feet trying to run away and fell with a thud on his behind. Luckily, the chain pulled taut and the dog choked to a halt just out of reach.

"Serves you right," said Bo, climbing to his feet and dusting himself off.

The dog strained against the leash and barked.

"*Woof, woof,* yourself."

The door to the inn swung open and the flush-faced Innkeeper clomped outside. "Quit your racket, you useless beast," he snarled, failing to notice Bo.

The Innkeeper had a habit of chewing tar-bark, which he'd spit on the ground in sticky globules; it stained his teeth black. The strings of his grimy apron looped several times around his stout frame, and his thinning hair was slicked across his scalp in weedy, silver tendrils. His pockmarked skin was the color of a slapped pig's hind.

Bo shrank back, trying to stay out of view. But the Innkeeper finally caught sight of him. His cheeks puffed and he turned a deeper shade of red.

"You! Devil-child! Come to set more Shadow Creatures on us, have you?" He grabbed a broom and poked it at Bo.

Bo stumbled back, rucksack rattling. "What are you on about?"

"Why d'you think this whole village is locked up tight? There were hundreds of Shadow Creatures roaming the village last night, scratching at doors. Why, Lucky Karl lost all his pigs!"

Bo couldn't care less if Lucky Karl's pigs had grown beards and done a jig, but he bit his tongue. "Always Shadow Creatures about," he said, but he knew the Innkeeper was right: Bo had heard the Shadow Creatures himself and had seen the claw marks. Galvin's warnings made more and more sense.

"People are scared out of their wits and half of them are leaving, scurrying with their tails between their legs to the Un-King. Who am I going to sell my beer to now, hey? You've cost me my livelihood." The Innkeeper stomped to the edge of the porch. "Away with you and your curse. Back to your forest and that Devil-man you live with."

Nix pawed at the ground, growling.

Bo opened his mouth but no words came out; the words had scattered, hidden, vanished. Like Star-children.

A thick globule of tar-bark splattered at Bo's feet. "Where is your master, anyway?" sneered the Innkeeper. "I'll have him locked in the Fuglebur for letting his Devil-spawn run wild in our streets."

Bo sucked down his grief; it burned his throat raw. "Mads is dead," he said, eyes on the splatter at his feet. "A wolf got him."

The Innkeeper stumbled back, shoulder crashing into the doorframe. "D-did you say w-wolf?"

"And it's after me, too, so —"

"You brought a wolf *here*? To the village?"

"But it's Light," argued Bo. Nix edged in front of Bo's shins, baring his teeth at the Innkeeper. "A wolf can't —"

The Innkeeper wailed and swung the broom. "You've brought a curse on us!"

Bo ducked as the broom went *whoosh* over his head. The Innkeeper swung again and again until Nix charged at him, biting down on his calf.

The Innkeeper howled. "Get this beast off me! I'll have you strung up!" The Innkeeper shook his leg, trying to dislodge Nix. "I'll set my dog on you both!"

As if hearing his master's threat, the dog reared, straining against the chain with hunger in his eyes. The Innkeeper struck at Nix with the broom. "I'll get you, you Devil-creature!"

"Leave him alone!" Bo swung his rucksack. The heavy pack connected with the Innkeeper's chin and he tumbled backwards. Nix finally let go; blood stained the white fur around his mouth.

"Come on, Nix!" shouted Bo.

They turned and ran, the pearly white huts blurring as Bo and Nix sped down the street.

"Nowhere to run, Devil-child!" called the Innkeeper, struggling to his feet. "You've no Mads to save you now. I'll have you strung up in the Fuglebur — see if you can escape the Shadow Creatures then!"

Bo and Nix hurried through the winding streets, circling closer and closer to the center of the village and the market square. More shouts joined the Innkeeper's. They'd have the whole village after them soon. Not to mention the Innkeeper's dog.

And then Bo saw a hedge of sneezewort, thick and tall and dense. Mads grew the foul-smelling shrub around their hut: *Keeps all manner of beasts and nasties away,* he used to say.

"Quick," said Bo. "Behind here." He didn't know if sneezewort kept dogs away but it was the only chance he had.

Bo squeezed through a break in the hedge, grabbing a handful of the small white flowers as he did so. Behind the hedge was a narrow yard filled with junk. Bo scurried into the gap between a wood heap and a broken old cart. Nix squished in behind, the pair of them pressed tightly into the hidden corner. Bo rubbed the flowers all over his skin and clothes; Nix whimpered as Bo rubbed the flowers over his fur, too.

They froze as heavy boots pounded past the hedge, villagers shouting: *This way, that way. The Devil-child ran through here!* Legs flickered between the slats of wood; the Innkeeper's dog barked but didn't come close.

Bo wrapped his arms around Nix.

"I'm sorry," he whispered. "I didn't think it would be this

bad." He should have heeded Mads's warning, should have known he'd find no help in this village.

Nix licked Bo's forearm.

"When it's safe, we'll go. We'll find somewhere before Dark. I promise."

After the shouting died down, Bo crawled to the end of the heap, and through a gap he saw the market square; it was deserted.

"We'll spend the night in the stables," said Bo, squinting at the mishmash of huts on the other side of the square. "I don't think they'll find us there. We'll grab more sneezewort and wrap ourselves in it." Bo pointed. "We make a run for the fountain in the middle first. There? See?" To the right of the fountain, a pole stretched into the sky, and from the very top hung an iron cage, creaking and groaning in the breeze: the Fuglebur.

For prisoners, Mads had told him the first time Bo saw it. *Not little boys who live in forests.*

The cage was empty, as it had been every time Bo peeked at it on his way into market — Mads said Squall's End was too far from everywhere else to be worried about enemies. There was just a pile of rags littered on the floor of the cage, as far as Bo could see from where he was crouched.

"We hide behind the fountain wall," Bo said, "and when we're sure there's no one around, we cross to the stables. There, see?"

Bo edged out from his hiding place, heart in his throat. But no one came running; the square was empty. "Don't wait for me, Nix. Run to the fountain and don't stop."

Bo sprang to his feet and pushed off, arms pumping and head down as he made for the base of the fountain. Nix ran ahead, looking back to make sure Bo was still behind him.

Bo skidded to a halt at the fountain and crouched, Nix at his feet. They listened for footsteps, for barking, for the shouts of angry villagers.

Nothing.

"You ready, Nix?" he whispered. "We'll be safe as soon as we get inside the stables."

"I would not be so sure of that," said an unexpected voice.

A zap of fear shot through Bo as he swung around. But there was no one behind him. His heart beat wildly.

"Up here," said the voice.

Bo craned his neck and found a pair of beady black eyes looking down at him from the Fuglebur. The eyes were attached to a feathered head with a thick, curved beak poking between the bars of the cage. The disheveled creature wrapped two large hands around the bars and heaved herself upright.

Bo gasped.

It was a Korahku.

THE TRUE HISTORIES OF ULV, VOL. XII

THE IRIN-KORAHKU WAR

———⊱⋆⊰———

he Irin and Korahku's hatred for each other is not just because the Korahku think the Irin are a primitive, piglike people or because the Irin believe the Korahku to be Devil-worshiping bird-beasts. Oh no, it is much deeper than name-calling and superstition.

It all started with an egg.

Five hundred years ago, a convoy of Irin royalty visited the great sky nests of Korak to forge stronger ties between the two provinces. At the welcome feast, a Korahku delicacy was served: stunklopog. (This is the egg of a kroklops — a large, one-eyed dragon-worm — buried in soft, peaty earth until rotten, whence it is dug up, boiled, shelled, pickled, rolled in a crust of fish scales and salt, and then served at room temperature. It is, shall we say, an acquired taste.)

To turn down a plate of stunklopog is the highest insult in

Korahku custom, so when the Irin royal family refused to eat it on the grounds that it was "repulsive," they were swiftly and thoroughly beheaded.

Thus began the Irin-Korahku War, a war that rages to this day, and should an Irin and a Korahku come face-to-face, well... it's best they don't.

CHAPTER SIX

B O SHUFFLED BACK, heart pounding like an axe against wood as the part-bird, part-woman stared down at him. His mouth was dry, his tongue sluggish and unwieldy as he tried to say . . . well, he didn't know *what* to say.

"Ah well, I see you know what I am," said the Korahku, her beak poking through the bars.

Bo had never seen a Korahku before. He'd heard the villagers talk — *The head of a bird! The body of a person! Monstrous wings with feathers like knives! Clawed feet to gouge out your intestines! So unnaturally tall and long-limbed! An abomination! A Shadow Creature!* — but all he could see from his vantage point was the birdlike head with unblinking eyes, a beak that curved into a sharp point, and the lightly feathered hands gripping the bars. The rest of her — including her enormous wings — was hidden beneath the tattered blue robe Bo had mistaken for a pile of rags.

She dragged herself closer to the edge of the cage, bringing down a rainfall of mottled reddish-brown feathers. "But what sort of thing are you?"

Nix snapped at the flurry of feathers.

"Irin of course," said Bo.

"Of course, of course." The Korahku laughed, a hearty sound that almost — *almost* — hid the heavy way she slumped against the cage bars. "An entire village of superstitious oafs are quivering behind locked doors and you are playing hide-and-seek in the market square. So, I ask myself: What kind of Irin are you?"

Bo tugged at the hood obscuring his eyes. "The cursed kind," he muttered.

"*Tsk, tsk, tsk,*" said the Korahku. "But I suppose every great story begins with a curse."

Bo squinted at the Korahku. She didn't *seem* evil but Bo knew Korahku ate their children, sharpened their beaks with Irin bones, and worshiped the Dark. At least that was what the villagers said. Perhaps he should use the spirit charm Galvin sold him? He kept his hand close to his pocket.

Bo craned his neck, trying to get a better look at the creature. "What did you do?"

"Do?"

"To be locked up. Why are you a prisoner?"

The Korahku chuckled softly. "Does an Irin need a reason to lock up a Korahku?"

Bo shrugged. "I'm not supposed to talk to you anyway. Come on, Nix."

"Ah, very sensible," said the Korahku. "And, of course, *I* shouldn't be talking to *you*."

"What?" Bo frowned. "Why shouldn't you talk to me?"

"Do you mean to say those villagers and their dog are not searching for you? Oh yes." The Korahku laughed at Bo's wide eyes. "From up here, I have quite a view. I can see the whole village . . ."

Bo's chest tightened; beside him, Nix whimpered.

"It's a mistake is all." Bo glanced at the stables. If he ran now . . .

"I have a deal for you, little Irin," said the Korahku. "Release me and I will take you to safety."

Release? A *Korahku?*

Bo snorted. "I don't —"

"Come now, little Irin." The Korahku glanced to the east, to dangers Bo couldn't see. "How long until that dog sniffs you out?"

"I've got sneezewort." Bo pulled the white flowers from his pocket; they were already limp and half-dead in his palm.

"Ah yes, dogs do not like it — you are right there." The Korahku leaned forward. "But Irin do not care if it is sneezewort or lindberry beer you are smothered in. They will skin you alive either way."

Bo sucked in a deep, shaky breath. He knew the Korahku was right. And now that he was closer, the stables looked *huge* and he had only three candles — how would he ever Light such a space and keep the Shadow Creatures from gobbling him up like one of Lucky Karl's pigs?

"If this is a trick you're playing on me . . ."

"No trick."

Nix pressed his snout to Bo's calf.

"I know," murmured Bo. "But it's not just villagers I have to worry about, is it? You heard what the wolf said." *You cannot. Escape me . . .*

He squinted at the Light making its slow crawl across the sky. If he freed the Korahku, perhaps she would take Bo and Nix safely out of the village. But to where?

The Korahku's hands strained around the bars.

"Promise," said Bo. "Promise you'll take us somewhere safe and . . . promise you won't eat me."

The Korahku snapped her beak — *tsk!* She held out an open palm and sliced it with the tip of her pointed beak, cutting deep into the flesh. She yanked a feather from somewhere beneath her robe, dipped it in the pooling blood, and tossed it through the bars. It floated down into Bo's hands. "Blood bind," said the Korahku. "Cannot be broken."

Bo didn't know what a blood bind was but he shoved the feather deep in his pocket. It was surprisingly soft — a delicate plume of reddish brown with creamy white spots, not a sharp edge to be found. Weren't *all* Korahku feathers tipped with razor-sharp metal? Hadn't the villagers said so?

Bo shook his head. There was an Irin dog with his scent, a wolf that wanted revenge, Shadow Creatures rampaging, a forest that was dying, and no Mads to keep him safe. He didn't have a choice.

"What do I have to do?" said Bo.

∞

Bo pulled and yanked and tugged until his palms were raw, but the chain holding the Fuglebur aloft wouldn't budge.

"Pull," said the Korahku. "Are you pulling?"

Bo muttered bad words as he tried again.

"What is 'Skugs fud'?" asked the Korahku.

Bo let go, tears stinging his eyes. "Deal's off. I can't do it."

"Typical Irin," said the Korahku, snapping her beak. "Always complaining, thinking the world is against you. But are *you* in a cage?"

Bo grabbed the chain with both hands and pulled. *Yes,* he thought, *a cage of trees and wolves and curses and Darkness. Twelve years in a cage with invisible bars.*

Nix bit the cuff of Bo's trousers, dug in his feet, and pulled too.

"You are not even trying," said the Korahku.

Bo growled as he pulled so hard he thought his arms would

snap off. "Always someone to boss me about," he said through grinding teeth. "Always someone to tell me I'm wrong, that I'm not good enough." He heaved, eyes scrunched. "Always someone to laugh at me. Call me names. Spit at me . . ." Bo felt ready to be torn apart and then . . .

Click!

"I did it!" But as the catch snapped free, the chain ripped through Bo's hands and the cage came crashing down. It broke apart as it hit the ground, iron bars twanging as they clashed against the stones. The Korahku tumbled free, a rolling ball of feathers, arms, legs, and beak.

Bo blew on his stinging palms. "That hurt."

"Arrows hurt more," said the Korahku, climbing to her feet, rising and rising and . . . she was twice the height of Mads! Bo shrank back, legs wobbling, guts twisted with unease. Perhaps he had made a mistake . . .

"Arrows?" he asked.

The Korahku pointed to the far side of the square. Reluctantly, Bo wrenched his gaze away from the strange and terrifying creature in front of him to follow her outstretched arm and gasped when he saw a large group of villagers nearing the square. A *very* large group. Some had brooms and rocks; others gripped axes and bows and arrows.

"I do not know why they wanted you before," said the Korahku, "but now they want you for setting a prisoner free."

As the villagers reached the edge of the square, they raised their weapons with cries of *Devil-child! Traitor! Shadow Creature!* The Innkeeper's dog barked and reared, desperate to escape his leash.

"Can you run?" asked the Korahku.

Bo looked at the giant bird-creature beside him. It was clear she had seen better days: she was hunched and molting and frail-looking. "Can *you?*" asked Bo.

The Korahku tilted her head. "Let us see," she said.

And then she ran.

Bo and Nix ran too, followed by the roar of villagers, the howl of the Innkeeper's dog, and the clatter of weapons. Bo could outrun the villagers with their bellies full of lindberry beer and jellied pig's trotters. But the Innkeeper's dog . . .

"This way." The Korahku veered right. Bo glimpsed the dog racing out in front of the pack before he rounded the corner.

They hurried up a steep path, huts too close on either side. Nix ran out front, looking behind again and again to make sure Bo was close.

He was.

But so was the Innkeeper's dog.

A searing pain shot up Bo's calf as the dog sank his fangs into his flesh. Bo howled as he flew forward, crashing to the ground.

His ears rang from the fall as he struggled to shake his leg free. But the beast had locked his jaws, fangs cutting deep.

Something flew overhead, colliding with the Innkeeper's dog, sending him tumbling down the hill with a high-pitched yelp. Bo gasped for breath, winded with worry — had Nix jumped in to defend him? He was no match for the Innkeeper's dog!

Bo struggled to sitting as a familiar wet nose pressed against his neck. "Nix? But you're —" Bo looked up and saw the Korahku crouched in a battle pose between Bo and the dog. She had saved him!

The Innkeeper's dog scrambled to his feet, baring his teeth with a growl.

"Silly beast," said the Korahku, flicking the corners of her robe behind her. "You think you can scare me?"

The dog gnashed his teeth and then sprang into the air, but the Korahku kicked out, landing a swift, hard blow to the dog's belly, enough to send him flying through the air again, and he landed with a thud and a whimper. Scrambling to his feet, the dog cowered, taking one look at the Korahku before scurrying away on unsteady legs.

"Quick. We must keep moving," said the Korahku, hauling Bo to his feet.

The villagers appeared at the bottom of the hill, waving their weapons and shouting. The Innkeeper jostled to the front and howled at the sight of his limping dog. "What have you done? I'll have your fox for dinner, Devil-child!"

Bo, Nix, and the Korahku turned and ran as fast as they could, shouts and curses growing louder behind them. Each time Bo planted his right foot, searing pain shot through his leg.

"The forest," said the Korahku, pointing up the hill. This was a side of the village Bo had never seen before — it was all new and curious. "We'll be safe in there."

Bo looked over his shoulder at the village mob: so close. He turned back to the strange glimmer of forest at the top of the hill. Far, far away and so very unfamiliar. Fear gripped his stomach, an icy iron claw.

There was no way they could possibly make it.

CHAPTER SEVEN

THE FOREST LOOMED AHEAD. Bo ran as fast as he could, though every step was agony, a lightning bolt of pain shooting up his leg. But when Bo took a hurried look over his shoulder, he saw that the villagers had stumbled to a standstill halfway up the hill.

"Go back, go back!" the Innkeeper was shouting, waving his arms. "They're leading us into the Forest of Tid! It's a trap!"

The villagers threw their weapons to the ground, a clatter of steel, wood, and iron. Bo ran on.

When the three of them were finally enveloped by the deathly quiet of the forest, Bo glimpsed the tangle of bronze, gold, and silver tree trunks as he rushed by. The air left a bitter, metallic sting on his tongue and the fallen leaves pinged, high and tinny, as Bo ran through them. The strangeness of it all made his head spin. Or perhaps that was because of the blood he felt trickling down his calf and into his shoe . . .

"Stop," panted Bo, throwing down his rucksack and shaking

off his cloak. He keeled over, pushing Nix away as his breakfast splattered over his toes.

Wiping his mouth clean, Bo crawled to the nearest tree and slumped to the ground with his back against the trunk, heart battering against his rib cage.

"You are hurt," said the Korahku, doubling back to crouch in front of him. Nix growled quietly as she inspected Bo's leg.

"Why aren't they following us?" panted Bo. He blinked slowly, trying to clear his woozy head: instead of rough, woody trunks, the trees were smooth like metal and glistened in the mottled Light. Was he seeing things? He had never been to the east side of Squall's End before, never known an entirely different forest from his own hugged the edge of the village.

"Lindberry, heldung, longthor leaf, and nokki paste," muttered the Korahku, reaching into the folds of her robe. Underneath she wore a tunic and fitted trousers. She pulled out a small leather pouch. "Does your creature understand words?"

Bo shrugged. "Seems to. The villagers think it's because he's a Shadow Creature but he's just always seemed to understand me. We understand each other."

With the end of a feather plucked from somewhere under her robe, the Korahku drew a shape in the dirt, a leaf with five sharp points. "Are you listening to me, strange little dog? I need longthor leaf for his calf. Looks like this." She jabbed at the dirt drawing. "Comes from a tree no bigger than your Irin friend here and just as scrawny. The color of half-Light in the Burning Season. Go!"

Nix sprinted off, his gold-red fur vanishing into the tangle of metal trees.

Bo tugged at the neck of his shirt. Despite the icy chill, the lack of a breeze was stifling, making the air feel thick and syrupy. "I asked you a question," he said. He dared not look as the Korahku gently rolled up his trouser leg. "Why didn't the villagers follow us?"

The Korahku mixed a foul-smelling paste from the berries, leaves, and potions in her pouch. She laughed. "You Irin. Scared of everything." She waved a hand at the trees. "This is the Forest of Tid. Your friends think it is haunted. Ha!"

"Not *my* friends." Bo cursed and balled his hands into fists, clenching his teeth as the Korahku slathered the paste on his calf.

"I think," said the Korahku, "that this 'Skugs fud' you speak of is not nice." She laughed all the same and Bo found he liked the sound — deep and rough and warm.

His brows drew together as he watched her work. She could have left him to be torn apart by the villagers and their dog but hadn't. And now she was carefully tending to his injured leg. Bo let out a long, shuddering breath — his fists unclenched and the knot of worry in his chest began to untangle itself.

Perhaps I will be safe after all, he thought.

"But why do the villagers think it's haunted?" he asked.

"You ask many questions, child. But I have one for you: How does an Irin boy know nothing of the Forest of Tid? Do not you live a hen's peck from here?"

Bo frowned. "Yes, but . . ." The paste was already soothing his pain. "The villagers think I struck a deal with the Shadow Creatures because I was left in the forest as a baby and didn't die. They think I cursed the land even though there's been Dark and Shadow Creatures long before I was born. Bunch of trollheads. And my guardian, Mads, never told me about the Forest of Tid —I didn't even know there was more than one forest here. He told me about cutting down trees and how to jelly pig's trotters. That's it. We never left our forest much—just into the village and back again to sell wood at market."

The Korahku laughed as she packed her things away. "But you never asked? You walked from forest to village and village to forest time and again and you never say, 'What is over *there?*'"

"At least I know the difference between a fox and a dog," snapped Bo. The truth was he *did* ask questions. Mads just never answered them.

The Korahku considered him with unblinking eyes. With a sigh, she picked up her feather and drew more patterns in the dirt. "Listen, because I only do this once, yes?"

Bo watched as she drew a map, an island shaped like a wolf's head—if you squinted. All throughout were villages, forests, mountains, lakes, and even a castle right where the wolf's eye would be.

"This is the land of Ulv," she said, retracing the outer edge of the island. "And this speck in the southwest here is your village. Your home is here." The Korahku jabbed northwest of the village. "The Forest of Long Shadows."

Bo didn't admit he never knew his forest had a name. All he knew was that the villagers thought it was where Shadow Creatures came from.

"East of Squall's End is the Forest of Tid." The Korahku jabbed the dirt. "Us. Right here. More Irin villages here, here, here, and here. Irin Un-Royal City is here." She stabbed the earth where she had drawn a monstrous-looking tree on top of a hill, its multitude of branches reaching for the sky like waving arms. "There, you will find your Un-King."

Un-King?

"And all the way over here is Korak, where the Korahku live." She pointed to the opposite side of the island, jutting out her beak, haughty and proud. "Seven provinces in total. Nev'en." She jabbed her finger in the center of the drawing. "And Lahesi. And Qirachi. And Rakoo. And Maledian." *Jab, jab, jab, jab* . . . The unfamiliar words bounced awkwardly around Bo's head, refusing to make sense. "The Seven Great Kin of Ulv."

"The Seven Great *what?*"

The Korahku glared at him with beady black eyes. She sighed. "They really never told you anything, did they?"

Bo's cheeks flushed — anger or embarrassment or both.

"Long ago there were two kin: the Elfvor and the Ulvians. Many years and conflicts and borders later, there are seven, but they are all related to one or both of the original two."

"But who were the Elfvor and the Ulvians?"

"Ulvians were ordinary folk and Elfvor were . . . not."

"What does that mean?"

The Korahku waved away Bo's query with a sharp flick of her hand. "I thought you did not ask questions but you ask *too* many."

"But what's that?" Bo pointed to the castle.

The Korahku sighed. "Aud. The Sovereign State. Queen of Ulv lives there."

"Queen? You said there was an Un-King."

"The Queen of Ulv rules all," she said. "But each province has its own ruler, who answers to her. Some are royal families, some are not. Irin had a royal family until my people beheaded them."

Bo spluttered with shock. "You *killed* the entire Irin royal family?"

The Korahku's shoulders stiffened. "Not me personally."

Bo shivered, folding his arms across his chest. Perhaps he wasn't so safe after all . . . "But what's an Un-King?"

The Korahku clicked her beak. "After the noble Korahku re-lieved your royal family of their heads, no one wanted to take their place because Irin are a superstitious people. So they de-cide it is safest to be ruled by a king who isn't a king — no crown, no throne, no glittering gold. The *Un*-King. *Very* silly business."

Bo frowned at the map. So much he did not know. He pointed to a cluster of squiggly lines in the middle of the Forest of Tid. "And that?"

The Korahku shook her head. "You don't want to end up there. Myling Mist — very bad place. We must walk around it."

Bo stared at the map. How had he spent twelve years in such a tiny corner of this land? Why hadn't Mads told him any of this?

"It's so . . . big," he said.

The Korahku laughed, deep and from the belly. "You are small, so everything looks big to you. Ulv is not big. Only a week's walk to cross from one side to the other. To fly is even quicker."

Bo scowled. "I'm normal-sized. *You're* abnormally tall." He huffed. *Why isn't there a flutter of wind in this silly forest?* he wondered. It was like being smothered in an icy cold blanket. "What I was *trying* to say," he continued, "was that this land is much bigger than I thought, bigger than my forest anyway. So how on Ulv did Mads think I'd be able to find the Stars among all *this?*" He waved a hand at the Korahku's drawing.

The Korahku grew stiff, pulling her shoulders back and cocking her head to the side. "Stars?"

Bo launched into his tale of Mads's death, the giant wolf chasing him, and his guardian's last words: for Bo to find and release the Stars. He shifted under the weight of the Korahku's narrow-eyed stare. "It's not as if I want to find them but now that I have nowhere else to go, perhaps it's —"

"A load of cluckity muck. Stars! *Tsk!*" The Korahku jabbed the feather into the dirt, at the base of a mountain west of a large inland sea. "Here is the Temple of the Silent Sisters, carved into the face of Lunaris Mountain, on the shores of the Sea of Widow's Tears. That is where we shall go. They will take you in and look after you, and I can return to my flock."

Suddenly it was hard for Bo to breathe—the knot in his chest constricted, a gnarled tangle of anxiety, hurt, grief. The Korahku was just going to *dump* him? On the doorstep of some temple? With people he did not know and who might be just as hateful as the villagers? He gripped the hem of his shirt until his knuckles were white.

"But—"

"Pish! We go this way." The Korahku raked the feather through the dirt, from the Forest of Tid to the Temple of the Silent Sisters. "Only three days' walk."

Bo couldn't believe his ears. He wanted to protest but all his words were suddenly too slippery to catch.

"I am sorry, child," said the Korahku, "but I cannot take you with me. If an Irin was caught on Korahku land, you would be fed to the kroklops, where you would slowly rot in the acid of its stomach. A more honorable death than the Fuglebur but unpleasant all the same."

Bo folded his arms across his chest, a stinging heat bubbling in his veins. It wasn't that he *wanted* to go to Korak, but to be cast aside yet again, like the runt of the litter that nobody wanted, was . . .

But what choice did he have? It was that or chase the Stars, which sounded impossible *and* dangerous.

Bo swallowed the lump in his throat. "If you think it's best," he mumbled. His shoulders slumped under the weight of all his troubles. "I'll go."

The Korahku nodded sharply before turning away. "It is for the best," she said.

Nix burst into the clearing and skidded to a halt, dumping a mouthful of leaves at the Korahku's feet. He waited, tongue flopped out the side of his mouth. But the Korahku said nothing as she wrapped Bo's calf with the leaves.

Bo gave Nix a scratch behind the ears.

"You are fixed, little Irin," said the Korahku.

Bo grabbed his bag and cloak and stood, easily putting weight on his injured leg. He looked up at the Korahku — strange how his "enemy" was the one saving him. Even if she was going to dump him the first chance she got.

"My name is Bo," he said, holding out his hand. "And he's Nix."

"I am named Tamira but you may call me Tam," said the Korahku, frowning at Bo's outstretched hand. "Do you have something for me?"

"What? No. You shake it. It's how you greet people."

Tam picked up Bo's hand by the wrist and jiggled it. "Like this?"

"Ah no. I mean, sort of."

Tam dropped Bo's hand. "Such peculiar habits you Irin have."

They set off through the forest. Shadows rippled and soft slivers of Light bounced off the metallic tree trunks, stinging Bo's eyes. He rapped his knuckles against one of the trunks — *ping!* Bo jerked back. "Are you sure this place isn't haunted?"

The Korahku chuckled. "You Irin. You think *everything* is haunted. When I was locked in that Fuglebur, I overheard a group of villagers discussing whether or not a goat was cursed because it had eaten the Innkeeper's rosebush. It took them three hours of argument to decide it was cursed. Poor goat."

"But there *are* witches," said Bo, thinking back to what Mads had said to the wolf, and what Galvin had said too. "I heard something about a Shadow Witch. Maybe she lives here." Bo kept his eyes low, stepping only in patches of Light. Just in case.

The Korahku clicked her beak. "So you know *some* things about the world, then."

"Do you know any witches?" asked Bo. "Why were you in the Fuglebur? How come your flock didn't rescue you? What do you know about Stars?"

Tam looked over her shoulder, large beady eyes narrowed. "I promised to take you to safety, *not* to answer one hundred and one questions."

As Bo passed a tree, it let out a long, low *ping*. He hadn't touched it! "Did you hear that?"

"I heard you asking more questions."

Bo scowled at the tree, daring it to make another noise. "I know what I heard."

Tam hurried on. "Typical Irin. Always with ghosts and ghouls."

But the *ping* rang out again, louder now; this time more trees joined in, creating a chorus. The Korahku swung around.

"See?" said Bo.

Tam and Bo stared at each other. Nix pricked his ears and whined.

"Perhaps," said Tam, "we should —"

The forest burst into a cacophony of earsplitting noise. *Ping, ping, pong, PING!*

The noise came from every corner of the forest, rattling Bo to his core. He covered his ears and crouched, Nix trembling by his feet.

Just when Bo could stand no more, the tree trunks split open and out flew hundreds — *thousands* — of tiny metallic creatures. Bo ducked and the creatures whooshed past his head, screeching and trilling as they swooped through the air.

"What is this?" he shouted.

Tam was huddled too, swatting at the sea of flying creatures buzzing by her. Birds, butterflies, dragonflies, moths, and bats — gold, silver, and bronze — all of them glinting and shining in the Light.

As the flurry finally began to settle, a small golden bird landed on Bo's leg. It hopped across the round of his knee, its little wings fluttering as it chirruped. It was made of gold, with tiny cogs and wheels whirring as it moved. *Tick, tick, clickety, click,* the bird whirred as it hopped along Bo's thigh, cocking its head inquisitively. Bo spluttered with wild, unexpected laughter. "They're . . . they're beautiful!"

"They are pests," said Tam, swatting a dragonfly buzzing by her face.

"They're amazing," whispered Bo. The little bird playfully nipped the back of his hand. "I can't believe I've never been here." Why *hadn't* Mads taken him to this place? It was merely on the other side of the village! His shoulders curled forward — he felt small, head full of fuzzy gray nothingness where things like golden birds and Un-Kings and temples and mists should be.

Tam scowled. "It should not be like this," she said. Her face was like thunder but her voice cracked with unease. "It should be dormant."

"Why?"

"Stop asking questions," grumbled Tam. She batted away a silver bird and stood. "We must keep walking. We need to find shelter before Dark." She turned and marched off.

Bo sighed and stood too. The little bird took flight, and he watched it *flap, flap, flap* high into the canopy, sending a scattering of leaves falling, bouncing off Bo's face and into his outstretched hand. He laughed until he noticed that several of the captured leaves were black and curled at the edges. Bo poked one lightly and gasped as it disintegrated into ash and slipped between his fingers, floating to the ground.

He brushed his hands and looked around. It didn't appear as if many other leaves had turned black. Perhaps this forest was just like that; perhaps some of its leaves often turned to ash. It didn't *have* to be the same thing as the gnarled old tree from his forest . . .

Bo shook his head. *No.* This forest was beautiful — it was *not* dying. It was full of life and strange, shiny creatures and trees that pinged. He had never witnessed anything so . . .

Magical.

THE TRUE HISTORIES OF ULV, VOL. I

ON THE STRANGE BEHAVIOR OF MAGIC

———

It used to be that magic was *everywhere*. In the trees, in the wind, in the flapping of a butterfly's wings. It was even found in bittersprouts, just like the ones you scraped off your plate and into the dog's bowl last night when your mother wasn't looking. (*She* wasn't looking, but *I* was — eat your bittersprouts or else.)

Mostly, however, magic was in the Stars.

Do you know how this world came to be? First, there was the sky and the Stars and the Moon. The Moon granted each Star a wish. The Stars wanted something interesting to gaze upon, so they wished for mountains and rivers and trees, and then they wished for people and animals and insects. Look around you now — everything you see was wished into existence by a Star! And each wish left behind a little sprinkle of magic.

But just as magic was found in the wind and the trees and

the wings of a butterfly, it was also found in lies and hatred and prejudice and all manner of nasty things. I did say magic was *everywhere*, didn't I? But those wonderful, *wonderful* Stars made sure there was always an abundance of good magic to keep the nasty magic a mere trickle.

Alas, when the Stars vanished (horrid business involving a wolf and a witch and a lust for revenge — for more, see *The True Histories of Ulv*, Vol. III, "The Origin of the Dark"), most of the goodness in magic vanished, leaving behind a creeping, malignant, evil kind of magic that knitted together to form violent, monstrous creatures made entirely of shadows and fear. They fed on the Dark, growing stronger and bolder and deadlier until a very smart witch or wizard decided to collect every remaining trace of magic and lock it away — this stopped the Shadow Creatures from growing stronger but did not vanquish them. And of course it meant there was no more magic in the world, not even in your bittersprouts (but they are still frightfully good for you, so eat up!).

Thus, many Shadow Creatures remained to torment us at nighttime, and all magical places became dormant, such as the Forest of Tid (it's made of clockwork magic — such fun!). At least the loss of magic meant the ghosts haunting the Myling Mist were suddenly too weak to get up to their old tricks (and by "old tricks" I mean "devouring those unfortunate enough to wander into the mist").

So you might wonder: *What would happen if magic returned?*

Oh, it would be brilliant! Wonderful! Magnificent!

Assuming, of course, the lock isn't broken *before* the Stars return, releasing mostly evil magic. If *that* happened . . . well, it's best not to think about it.

CHAPTER EIGHT

THEY WALKED FOR MILES and all the while Bo could not keep his eyes from wandering to gaze with awe at the creatures fluttering around him. He was so enraptured he hardly noticed that his chest had begun to feel hot. He paused to look down, letting Tam and Nix walk ahead.

Bo clutched his chest over his shirt and sure enough it was uncomfortably warm. He scrunched up his nose as he stretched out the neck of his shirt, peering down. "What on Ulv?"

"Keep up," called Tam, somewhere ahead. Bo could no longer see her, just rows and rows of metallic trees.

He hurried along, still with his eyes down. It seemed as though Mads's crystal pendant was the culprit — why would it have begun to burn? And *how*?

As Bo reached down his top to grip the pendant for inspection, he was suddenly yanked to the side. He lurched, arms swinging, grasping for something — anything — to hold on to.

He steadied himself against a tree and looked down: a small tendril of mist had curled around his calf.

"What on —"

A second tendril joined the first, wrapping around Bo's other calf. He tripped and stumbled toward a steep embankment. His foot caught on the edge, and he rolled his ankle on the uneven ground. He stumbled, unable to right himself before he was falling.

He tumbled.

Down and down and down.

Bo landed, battered and bruised, flat on his back in something wet and sticky, rucksack digging into his spine. He opened his eyes and saw a blinding gray mist swirling around him, thick and impenetrable.

"Nix?" he called. "Tam?"

His head spun as he stood — he hardly knew which way was up. He waited for an answer but there was silence. Suffocating silence.

With arms outstretched, Bo felt his way forward. The pendant around his neck was still burning but he couldn't focus on that now. The mist licked and suckled on his fingers, and he found no embankment to climb back up. He wondered if he was heading in the right direction; maybe he had been turned around in the fall. So he turned again — it was hard to tell how far — and headed back the way he'd come. The mist grew thicker.

Mist . . . The word throbbed in Bo's head.

Suddenly, the truth clipped Bo around the ear: he was in the Myling Mist, the place Tam said he definitely did *not* want to visit. But how? They were supposed to walk around it. And what *was* this place?

Bo spun as he heard a giggle behind him.

"Hello?" he called.

Silence answered him.

The mist was so thick that breathing felt like an icy, swollen fist being forced down his throat. He wished he could see something, *anything*.

Bo pushed forward until a cold object clipped his arm. Was that another noise? Yes! Laughter. Light, childish . . .

And close.

Bo waved his hands, trying to part the mist. "Who's there?"

An icy hand clasped his arm, spinning him in a full circle. He fell — *thump!*

"Show yourself!" cried Bo, scrambling upright again. The sound of his own rasping breath pounded in his ears as he waved his hands again and again. But the mist was only growing thicker, wrapping around Bo's skin, damp and suffocating.

Cold hands closed around his ankles as his feet were swept out from under him, and he fell — *splat!* He groaned as he lay in the sludge. Peals of laughter tinkled around him.

"Come play with us," said a child's voice, wet against his ear. "You can hide and we'll seek."

Bo stood, his heart beating wildly. "Who's there?" he called. His voice cracked. He reached into his pocket and drew out the spirit charm Galvin had sold him, squeezing it tightly in his clammy fist.

The mist swirled. It spiraled, faster and faster, then broke into one, two, four, eight whirlwinds! Each whirlwind settled into the shape of a child, formed entirely of the gray mist. What were they? Ghosts?

The fog behind them was softer now, see-through like a scrim of gauze behind which loomed hazy, shadowy shapes that could be trees or people or houses or perhaps they could be Shadow Creatures . . . The hair on Bo's arms stood on end.

"What — what are you?" he stammered.

"We're your friends," the mist-children chorused.

He was surrounded. They grabbed his cloak, his hair, his arms, begging him to play. Bo's knees wobbled.

"Let's play Wolf and Stars," said one mist-child. "You'll be the wolf and we'll be the Stars. But you're not going to eat us. We're going to eat *you*."

The mist-children opened their mouths, revealing rows of razor-sharp fangs. Bo threw the spirit charm to the ground: the glass broke and a puff of green smoke mushroomed in the air, stinking like old socks and rotted meat. He coughed into his fist, crying out: "Be gone! Be gone! Be gone!"

Nothing happened.

The mist-children moved closer, reaching for him. Had he done it wrong? Why wasn't it working? Bo flung his arms over his head with a sob of fear.

A deafening *whoosh* ripped through the mist, and the children were shot screaming through the air, sucked into nothingness. Shivering with fear, Bo lowered his arms and saw the mist had all but vanished and he was ankle-deep in a desolate wasteland. Nothing but swampy mush and blackened, clawlike trees as far as he could see.

Then in front of him appeared a Light, bobbing in the air. Bo watched, frozen, as the Light transformed into a floating glob of liquid silver, which then slowly poured itself into the shape of a tall man, a *familiar* tall man . . .

"Mads?" Bo stumbled backwards. "But you're . . . ?"

"Don't be afraid, little one," said the silvery apparition in a wispy, floaty voice. The apparition rippled as it drifted toward Bo. "I'm not here to harm you."

Every nerve ending in Bo's body prickled with fear. Because Bo *knew* Mads was dead; he had seen him die. So this . . . *creature* . . . couldn't be his guardian. It *looked* like Mads—a see-through, silvery, shimmery version of Mads. But it couldn't be him . . . could it?

"What are you?" said Bo, inching away. His eyes darted, but every direction looked the same — no embankment, no way out as far as Bo could see. "Are y-y-you . . . a ghost? Is that what those children were?"

The apparition looked down, inspecting its arms and hands and fingers. "Perhaps," it said. "I am here, but I am not. Not yet. Not fully." It radiated so much heat that beads of sweat dribbled between Bo's shoulder blades. The center of his chest burned — a ball of fire directly over his heart. Was it the pendant still?

"What are you doing here?" Bo asked.

"Magic is returning," said ghost-Mads. "The lock was broken and magic is seeping through. It gives me the strength to return too."

There was a flutter in Bo's belly. This time it wasn't fear — it was hope.

"You're coming back? For good?" Bo licked his lips. "Because the Shadow Creatures have been running wild and Galvin said it was because of the Shadow Witch and everybody's leaving the village and I think the forest is dying and the Innkeeper chased me out of town because I met a Korahku and she says I have to go to the Sisters to be safe, so I'm sorry but I can't look for the Stars — I *can't* — not on my own."

Bo could see through the shimmery apparition to the swamp and the claw-trees and the bleakness beyond. The ghost of Mads looked so temporary, so fragile, so vulnerable. Like a flame — all you needed was a puff of wind and it would be snuffed out.

"But you *must* find the Stars," said ghost-Mads. "I need Star-magic to be powerful enough to return. Don't you want me to come back?"

"But you said magic was already returning. Why do you need me?"

Ghost-Mads flickered, like a candle dancing in the wind. "Without the Stars, magic is wild, untamed, a tangle of chaotic forces at war with one another — it makes magic so much easier to corrupt. Why do you think the Shadow Creatures are growing in strength? They feed off this chaos and only the return of the Stars can stop them. Soon, they will be strong enough to hunt in the Light. Do you want that?"

"But you said Stars were a myth! You said . . . you said . . ." Bo stopped, breathing deeply, trying to untangle his tongue. "I don't know *anything* about the world," he said finally. "Why did you never tell me anything?"

The ghost knelt, placing a warm hand on Bo's arm. Bo startled at the unexpected softness.

"There was a wolf," explained ghost-Mads, "a greedy, magical wolf who climbed into the sky and ate the Stars because he wanted their power all for himself. He was captured by a wizard, who worried that the wolf had proven how easy it was to steal the Stars. So he hid the wolf in a cage far, far away where no one could find him and use the Stars for their own selfish needs.

"But that was a mistake, you see? Because without the Stars to maintain a good balance, magic was corrupt. *All* magic had to be locked away to save the land from being overrun with Shadow Creatures. But the lock broke and now magic is returning. Except, without the Stars, there is no balance again. So much evil magic is coming." Mads tightened his fingers around Bo's arm. "There are three keys needed to open the wolf's cage. Find the keys and then find the cage."

Bo pulled at his shirt uncomfortably. His chest still burned — why was the pendant so hot?

"You said something about a witch before you . . . a Shadow Witch who was after the Stars. It was her that broke the lock, wasn't it? And —"

Mads squeezed tighter. "Listen to me, child! Magic is returning but the Shadow Creatures are feeding off it and growing stronger. We need the Stars to defeat them once and for all. You will be a hero!"

Uncertainty prickled at the bottom of Bo's belly. The land was so big and he knew *nothing*. And who would help him? Tam couldn't wait to get rid of him, and the villagers wanted to feed him to the Innkeeper's dog. He was nothing. No one.

Mads pulled him close and placed his palm against Bo's

forehead. Suddenly, Bo could see himself running through his forest home, laughing and carefree. He ran, weaving through the trees and jumping over fallen logs, until he saw her.

His mother.

He knew it was his mother even though they had never met. Not really. He could feel it, deep in his heart, deep in the part of him he kept hidden, the part that ached with need and loneliness. His mother's face was hazy but he knew she was smiling as she knelt and opened her arms wide. Bo ran into her embrace with such force that they both fell over, giggling and giddy and holding each other tight. "I've missed you so much," his mother told him. And Bo believed her. Because this was how things *could* be; with a wish, Bo would finally have a mother who wanted him.

Mads withdrew his hand and the vision was gone. Bo felt heavy with the loss; never had something tugged so tightly on his heart. All those years of longing to know her, to run into her welcoming arms, to have what every other child in the village had . . .

"The Stars will give you what you crave," said Mads. He was beginning to flicker in and out of focus. "Any wish will be granted."

The hairs rose on Bo's arms and nape. His fingers ached with the need to reach out and touch the vision Mads had shown him. He wanted it *so* much.

A shadow passed over Mads's face, twisting his features from soft to hard. He shot out a hand and gripped the leather strap of Bo's necklace, pulling it out from under his shirt.

Bo whimpered as he was jerked forward, the strap cutting into his skin as Mads examined the necklace closely. "You gave it to me," explained Bo. "Before you . . . I thought you wanted me to have it. I'm sorry. I'll give it back. I'm—"

Mads shook his head. "There are words," he said. "Ancient Ulvish carved into the leather. See? 'The first shall be found with the king who has no crown.'"

Bo squirmed, trying to wriggle free of Mads's grasp. "A riddle? You said—you were talking about the keys and you said something about a riddle leading me to them and—"

"Yes!" cried Mads, the shadow finally clearing from his face. "Yes, I did, didn't I?" He let the necklace drop; Bo's hands flung to his neck, and he pressed the cool of his palms where the leather had rubbed his skin raw. His eyes pricked with tears but he said nothing. He did not understand what had just happened, but it sat like a cold lump of pond scum in the pool of his belly.

Mads turned his keen gaze on Bo, clamping his hand on Bo's shoulder. Bo hissed as the old man's fingers dug into the flesh—he was a ghost! How was that possible? "The answer is where you will find the first key," said Mads, excitement carrying his voice loud and raw-edged through the marsh.

"But what does the riddle mean?" asked Bo.

Mads flickered, his edges fading; the hand on Bo's shoulder was little more than a wisp of silver mist. "Curse the Moon," he snapped. "Not enough magic to sustain me." He bent close; when Bo huffed out a breath, parts of Mads floated away. "Solve the riddle and find the first key," Mads implored, but his voice was weak.

Bo tried to grab Mads's hand as the old man was suddenly turned from mist to liquid silver, then sucked back into a ball of Light, which hovered in the air in front of Bo.

"Wait!" he cried. "Mads! Please! You can't go."

But the suffocating mist was returning.

Bo coughed and spluttered — the mist was filling his lungs and he couldn't breathe. And the heat! Why was there still a ball of heat against his chest? Bo gripped Mads's crystal pendant. It was on fire!

"Don't go!" cried Bo. "Don't leave me!"

But the Light flickered once, twice, three times, and then it was gone.

Bo stumbled back, gasping for air. "Help me," he wheezed.

And then he fell.

Bo braced himself for the impact that didn't come. He just fell and fell and fell. Where was the ground? The world grew Dark, and the last thing he heard was a light peal of laughter and somewhere, in the distance, a wolf's howl.

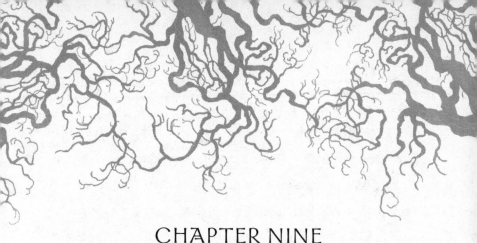

CHAPTER NINE

LAUGHTER ECHOED IN BO'S EARS as he woke, lying in the dirt with no idea why his head ached. A cold, wet nose pressed against his cheek, followed by a familiar bark.

"Careful, Nix," said Bo, gently pushing the fox away as he sat up. "You'll lick me to death."

Rubbing his tired eyes, Bo glanced around: behind him the Forest of Tid shimmered gold, copper, and silver, and in front, fields of green stretched for miles. His brow wrinkled; the last thing he remembered was falling through the mist, so how could—

"Come eat," said a curt voice.

Bo swung around and saw Tam sitting on a rock, stoking a fire. A rabbit sizzled in the flames, skewered on a branch. Bo's cloak was neatly folded on the ground, his rucksack resting on top of it.

"How did you find me?" Bo hobbled over and sat cross-legged

in front of the sparking fire. The smell of roast meat made his mouth water. "I was in the mist and —"

The Korahku's eyes shone with mirth. "I bound myself to protect you, remember?" She carved sinewy strips from the rabbit's carcass and tossed a handful into Bo's lap. "But it was Nix who found you." Tam jutted her beak at the fox, whose golden eyes had locked onto the meat in Bo's lap. "But not in the mist. Here. On the edge of Tid. A little Irin like you would never survive the mist."

Bo shook his head as the memories came flooding back at once. "No, I *was* in the mist and there were ghost-children and ghost-Mads told me about the wolf who ate the Stars and how the Dark can be destroyed. All I need to do is figure out the riddle and —"

"Nonsense, child. You simply hit your head and wandered off for a moment. You must have been dazed." Tam flung a chunk of meat into the air, caught it in her beak, and jerked it down. "You need to watch where you are going and you need to forget this silly business with the Stars. We go to the Silent Sisters and that is final."

Bo winced, all his hopes for finding the Stars vanishing with a *whoosh* like the ghost-children being sucked into nothingness. He reached around and felt the back of his head: there *was* a lump there — had he dreamed it all? He gave half his meat to

Nix and ate the rest, frowning to himself. *No.* It had been real. It had been *real.*

He was certain he had fallen into the mist.

He remembered everything Mads told him.

He remembered the riddle and the cage and the wolf and the Stars.

And if he tried very, *very* hard, he remembered how it felt to be held in his mother's arms, even though it was only a vision. And there was nothing he wanted more than to feel that warmth again.

To feel it for real.

Tam kicked dirt over the fire, extinguishing the flames, and stood. "I have been around a long time, so perhaps you should believe what *I* have to say over a ghost you dreamed up. Now we leave, yes? Or do you wish to be gobbled up by Shadow Creatures?" She marched away, not even checking that Bo was following.

It was clear.

Tam may have saved him from the Innkeeper's dog and looked for him when he was lost in the mist, but she wasn't Bo's friend; she was just someone else who didn't want him around.

Bo packed up his things and hurried after the Korahku. "Come on, Nix," he said.

They hiked for miles, keeping away from the main roads and

the Irin soldiers who patrolled them. It was a cloudless day, the air warm and spicy with the end of the Burning Season; soon, it was hot enough for Bo to remove his cloak and tuck it into his rucksack. In the distance, the grassy plains swept into undulating hills — it was going to be a long, hard walk.

"Wouldn't it be quicker to fly?" he asked.

Tam strode ahead.

Silence.

"Guess not," said Bo.

He hitched his rucksack over his shoulder, stumbling through the unfamiliar grass — it was long and sharp and made his nose itch.

He never thought he'd miss the forest — the shadows, the crunchy mulch underfoot, the fir trees, and air so cold Bo swore it had teeth to bite him. But he missed it so much he ached.

If he was brave enough and if he was smart enough, he would find the Stars, and Mads would come back and Bo could wish for his mother and it would all be worth it. He would return to his forest a hero — perhaps the village children would invite him to play with them. Everything could go back to the way it was, only better. And no one would leave him again.

He dawdled, letting Tam march out front so he could discuss the riddle with Nix.

"The first shall be found with the king who has no crown,"

recited Bo, an idea already tickling the back of his mind. There was something he had heard . . . "What do you think it means?"

Nix barked.

"There is so. Well, actually there's a *queen* of Ulv — Tam said so — but there *is* a king of Irin, too. Or, no. It was an *Un*-King because no one wanted to be beheaded and *oh* —" Bo pulled up short, face alight. "The Un-King doesn't have a crown. That's what Tam said. Could he have the first key?"

Nix nipped at Bo's ankle.

"Yeah, but he *could*. It's worth a try. I mean, do *you* have a better idea?"

Nix trotted ahead, snout lifted to the sky.

"Just what I thought," said Bo with a snort.

Bo's excitement cast a long shadow over his insecurities — *Take that, Innkeeper! Take that, village children! Take that, everyone who ever called me a curse!* If the Un-King had the first key and Bo had worked out the riddle all on his own, then surely he could find the Stars and put everything back to rights.

"But how do we convince Tam we need to see the Un-King?" he said.

Nix scooted off into the undergrowth, snout to the ground.

"Fine," grumbled Bo. "I'll work it out myself, shall I?"

Bo trudged on. With his eyes scrunched shut, he pictured the gnarled tree and its maze of branches that marked the site of the Irin Un-Royal City on Tam's map. It was in the northeast of the province, wasn't it? Bo opened his eyes and tilted his head to the Light — it was straight ahead, nudging the end of the third quadrant. So they were already headed in the right direction. Perhaps if —

Nix appeared with a bird wedged between his jaws and dropped it at Tam's feet — a gift. He sat back on his haunches, waiting to be fussed over.

Bo snorted. But then he realized it was a bird Nix had just offered Tam. A *bird*. "Nix! You can't —"

Tam clicked her beak. "You eat pig, do you not?"

"Yes, but —"

"Then I can eat bird."

"Wait. Are you saying Irin come from *pigs?*"

Tam laughed as she walked away. "Alas, they do not. *But* the resemblance is uncanny. For instance, Irin are small, round, and beady-eyed. And to me, Irin language sounds like a pig squealing and —" She stopped suddenly, lifting her foot to glare at the green gunk dripping from her talons.

Bo laughed until his belly hurt. "That," he said, wiping his eyes, "is Skugs fud."

With her beak held high, the Korahku scraped her foot clean on the grass. "We best keep walking, little Irin," she said. "After all —"

Tam stopped abruptly and when Bo heard voices on the

other side of the hill, he understood why. She dropped, motioning for Bo to lower too.

"It's dead," said a woman.

"Time of year for it," said another.

"Not like *this*," said a man. "I'm telling you it's the work of Shadow Creatures, maybe even the Shadow Witch herself."

Bo hugged Nix close to his side and parted the grass. He peered down the gentle incline that led to a road snaking through a scatter of trees. A convoy of Irin pushed their carts, loaded high with possessions.

The voices belonged to three who had stopped, their cart leaning precariously on the edge of a ditch on the side of the road. They were nervously inspecting a charred, leafless tree.

"You don't think—" The man snapped his mouth shut and gave a passing family a narrow-eyed glare. Once they had trundled out of hearing distance, he leaned in and lowered his voice. "You don't think *she* could be around here, do you? You don't think *she* could be one of *them*"—he jerked his chin at the family—"in disguise?"

"Who cares about a tree?" exclaimed one of the women. "There's Shadow Creatures slaughtering whole families in the half-Light! They'll kill every one of us!"

All three startled as another nearby tree lost its leaves in a single violent shiver. The Irin clutched one another as the leaves floated to the ground in a cascade of ash.

"She's here! She's here!" The man rushed for his cart, gripped the handles, and pushed it away from the ditch. "Hurry! To the Un-King! Before she turns us all to ash!"

They disappeared around a bend in the road, wailing and whimpering.

Beside Bo, Tam snorted. "See? Superstitious."

Bo's heart beat so hard against his ribs the sound echoed in his ears as he stared at the charred trees. "You don't think that's strange?" he said.

"Everything in this province is strange to me."

"What about Shadow Creatures attacking in the half-Light? That's not normal."

Tam clicked her beak and said nothing.

When the last of the traveling procession rounded the bend and disappeared from view, she stood, rolling back her shoulders. "Come, child. We must find a safe hut for the night. There are many situated near the roadside for travelers caught in the Dark." She stalked away before Bo could even open his mouth to respond.

"This is *exactly* like being with Mads," Bo hissed to Nix. "Except Mads never had plans to dump me the first second he could."

Nix barked.

As Bo chased after the Korahku, his rucksack bounced

against his back with a *thump, thump, thump* and the sharp, reedy grass whipped his legs.

Tam led them to a rickety hut beside a tree, bare and wind-swept and bowed. The hut was set back and away from the others, those closest to the road and crowded with Irin travelers. "There is our safe hut," she said. "You will get a good night's sleep and tomorrow you will understand that I am right."

The air was chill and the Light was a murky gray and the world so unfamiliar and frightening; Bo had no other choice. So he followed Tam inside and lit candles and ate stale bread and checked his wounded leg and crawled beneath the blankets and closed his eyes, biting his tongue the whole time.

It wasn't fair.

Why didn't Tam listen to him?

Why was she set on turning him over to the Sisters?

Why did everyone always leave him?

Dark fell quickly. But Bo did not sleep. The Shadow Creatures howled all night.

༄

The next day was the same as the last.

Bo chased Tam's heels, his head filled with what-ifs and why-nots. He tried to argue with the Korahku, but Tam waved away his words as though they were bothersome gnats buzzing around her head. Every time they weaved close to the road, they heard hushed voices and squeaky carts and wailing children and the same stories over and over: *Shadow Creatures. Attacking villages. Growing stronger. Everyone in danger.* They passed safe huts — doors swinging open in the wind, scratches on the walls, no one inside them.

Bo's insides twisted with worry.

As they crested a hill, Tam paused. She sat on the grass and with a wave of her hand motioned for Bo to do the same. Bo peered into the valley below: circling the valley was a forest and in the center was a cluster of wooden huts. A village.

None of the chimneys smoked; not a single soul stirred.

"We need more water, so I'd better go," said Bo. There was no way Tam could wander into an Irin village without finding herself locked in a Fuglebur. Besides, Bo wanted to ask about the Un-King. Perhaps he would meet someone who would agree to take him — a woman with a braid like a golden crown, and she would smile and laugh and ruffle his hair, and she would never want to leave him . . .

Tam waved again at Bo to sit down. "It is dangerous for you."

"They don't know me in this village. I'll be fine." Bo took out his cloak and wrapped it tightly around himself, tugging the hood low. "Nix, you stay with Tam."

Nix barked.

"I mean it. People here aren't going to know you're tame. They might try to hurt you."

Tam gave Bo a narrow-eyed stare. "I do not like—"

"I won't be long," insisted Bo, and with a deep, steadying breath, he started down the gentle incline.

The fox followed.

"This isn't like at home, Nix," said Bo as he rounded on his friend. "I'm not playing. You stay."

Nix pawed at the ground, whining.

"Stay."

Bo hurried down the hill. He heard Tam chuckle as four little paws padded after him, swishing through the long grass.

"Fine," snapped Bo with a glance over his shoulder at his disobedient friend. "But if you end up fox stew, I'm not saving you."

Nix trotted happily next to Bo, yipping and barking.

Bo sighed. "I wasn't going to leave you. I'd have come back for you. Always."

When they reached the village, Bo peered into every window but they were all the same: not a villager to be found. He knocked on doors; no one answered. Even the market square was deserted. Bo peered up at the Fuglebur — not a scrap nor a bone.

"They are gone," said Tam. Bo jumped, crashing into the Korahku's rock-hard body.

"Does nobody listen to me? I said to stay put." Bo rubbed his shoulder.

"I made a blood bind," said Tam. "Korahku always keep their promises."

Bo folded his arms across his chest. "Well, where is everyone? Should be a hundred villagers with this many huts." *Should be braids like golden crowns and smiles and laughter and ruffled hair . . .* Bo pressed his lips tightly together.

"Let us explore, shall we?" said Tam.

The Korahku crossed the square to the nearest house and sliced open the wooden lock with a silver spike on her forearm. She forced the stiff door inward with a bump of her shoulder, revealing a small single-room hut much like Bo's forest home.

It was chaos: bedsheets flung across the room, pots and pans in tumbling piles, furniture broken.

"And Mads thought *I* was messy," said Bo, taking a cautious step inside, followed by Nix. He pulled back his hood.

Tam stooped as she moved about the room, poking and prodding and peering. "This is not normal for Irin?"

"For the last time, we're not pigs!"

Tam clicked her beak, unconvinced. "Perhaps you are the exception to the rule. After all, you were the only one who dared set me free. And I do not think you would be the kind of person to lock me in such a prison in the first place. So." Warmth shone in the Korahku's eyes.

Bo frowned — he didn't know what to say.

He watched as Tam crouched by the entrance, peering at the earthen floor.

"The Light is almost to the fourth," Bo said. He toed a broken cup. "We'll need to find somewhere to stay. I don't want to be outside when it's half-Light. In case you forgot, there's a wolf after me."

"Tracks," muttered Tam, and ducked out of the hut, beak to the ground.

Bo hurried after her, Nix snuffling along behind, whining and growling.

"But I want to know what she's found," he said. He followed Tam into the forest. As he zigzagged around the trees, he noticed many of them were drooping — the leaves turning black and shedding. He swallowed down his unease.

The Korahku came to a sudden halt on the edge of a small clearing. "What do you mean 'tracks'?" Bo asked.

And then he gasped. For the Korahku had led them to a macabre discovery.

There, in the clearing, was a mound of bones, twice as high as Bo and glistening like the fangs of ghost-children.

"Is that . . . ?"

"Now we know," said Tam, turning away from the ghastly sight.

But Bo was frozen.

It wasn't just bones he saw. On the very edge of the mound was a straw doll. A child's toy, blond and wearing a dress that might once have been blue but was now stained red.

"Now we know what?" croaked Bo.

There was a tremble in Tam's voice as she spoke. "Now we know what happened to the villagers."

CHAPTER TEN

THEY RAN FROM THE CLEARING, Bo shooting a desperate glance over his shoulder at the glimmering bones. He couldn't help picturing the child who had held that little doll in their hands; his stomach lurched.

"Who ... *what* did that?" The blackened leaves crunched underfoot as they dashed through the forest. Bo hurried behind Tam, panting and sweating from effort, Nix rushing out ahead. "They should have been safe in their huts. They had candles. And fires. It can't have been Shadow Creatures. It *can't*."

But his protests sat uneasy. He had heard the villagers on the road. And now he had seen the proof. The ugly, terrifying truth.

The Shadow Creatures were on the rise, their power growing, their hunger insatiable.

When they reached a safe hut, relief surged through him. But as he sat panting on the floor, he felt sick. Were they really safe here?

A whole village.

All those people.

And Bo knew how to stop it.

He set his jaw, pushing down all the doubt, all the voices he carried with him, the sneering, jeering, snide voices of the people back home who had called him names and made him feel small. It didn't matter whether he *could* do it; he *had* to do it.

"Are we close to the Un-Royal City?" he asked.

Nix pressed close to him, his scar beginning to weep.

Tam lit candles around the hut. Bo stared into their flames, small and flickering; would they be enough to keep the Shadow Creatures out?

"The city is a hen's peck from here," said Tam. She blew out the match; smoke wafted, the sharp, bitter smell tickling Bo's nostrils. "To the east, just over that hill. Why?" Tossing the match, she began to explore the hut, sitting back on her haunches as she pulled out water, dried meat, and stale bread from a box hidden under one of the cots.

Bo clenched his jaw, twisting his fingers in Nix's fur. "Because I'm going to find the Stars and I think the first key is there." He fixed Tam with a determined look. "You should come with me."

"Ah yes, the Stars," she muttered. She slammed the lid of the box and hung her head. "Just come with me to the Sisters and you will be safe. What more could you want?"

More? The word rumbled through him. There was so much

emptiness inside him that it bounced off the walls and echoed. He wanted *so much more*. He wanted what the ghost had shown him in the Myling Mist—his mother and a future where he was loved and taken care of and wasn't treated like a curse. He wanted Tam to help him, not to throw him away the second she could. He wanted the village children to play with him. He never wanted to see anything like that straw doll again.

Tam sighed and stood. "We sleep and then tomorrow we walk to the Temple of the Silent Sisters. There you will be safe. That is all that matters."

Bo climbed under the thin blanket, tightened his cloak around him, and closed his eyes. But all he saw was the straw doll. He shook his head but the image stayed there. It stayed there while he listened to Tam shuffle about, the creak of the cot as she finally settled for the night. It stayed there as it grew Dark outside and Shadow Creatures stirred and an all-consuming fear turned Bo's insides to ice.

And as he lay awake all night, turning Tam's blood bind over and over in his hands, Bo realized what he had to do.

ॐ

In the end, it was easy to slip away at first Light while Tam, perched on the edge of the bed even in sleep, slumbered on. Bo did not want to leave the Korahku behind but what choice did he have?

At least he had Nix.

The fox trotted beside Bo as they followed Tam's directions to the Un-Royal City. It was a long walk, weaving through the growing number of Irin villagers with their overflowing carts and bundles and scowls. He kept his head down, thumbs hooked under the straps of his rucksack, hood low.

He nudged Nix with his toe. "Do you think the Un-King will be nice?" he asked. "Perhaps I'll only have to ask for the key and he'll —"

Bo crashed into someone's back. All the air in his lungs whooshed out in one go as he stumbled backwards.

A woman with her arms folded turned to give him a filthy look. "Mind where you're going, child."

His chest smarted. He rubbed it and peered around the woman: a thick crowd had gathered on the road; people and their carts and their wailing children were stuck and unable to move forward. Bo climbed onto the wheel of a nearby cart for a better view.

"Get down off my cart, you guttersnipe!"

The villagers were fighting their way toward the grand arched entrance in a city wall. But while everyone on Bo's side tried to squeeze *in*, on the other side more were trying to squeeze *out*.

Beyond the arch was a hill teeming with huts, tall and imposing and leaning precariously. "Must be the Un-Royal City," he called down to Nix.

"Of course it's the Un-Royal City," cried the owner of the cart. "Now hop off before you squash my husband!" Bo looked down at the cart, and a frail-looking man lying on a bed of potatoes scowled up at him.

Bo hopped down and pushed through the crowd: sniveling kids and overflowing carts and red-faced adults shouting and shoving and surging.

"Come on, Nix," he said. "We need to get inside."

Bo got as far as the gate, where two burly men were facing off.

"And I said there's no point!" shouted a heavy-browed redhead with a scar that ran from the corner of his eye to the tip of his chin. "Shadow Creatures have been tormenting the city for days, so we're leaving! Get out of my way!"

"And I said we don't have anywhere else to go," spat a stout man with scruffy black hair. He looked strangely familiar. "What's the Un-King going to do about it? We're his citizens! He's supposed to protect us!"

The redhead hooted. "Oh, that's precious! You must be from the south. How else could you be so ignorant?"

"Why, you —" The stout man swung a fist wildly. It slammed into the other man's jaw with a *crack*.

In the ensuing silence, the redhead slowly wrapped a hand around his jaw and moved it from side to side, checking for a break. Blood trickled down the side of his mouth; he wiped it with the back of his hand and looked at the smear. He fixed the stout man with a hard look. "You'll pay for that."

The two crowds suddenly surged at each other, faces wild with unbridled rage as they swung their fists and spat curses. An errant elbow knocked the wind out of Bo and he fell forward, landing on his hands and knees beside the two brawling men. Nix bit Bo's trouser leg and tried to drag him out of danger just as a blinding Light shot through the air, and every person stopped in their tracks.

When Bo looked up he saw the stout man on his knees, gawking at his still-sparking hands. Bo remembered Mads in the forest and the Light that had hurled Ranik through the air — magic. This man had just used *magic*. Bo's skin tingled, his body thrumming with energy. He knew magic was returning — Mads had said so — but to see the sparks of it right before his eyes was . . . awe-inspiring, terrifying, overwhelming. How many more people were capable of wielding it?

"Witch!" someone shouted. A chorus of voices agreed: "Witch! Witch! Witch!"

The stout man shook his head. "No! It wasn't me! It was . . ." His wild eyes met Bo's, suddenly turning cold and hard.

Now Bo recognized him: it was the baker's cousin from Squall's End. He used to pitch the stale loaves at Bo's head whenever Bo passed the baker's stall.

He jabbed a finger at Bo. "It was him! He's from my village. He lives in the Forest of Long Shadows, where they say Shadow Creatures are born! Everyone knows he's in league with them! It wasn't me — it was him!"

A hundred eyes fell on Bo.

He shrank in on himself, crawling backwards. "It wasn't . . ."

Soldiers elbowed their way through the crowd, waving their swords. "What's going on here? Who's causing trouble?"

"Witch!" shouted the crowd.

"It wasn't me!" cried the baker's cousin. He hid his hands behind his back. "The boy! It was the boy!"

"Both of you can come with us," said the captain, and several soldiers stepped forward to grab the baker's cousin and Bo. Nix snapped at their boots, earning a kick to his gut.

"Leave him alone!" shouted Bo, struggling in a soldier's grip. He tried to kick her but couldn't reach.

She dug her nails into his arm and sneered close to his ear. "Call off your dog or he'll get worse than my boot."

Bo told Nix to calm down as he was led through the parting crowd and the gate.

The baker's cousin howled with indignation as they were dragged against the flow of traffic while more and more people from the city hurried down the main road with their overflowing carts, joining the bottleneck at the gate. Bo didn't have to wonder why; he saw the deep claw marks in the walls of the rickety double-story huts that slanted toward the road as if peering down curiously at the people. Doors and shutters hung off their hinges; window cracks looked like creepy, toothless smiles. The Shadow Creatures had been here.

He was gasping by the time they reached a plateau at the top of the hill, where a large garden wall hid everything from view, everything other than the gnarled branches of a monstrous tree that stretched high above the top of the wall. Bo was pushed through a wooden gate, bashing his shoulder against the frame. He cursed and turned to give the sneering soldier his best glare.

The soldier laughed, pale green eyes glistening. "None of that, boy. You're about to plead for your life in front of the Un-King. Tears will work better than scowls."

He was shoved forward and fell to his hands and knees, Nix rushing to his side. Bo gently nudged the fox away and looked up to find the shadow of an imposing structure looming ahead of him. He looked up and up and up and . . .

The Un-Royal Palace.

It was a hodgepodge of interconnected buildings, as though a giant had scooped up an entire village and dumped the huts here, one on top of the other. The tree Bo had glimpsed from the other side of the wall appeared to be growing *inside* the palace; all Bo could see were its bare, curled branches breaking through the rooftop, as though the palace were a giant mouth swallowing the tree whole.

The soldier gripped Bo's cloak collar, hauled him to his feet, and dragged him into the palace — dirt floor, crooked walls, a maze of corridors, soldiers pushing past with red-faced fear and calls of *Hurry! Pack your things!*

"Cowards," sneered the green-eyed soldier.

"What's happening?" said the baker's cousin somewhere behind them. His voice wobbled with fear. "Where are they all going?"

No one answered him.

Nix snuck in behind the soldiers as they led Bo and the baker's cousin into a large room. In the center was the tree — thick trunk, jagged bark, knots that looked like giant warts. It grew out of the floor and spread high up through the space where the roof *should* have been but wasn't — there was no ceiling in this room at all!

The four walls were painted with colorful scenes: farmers and their pigs, bakers in the kitchen, woodcutters chopping trees, markets overflowing with people. Hundreds and hundreds of candles burned brightly in every nook and cranny. The only furniture was a threadbare floral armchair nestled against the base of the tree. Above it, a wind chime dangled from a branch, tinkling in the mild breeze.

The room's only occupant was a . . .

Bo tried to scramble back. "What on Ulv is *that*?" he gasped, pointing at the . . . the . . . the *thing*. It was a wormlike creature the size of Nix. Its thick, slimy body was translucent white with a long strip of orange down its spine, a horn jutting from its head, and a trumpet snout that fish-mouthed steadily, making little *pop, pop, pop*s. It crawled slowly along the floor toward Bo, leaving a trail of luminous, steaming sludge in its wake.

"There you are, Patrice!"

A man stepped into view and scooped the creature into his arms. Over ratty clothes the man wore a leather apron, chunky boots, and bright yellow gloves that reached all the way to his elbows. His glasses were thick like the bottoms of the jars Mads stored his pickled lindberries in, and his beige skin was weather-worn and wrinkled. "You must not run off, Patrice," he said, stroking the creature's spine. "No telling what those blasted owls will do."

"Prisoners for you, Your Un-Highness," said the other soldier. He shoved the whimpering baker's cousin to the ground.

The man—the *Un-King?*—startled, surprised to see he was not alone. He blinked at Bo.

"Is it Tuesday?" he asked.

The soldiers shared a look. "Er, no, sir," said the green-eyed soldier.

"Ah well, you are out of luck. I only see to Un-King business on Tuesdays. Between eleven and seven minutes past. And oh dear, look." He glanced up at the sky through the tangle of branches. "It's much, *much* past that time now, and besides, it's Thursday. So. Toodle-oo!"

"But they're prisoners, sir. One is a suspected witch and the other is rumored to be in league with Shadow Creatures. It might explain why the city has been under attack."

The Un-King grumbled, shuffling to the armchair. Another slimy *thing* had appeared, crawling across the back of the chair. He sat, index finger stroking the spine of the creature cradled in his arms, its trumpet mouth opening and closing: *pop, pop, pop . . .*

From somewhere overhead, an owl hooted; the Un-King glowered at the branches.

"This job is such a chore," he moaned, and turned his look to Bo. "The Queen sends for me *constantly*. She expects monthly meetings in the capital for all the province leaders, but I can't leave my slugs, you see? They're colossal spit-mouth slugs — fascinating creatures, don't you think? Very rare and *very* temperamental. So, I can't leave them, not even for a second. Too many owls flapping about. And Patrice gets lonely." He cooed gently at the slug cradled in his arms. "And now I'm expected to deal with prisoners and it's not even Tuesday!" Patrice shot out a long slick of steaming white sludge from her trumpet mouth all over his leather apron. "See? Patrice agrees." He cleaned the sludge with a cloth, hissing when a spot landed on his trousers and burned through the fabric. Bo tugged his cloak tightly around him as Nix edged closer, whimpering softly.

A door on the west side of the room slammed open and five more soldiers burst in, panting and faces red.

"Shadow Creature sighting at the eastern wall," wheezed one, hands on knees.

"And more skirmishes at the west gate," said another. "Too many people trying to leave at once. More still fighting to come into the city."

A young soldier — lanky and freckled and wide-eyed — gripped his own hair and pulled. "We should be leaving too," he cried. "Why aren't we leaving?"

"It's him," sneered the baker's cousin, jabbing a finger at Bo. His teeth were bared. "He leads the Shadow Creatures."

The soldiers murmured, turning to Bo with distrustful eyes.

Bo shrank back, the warm press of Nix beside him like a tether. "I'm not —"

"Lies!" spat the baker's cousin, face twisted. "It wasn't even my magic — it was him! I'm innocent."

Bo bit his lip, sneaking a glance at the Un-King. With one hand he stroked Patrice, and with the other he tapped an impatient beat against the armrest. Did he think Bo was guilty? Would he sentence him to the Fuglebur? Bo jerked back as his foolishness hit him hard — *I should never have left Tam. I failed before I even started. I am cursed.*

The soldiers' worried murmurs grew louder, a buzz of nervous energy sparking all around them.

The Un-King sighed loudly. "Oh, all right, then. Bring the boy here," he said. "Not even Tuesday . . ." he muttered under his breath.

A boot to his behind sent Bo flying forward; he landed in a crumpled pile at the Un-King's feet.

"Stand up, boy," said the Un-King.

Bo stood, straightening his tattered clothes. The Un-King leaned forward, peering into Bo's face.

"He doesn't *look* evil," he muttered. The slug in his arms turned her trumpet to *pop, pop, pop* at Bo. "Looks like an ordinary boy to me."

"I am," Bo said. "I'm just here to look for a —"

A sudden gust of wind chased through the room, and the chime in the tree tinkled loudly. Bo glanced up and saw it was made out of a strange assortment of items: a bejeweled scepter, necklaces and bracelets and . . .

"A key!"

"I've no need for any of that old royal junk," explained the Un-King, following Bo's eye line. "Far more useful as a wind chime. Patrice has a nervous disposition, you see, and the sound calms her. She's less likely to shoot poisonous mucus everywhere if she's happy."

As if to prove the Un-King wrong, Patrice shot a spear of

white mucus from her trumpet; it landed on the armrest and dribbled down the side, burning holes in the fabric as it went. But Bo was mesmerized by the key.

It was large and gold, one end shaped like a teardrop. *This has to be it,* he thought. *The first key! I was right. I was actually right!*

His fingers itched to reach out and grab it.

"Well?" shouted the baker's cousin. Bo jerked at the sound, quickly lowering his head again. "Aren't you going to lock him in the Fuglebur and set me free?"

With a scowl, the Un-King stood. "I do hope you're not telling me what to do," he said, bearing down on the baker's cousin. "It's not even Tuesday! Do you know how distressing this is for my slugs? Honestly!" He turned to the soldiers. "Why would you bring me such nonsense? I have enough to worry about as it is. Don't you know there's another owl infestation?"

"Owls?" spluttered the green-eyed soldier. She threw her hands up. "Who cares about blasted owls? There are Shadow Creatures attacking the city. In the *Light!* You're the Un-King — what are *you* going to do about it?"

Everyone started shouting at once: *Witch! Shadow Creatures! Leave! Attack! Tuesday! Arrest! Slugs!* The young freckled soldier pulled at his hair, crying.

The baker's cousin shouted louder than all of them, the air electric around him. Suddenly, above the din was an almighty *crack!* A flash of white Light shot through the room, severing half the tree branches above Bo and sending them — and the wind chime — to the ground. Bo barely jumped out of the way in time, and Nix barked once at the fallen branches, then hid behind Bo's legs. The room was silent save for the quiet whimpering of the freckled soldier. The baker's cousin stared open-mouthed at his hands, once again the source of the strange Light.

And then the shouting started up anew, louder this time, urgent. Some soldiers threw their weapons down and fled from the room; others ran for the baker's cousin and pinned him to the ground.

"Witch!"

"Get out of here! Save yourselves!"

"Protect the Un-King!"

"Leave the city at once!"

"Don't hurt Patrice!"

In the chaos, Bo crawled to the fallen branches and sifted through the teetering pile. The splintered wood cut into his hands, but he ignored the pain. *Where is it? Where?* A glimmer of gold at the bottom of the pile set his heart racing. He tossed branches aside and finally clasped the buried wind chime. Bo reached past the scepter and the other glittery objects, then unhooked the key and slipped it into his pocket. "Come on, Nix," he whispered. "Let's get out of here."

They edged along the wall as soldiers dashed around the

room — the baker's cousin was dragged along the floor, wailing and cursing and screaming at the sparks still firing from his hands.

Bo made a dash for the door. "Now, Nix! Now."

But a firm hand gripped his cloak and yanked him back. He gasped for air as his collar dug into his throat.

"Where do you think you're going?" said the green-eyed soldier, a cruel grin twisting her mouth. In her other hand she had Nix by the scruff. The fox twisted around, trying to snap at her. "The Un-King might not have plans for you, but I do," she said. "You *and* your witch dog."

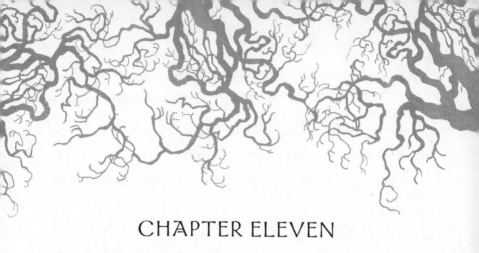

CHAPTER ELEVEN

B O PEERED THROUGH THE CAGE BARS — it was a long way down.

He had been strung up in the city's elaborate Fugle-bur: ten iron cages hanging from the branches of a tree whose blossoms made Bo's nostrils itch. His rucksack had been confiscated, and although the key and Tam's blood bind were safely tucked away in his trouser pocket, all his supplies — candles, matches, water, food — were gone.

Nix was in the cage beside him; if Bo poked his arm through the bars and strained until his shoulder burned, then he could just press the back of his hand to Nix's snout and reassure the whimpering fox. On his other side, the baker's cousin was cursing and rattling the bars so hard the whole tree shook.

"This is your fault, Devil-child," he growled.

Bo ground his teeth and ignored him, scouring the market square for a way out, an idea, a friendly face. Anything.

But no one looked up; villagers pushed their overflowing

carts and threw fearful glances over their shoulders at the homes they were leaving behind. Soldiers stalked the cobblestones, shouting orders and breaking up fights. But Bo saw plenty of them pushing carts too, tearing the yellow insignia of the Irin Army from their breast pockets and tossing them to the ground.

He was stuck.

And when the Dark came . . .

All those times walking through the village market square and Mads had said: *For prisoners. Not little boys who live in forests.*

How wrong he had been.

Bo gripped the bars and pulled but they would not budge. He gritted his teeth and kept pulling, a growl fighting its way through his gut and into his throat before exploding from his mouth as a wail.

Why had he left Tam's side? *Why?* Hadn't the villagers told him for years how useless he was? He panted heavily, dropping his hands from the bars.

"Got you, too, did they?" said a voice somewhere behind him.

Bo jerked around all the way until he saw a familiar face with a gold-toothed smile peeking from behind the tree's thick trunk from a cage on the other side.

"Galvin? What are *you* doing here?"

"Darn soldiers," said the wish-seller. "Made up some

gippitty-gunk about my goods being stolen and locked me in here." He sniffed sourly.

"Who is it? Who's there?" snapped the baker's cousin, twisting until he could settle his distrustful glare on the wish-seller. "Oh. Is this a friend of yours, Devil-child?"

"He's only a . . ." started Bo before he remembered the mist and the ghost-children and the mushrooming green smoke that stank of old socks and rotted meat but did *not* fight off spirits. ". . . a cheater!" he said. "You cheated me! That spirit charm was a load of old trolldung!"

Galvin huffed. "Never! I'm the most honest salesman in the whole of Ulv."

"You charged me twelve Raha for that charm and it didn't work. I almost got eaten by ghosts! And I bet that wasn't a real wish you had either."

"*Tsk!*" said Galvin. "Of *course* the charm didn't work on ghosts! You need a special ghost charm for them. I have one I can sell you for twelve . . . eh, *fifteen* Raha. Well, I *did* have one. The soldiers took all my things."

Bo turned around again, folding his arms across his chest. "I don't believe you," he said. "And I'm not talking to you anymore."

Galvin snorted. "Fine. I'll talk to your friend here instead."

"I'm not *his* friend," said the baker's cousin. Bo could hear the revulsion in his voice. "This child is a curse!"

"Well, in that case you'll need a honkypokey charm — stops

curses from taking hold. I can sell you one for twenty-five Raha. When we're free, that is, and I get my goods back."

It was Bo's turn to snort. *When we're free . . .*

"Fifteen and you've got a deal."

"Twenty."

"Sold!"

A swirl of wind plucked a handful of blossoms from the tree and tossed them at Bo. He shook them off, sneezing once, twice, three times.

Nix whimpered again; Bo shot him a reassuring smile. He longed to reach out and run his fingers through the little fox's fur.

I'm sorry, he wanted to say. *I'm sorry I led you here. I'm sorry I wasn't smart enough, quick enough, brave enough to keep us out of trouble.* And as he looked down at the scattered villagers — only a handful now — he felt sorry for them, too. He was certain it was the Shadow Witch who had caused all this chaos, and it had been within his means to stop it. Not from behind the bars of a Fuglebur, though.

He reached into his pocket and fingered the key, cool against his skin.

"Squall's End is abandoned now," the baker's cousin was saying to Galvin. "Won't be a single soul left in Irin soon. Anyone who remains might as well start carving their headstone." He shook his head. "There's no hope. None at all."

"You could use your magic to free us," said Bo.

The baker's cousin whipped his head around so fast the bones cracked in his neck. "I haven't got magic!" he sneered. "There's no such thing!"

"There is," said Bo. "Why do you think the Shadow Creatures are getting stronger? It wasn't me — it was because the Shadow Witch released magic and now the only way to stop her is to free the Stars. Tell him, Galvin. You agree with me."

"Stars?" said Galvin. His eyes danced. "*Real* Stars?"

The wish-seller pressed himself against the bars; the cage swayed in the breeze.

Bo rolled his eyes. "Yes, *real* Stars. Not like the fake ones you sell." He frowned at Galvin's growing smirk. "I thought you knew about this," he said. "You were the one who told me about the Shadow Witch."

Another handful of blossoms landed in Bo's lap. He supposed they were quite pretty — tight blue buds with wispy white hairs that fluttered away on the wind when Bo sneezed.

The baker's cousin threw back his head and laughed. "Stars? Only babies believe in Stars!"

Bo shook his head. "The Stars were stolen by a wolf a long time ago. He's still got them."

"Where?" said Galvin. His eyes glinted with barely concealed hunger. "You know, don't you?"

Bo shrank back against the bars. A prickle of unease danced up his spine as he shook his head. "No, I don't —"

A single blossom landed on the back of Bo's hand in his lap; it was black. When he gasped, the movement of air was enough to cause the blossom to crumble; the resulting ash blew away on the wind, leaving behind a Dark residue on Bo's skin. He rubbed it clean against his trouser leg and looked up.

Bo watched in horror as, slowly, every blossom on the tree turned black and rained down on them, coating their skin and their clothes in ash.

"What witchcraft is this?" cried the baker's cousin. He slapped at his arms, his legs, his face, trying to wipe himself clean of the black dust.

The sickness spread to the branches, too — the wood shriveled and blackened. The branch above Bo splintered with a shrill *crack* and his cage jerked.

"Oh no," he whispered.

Nix barked and Bo looked down — so far to fall.

There was another shrill crack and then a split second where nothing happened — just Bo suspended in the air, ash raining down around him. But then the branch broke clean and tumbled to the ground, Bo's cage with it.

Pain shot through him as he landed. He hit his head, his elbow, his knee. More crashes and cries for help echoed around him. Nix barking, metal clanging. *Bang, bang, BANG!*

When his ears stopped ringing and his vision cleared he was on his back, tangled in his cloak, and broken iron bars littered the ground around him. He sat up and got a face full of excited fox, the fur tickling his cheeks.

"I'm glad you're okay too, Nix."

The baker's cousin groaned and Bo looked around: all the cages had fallen and the tree was nothing more than a charred stump, clumps of ash wafting away on the wind.

"Quickly," said Galvin, suddenly at Bo's side, grabbing his arm and hauling him to standing. "Noise like that is bound to attract the attention of—"

"Halt!" The soldier's cry shot through the market square. "Prisoners escaping!" she yelled, waving her sword at them, more soldiers rushing toward her calls.

"Run!" shouted Galvin.

They all ran, weaving through the crooked city streets, the soldiers hot on their tails, boots stomping and cries of *Halt! Stop them! Traitors!*

"Sacrifice the boy," panted the baker's cousin. "He can lure the soldiers away while we escape."

"What an excellent idea," said Galvin, but it was the baker's cousin he pushed, sending him flying. He tumbled before coming to a halt against the wall of an inn. The baker's cousin sat up with a snarl and a red face. Bo felt the telltale sparks zapping through the air before the explosion of Light.

"Duck!" he called, and dived down an alley, Nix and Galvin close behind. There was a crash as the magic connected with something — a wall or a window. A chorus of voices rang through the air as the soldiers caught up; the baker's cousin was howling: "It wasn't me! I'm not a witch! Take the boy — he's down there!"

Galvin grabbed Bo's sleeve. "This way!" he hissed. "I know a secret exit — I'll see us free." He swerved a sharp left, herding them toward a narrow gate in the city wall, half-hidden by a creeping vine. Despite Nix's urgent barks, Bo had no choice but to follow — he could still hear the other man's screams as the soldiers hauled him back to the Un-Royal Palace.

They ran through the gate and out onto a flat, marshy wasteland that stretched as far as Bo could see — mud and patchy grass and a handful of spindly trees, their meager branches bare of leaves. Galvin led the way, weaving a path that Bo tried to follow.

They were well away from the city wall when Bo's foot became stuck in the mud and he was flung forward, landing on all fours. His hands sank into the sludge.

What on Ulv?

Bo pushed himself to standing; there was a loud, slurping *pop* has he yanked his hands free of the gooey mud. He looked down at his feet; they were sinking too! "What is this?" he cried. He tried to lift his feet but they were stuck.

"The quagmires," announced Galvin, voice smug. He was standing on a large green island to Bo's left, one of many bursts of green scattered about the quagmires. Bo looked around wildly. Nix was safe on a grassy tuft, barking at Bo's sinking feet.

Galvin's smile stretched wide as he rocked onto his heels. "You need to grow up around here to know which bits to stand on and which will suck you down forever," he said.

"Help me out, then," said Bo, his stomach tying itself in knots of worry. "Quick!"

"Oh, I would," said Galvin. "Really, truly I would. Except . . . those Stars you mentioned. I would *very* much like to get my hands on them. I'd get *ever* so much money for them on the Dark Market."

Bo's heart sank. The Irin was trying to cheat him. Again.

"But I made it up," lied Bo. "There are no such things as Stars!"

"*Tsk, tsk, tsk,*" said Galvin. "Do you think I am as dull-witted as a troll? Do you see *me* stuck in the quagmires? I *know* it's true. My Ooma told me all about the Stars — she rules the Dark Market and she knows *everything*. So if you don't tell me where they are, then I won't be able to rescue you, and that would be very sad. For you. Not for me."

Even if Bo knew where the Stars were, he could never tell someone as unscrupulous as Galvin. But there was no way he could escape the sinking mud on his own.

"All right," said Bo. "You promise to set me free if I tell you?"

Galvin nodded. "Oh yes," he said. "Of course."

Nix yapped but Bo told him to stay quiet. "The Myling Mist," he said.

Galvin narrowed his eyes.

"You can't see anything because of the fog — that's why it's the perfect place to hide them," Bo added. "The wolf guards them but if you wait quietly by the edge of the marsh, the fog clears for an hour every . . . um . . . once every day at mid-Light, so the wolf has to hide or he'll burn, and you can see the Stars just hovering there. You'll need a net and a large sack to catch them." Bo's face stung hot and raw with the lie but he hoped the Irin believed him. "It's true. Cross my heart and hope to be gobbled whole by Shadow Creatures."

Galvin stared at him and for a long time there was silence. Except for the slow *glug, glug, glug* of the mud sucking Bo under.

"You *could* be telling the truth, I suppose," said Galvin eventually. "Everyone says the Myling Mist is haunted and that you should never, *ever* enter it, so it would be a good place to hide such a treasure . . ." He chewed on the inside of his cheek thoughtfully.

Glug.

Glug.

Glug.

By now the mud was up to Bo's chest. He held his arms

above his head, and the more he struggled, the tighter the mud enveloped him. Like being squeezed in a giant's fist.

After more excruciating silence, Galvin finally spoke. "I have decided you are telling the truth," he announced.

Bo heaved a sigh of relief. "Good. Now please help me out."

Galvin shook his head wildly. "Oh, I'm afraid I can't do that. *Tsk, tsk, tsk.* Absolutely not."

Anger shivered through Bo's body in hot, tingly waves. "What?"

"If I set you free, you'll attempt to steal the Stars before me and I can't have that," said Galvin. "They're going to make me ever so much money on the Dark Market."

"You lied!" cried Bo. He tried to wriggle forward but the mud had locked him in place. He cursed his naivety — he should have known a promise from the Irin who'd sold him a fake spirit charm was worthless.

Galvin laughed and waved. "I'll be off, then," he said brightly. "It is a shame I have to leave you but such is life." He bowed to Bo with an elaborate flourish. "I'd say 'see you soon' but I doubt I will. So I'll say 'goodbye' instead. Goodbye!"

As the Irin skipped away, Bo called for him to stay, to come back, to save him. Nix barked loudly from his little tuft of safe green grass. But Galvin did not come back.

The mud gurgled up to Bo's neck.

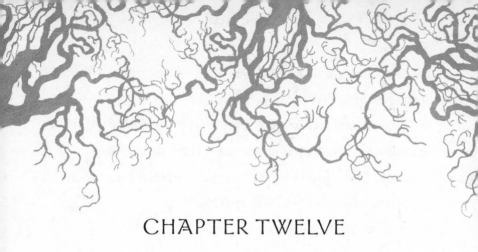

CHAPTER TWELVE

Y OU, DEAR BOY, are up to your neck in trouble," said a voice behind Bo.

Bo tried to locate the owner of the voice, but he was locked in place by the gurgling mud. Fear danced up his spine, making his hair stand on end. Was it a soldier? The baker's cousin?

Nix barked, hackles rising, as footsteps approached from behind Bo, squelching in the soggy grass.

"Oh dear, dear, deary me," said the Un-King, coming into view. The fear that had been slinking up Bo's spine now danced a frenzied jig — he would be dragged back to the palace for sure! "That's quite a pickle you're in."

Patrice was tucked under the Un-King's armpit, and another slug was draped across his shoulders. He set a bucket on the grass beside his feet and calmly looked Bo over. The mud was squeezing the air from Bo's lungs; it felt as if a troll had sat on his chest.

"Do you think you could help?" Bo wheezed.

The Un-King sucked on his gums. "Perhaps," he said. "It's still not Tuesday, though."

With an angry yelp, Nix shot off, tearing back the way they'd come. Bo's heart lurched as if to follow him. The troll sat heavier, crushing Bo's ribs and his lungs, and it had *nothing* to do with the mud. Was Nix *abandoning* him?

But then Nix came charging back, a long stick clamped between his jaws. Relief flooded through Bo.

"Oh, what a smart fox you have," said the Un-King. "Doesn't hold a candle to my slugs, of course."

"But I'm locked in place," said Bo, gasping for air. "The mud is too tight."

"Perhaps Patrice can help with that," said the Un-King, placing her on the ground.

Immediately, the slug began to creep toward Bo and for a moment he wondered if this was it, if this was how the Un-King planned to end him. The slug's trumpet mouth went *pop, pop, pop* as she crawled closer and closer until *blergh* — sizzling white mucus shot out, spilling all over the mud. The mud steamed and an acrid stench poured from the earth. Bo coughed and spluttered, his eyes scrunched shut as he tried to squirm away from the noxious smell.

But when he felt air on his neck again, his eyes opened — the mucus was melting the mud! Patrice vomited again and again until the mud had abated to Bo's waist.

Nix dropped the stick on the ground and gripped one end in his strong jaws as Bo grabbed hold of the other. With surprising strength, the little fox dug in his paws and pulled until Bo slid out of the sludge and onto a patch of soggy grass.

Mud and gunk dripped from Bo as he sat up, sucking in great lungfuls of air. But before he could relax, the mucus began to eat through his cloak. He flung it to the ground and watched it disappear into a cloud of noxious smoke. He ripped a canteen of water from the Un-King's belt and quickly doused himself with the water — he didn't want his skin to end up like his cloak!

"Um . . . sorry," said Bo, handing back the empty canteen once he was completely free of mucus — the mud seemed determined to stick to him, however.

"Quite all right," said the Un-King. "Patrice doesn't know her own strength sometimes."

Bo bent over and ruffled Nix's fur, hugging him close to press a kiss to his head. "I knew you wouldn't leave me," he murmured. Nix licked his cheek.

Bo looked up at the Un-King. "Thank you," he said. "And thank *you*," he told Patrice.

Pop, pop, pop, said Patrice.

The Un-King waved Bo's acknowledgment away and scooped up the slug, tucking her back under his arm. "You're lucky I decided to escape the palace madness to collect mudmygs for my slugs to eat."

Bo peered into the bucket; a writhing mound of mud-mygs peered back. He shuddered.

Bo stood, trying his best to wipe himself clean of the mud. His skin felt uncomfortably tight as the mud dried, not to mention the rancid stench. He cast a mournful eye over the strip of grass where his cloak had been. No cloak and no rucksack. What would he do without candles and matches and food and water and warmth? The only things he had left in his pockets were the key and Tam's feather—he could hardly chase away Shadow Creatures with them!

The Un-King retrieved his bucket and turned. "Well, toodle-oo," he said, and started to walk away. "Remember to stay on the grass."

Bo blinked. "You're just letting me go?" he blurted, but quickly covered his mouth—perhaps he should not have reminded the Un-King he was a fugitive.

The Un-King snorted as he turned back. "Were it Tuesday perhaps I might feel differently, but as it is I have my mud-mygs and Patrice is hungry." He grinned, delightfully crooked teeth on display. "So off you hop."

"But aren't you all leaving?" said Bo. "The city is under attack and—"

"What care I about Shadow Creatures? I have fire and candles and Patrice. At least with everyone gone I won't have to worry about tedious Un-King business: *Humphrey Hovington stood on my front lawn and now the grass won't grow — he must be a witch! Lucy Worth has a cat with one green and one blue eye — it's a Shadow Creature!* It will just be me and my slugs." He smiled down at Patrice. "Isn't that right, my precious?"

Pop, pop, pop, said Patrice.

Bo shifted from foot to foot. "Thank you, then," he said. The unexpected kindness made his heart squeeze in a funny way.

Again, the Un-King waved Bo's thanks away. "Not to worry. But if you happen to spy any owls flapping about, send them on their way — Patrice and I would be ever so grateful."

"Owls?"

The Un-King's face clouded over. "Oh yes, a plague of them. It's the Scribe, you know? She sends them to the Un-Royal City *constantly* — says it's research for her blasted scrolls but I know it's to eat my slugs." He scowled at the empty sky. "I know you're there, owls! Go back to your mad mistress and tell her I'll be writing another sternly worded letter to the Queen."

"The Scribe?" Bo's back straightened, a flutter in his stomach. Hadn't Mads mentioned a Scribe before he died? *The Scribe can help* . . . Bo dug a hand into his pocket and felt the smooth, cold metal of the key. He needed help now that he had a key but no idea what to do next. "Do you know her?"

The Un-King clucked his tongue. "Horrible, horrible creature. Her and that army of owls — they're a natural predator to the colossal spit-mouth slug, you see?"

"But where can I find her?"

The Un-King's face soured. "Oh, very well. If you must know, she's at the Temple of the Silent Sisters."

Bo's heart stuttered. The Temple of the Silent Sisters? That was where Tam had wanted to take him before he ran away.

Bo thought about Mads — all the harsh words, clips across the ear, and disappointed looks each time Bo failed to meet his expectations. Would Tam be the same? Would she be waiting at the temple, angry and disappointed and spiteful?

No. Tam would have returned to her flock the minute she discovered that Bo had left. She would have been relieved. Glad to be rid of him so soon. No one ever cared enough about Bo to miss him.

Bo swallowed over the lump in his throat, blinking hard and fast.

"But I wouldn't advise going anywhere near her," continued the Un-King. "Then again, I wouldn't advise bothering with anyone! Much better off with slugs." He turned away and hopped from one patch of grass to the next. "Toodle-oo!"

As the Un-King bounded away, Bo pulled out the key. At least Galvin hadn't known about *that*.

The key was cold and heavy in his palm. Mads had told him that riddles would lead him to the keys, so he peered closely for clues but saw nothing. He ran his fingers along the gold metal;

it was smooth until his fingertips reached the teardrop and he noticed rough indentations under his touch. "What's this?"

Small marks had been carved into the key, but Bo could not work out the pattern. He frowned as he shoved the key back into his pocket. "Let's just hope the Scribe knows," he said.

Nix barked.

"Then I guess it's a good thing we know the way. Let's go."

∽

Bo had not been expecting a wall.

It was tall enough for him to wonder if giants had built it, with thick, coarse bricks carved from river rock that glimmered red and silver in the fading Light. It stretched as far as he could see — a barrier between this province and the next.

Nev'en.

From his hiding spot at the side of the road, Bo peeked through low-hanging branches at the wall and the cluster of stone huts — elegant, round, and blue — that he could see through an archway where the road cut through the wall.

Bo had hidden at the edge of the forest and watched the village for some time, waiting for signs of life. But he saw no one. Around him the trees shed their blackened leaves, the trunks wilting and charred.

Nix growled; the scar along the bridge of his snout was beginning to weep. Bo was already on edge — it was half-Light and he expected every rustle of wind or creaking tree to be the wolf come to eat him. But he had heard and seen nothing of Ranik.

Bo straightened. "What do you think?" he asked Nix. "We need supplies and somewhere to stay and it looks deserted." He fought back the memory of the last deserted village he had seen and the little straw doll.

With clammy hands and small, careful movements, Bo stepped out of the forest and approached the village on the other side of the wall. As he neared the first hut, his knees grew weak at the sight of the telltale claw marks.

Shadow Creatures had been here.

Bo crept through the village, peeking through windows at the chaos inside each hut: clothes and belongings tossed about, tables and chairs and beds overturned, dishes smashed. All the while, the Light crept closer to the horizon and the scar on Nix's snout wept.

"We'll take one of the huts closest to the square," said Bo. "Should be the safest. Farthest from the forest. We don't have time to look for anywhere else."

Once inside, he lit a fire and as many candles as he could find. Somehow, they slept through the night; it was surprisingly quiet — not a creature stirred. But Bo still woke tired and restless.

And hungry.

All his food had been confiscated by the soldiers and he was not a hunter like Tam.

Tam.

Bo dipped his hand into his pocket and brushed his fingers against the soft feather, ignoring the way his heart stammered at the thought of the Korahku. He shook his head and refused to feel bad about leaving her.

Bo scrubbed himself clean with water from the village well, then scrounged together a meager breakfast from the abandoned huts. The food was strange — pale, salty bread and preserved meat that set his tongue on fire. It sat heavily in his gut.

Soon, Bo was trekking through the unfamiliar landscape of Nev'en, equipped with a new rucksack, plenty of supplies, and a cloak that actually fit him. But he was still on edge — the silence, the blackened trees, the craggy ground, the steep hills, the wind that pushed and pulled at him from every angle. He kept the Light over his left shoulder to ensure he was going the right way.

Nix barked.

"I do not! I bathed this morning," he insisted. But he sniffed his shirt and recoiled. "Well, so do you."

Nix nipped at his ankle.

"It's hot and we've been walking for miles, so it's hardly unexpected. Besides, we're not likely to meet the Queen, so who cares what state we're in?"

Nix barked again.

"You are *not* more important than the Queen of Ulv, Nix. If you think —"

Suddenly, a bloodcurdling howl pierced the air. Fear shot through Bo like the icy wind of the White Season.

The wolf.

But it was Light!

Bo whipped around, scanning the landscape, and there he was.

Ranik.

Bo saw he was moving quickly, bounding over the crest of a hill. There was nothing but a small valley between them. Bo wanted to throw up, to cry, to run away, to run headlong at the wolf and make him pay for what he'd done to Mads.

But he was no match for Ranik. "Hurry," he said to Nix. "Run!"

They ran, jumping over rocks and scrambling up hills. The wolf's howl followed them, haunting their steps.

Bo glanced over his shoulder and saw the wolf not far behind. "He's coming!" shouted Bo. Was there anywhere that was safe? There was no way he could outrun a wolf.

Just then, something grabbed Bo by the arm. He spun around, fear choking off his scream.

But it was Tam.

Bo's shock turned to relief — his whole body sagged with it. He knew the Korahku would be angry with him, that his heart had no right to swoop at the sight of her, but he couldn't help it. His relief was bone-deep.

"Quick," said the Korahku, and before Bo could ask where she had come from, Tam pushed him toward a tree. "Stay out of sight."

"But —"

The Korahku threw off her robe. "I will fight. You hide."

Without her tattered blue robe, Tam was a fearsome sight: tall, muscular, a sprinkling of silver-spiked feathers along the edges of her wings and forearms — far fewer than the villagers claimed — and tail feathers like a metal fan. Bo guessed Tam's wings would be more than three times her height if she spread them fully.

But she couldn't.

Bo finally understood why they couldn't fly to the Silent Sisters: Tam's wings had been clipped.

Despite his fear, despite everything, Bo's heart sank with shame: What had his people done to Tam? But he didn't have time for shame; the wolf was bounding up the hill, gnashing his fangs.

Tam snapped her beak at Bo. "I will not lose anyone else — do you hear me? Hide behind that tree or I will kick you there myself."

Though Bo didn't understand Tam's concern — shouldn't she be angry with him instead of saving him? — he and Nix hurried behind the trunk and peeked around the side. Bo had seen the Korahku fend off the Innkeeper's dog, but a wolf? When it was clear she couldn't use her wings?

Ranik bounded to a halt in front of Tam, and Bo recoiled from the stench of burnt skin and hair; had the wolf really been traveling through the Light all this time?

"Boy," the wolf growled, clawing at the dirt. "Is mine. He knows. Where key is. He will. Tell me. Or die. The truth. Is in his heart. I will. Know it. When I devour it."

Tam flexed the silver spikes along her forearms. "You will have to come through me first, beast."

"Very well," said Ranik. "I need boy. Do not. Need you."

The wolf lunged but Tam dodged, clawing five bloody gashes along the wolf's side. Bo clamped a hand over his mouth to stem his whoop of joy.

Perhaps . . . perhaps Tam would win!

But Bo's hope was short-lived. Though Tam was fast — her claws and talons deadly sharp — the wolf was stronger and soon he had overpowered the Korahku. Tam roared with pain as the wolf sank his teeth into her already mangled wing and tore. Suddenly, Tam wasn't moving at all.

The wolf's head jerked at the sound of Bo's strangled cry.

"Why are you doing this?" said Bo, stepping out from behind the tree, Nix by his side. There was no point hiding anymore. "What do you want from me?"

"Answers," said the wolf with a bloodstained grin.

Bo shook his head. "But Mads never told me anything." His eyes flicked to Tam on the ground—her chest rose and fell with shallow, labored breaths. She was alive. *Alive!* If only he could keep the wolf talking. Maybe he could distract him long enough for Tam to wake up. "But . . . but . . . I *did* overhear something," he said. "About a wolf who ate the Stars."

Ranik towered over Tam's inert body. He blinked slowly but did not interrupt; clearly, he was listening.

"He's locked in a cage. Don't know where," said Bo. "But I know there are three keys needed to open the cage. You said you were looking for your brother—is it him? Is he the wolf who ate the Stars?"

The wolf inched forward. "Very good. Very smart."

"Then I can help you. You want to get your brother back. And I need to find him so I can set the Stars free. We can help each other."

The wolf shook his head.

"We were tricked," he said. "Were promised. All of Ulv. To rule. That Stars would. Give us power. But she lied."

"She?"

"The Shadow Witch. She wants Stars. To destroy. No more good magic. Just chaos and Darkness. But Stars belong. To brother and me. So we can rule. Rule this land. Have our revenge. The Shadow Witch. Rises again. But I will. Get to Stars. First. You will not. Steal them."

Bo edged back. "I don't know where your brother is and I don't know anything about the witch," he said. He collided with the tree trunk, trying to back away. "And I don't want the Stars for myself. I just want to set them free."

"They will not. Go free. They belong. To brother. And to me. We will rule. With their power. Tell me. The truth. Or die."

"But I don't know any more."

Ranik laughed. "I can. Make you. Tell me." He inched closer. Beside Bo, Nix growled. "Or I can. Just kill you. And find brother. Myself."

Bo swallowed hard as he slid down the base of the trunk and pulled Nix in tight. Tam lay motionless on the ground and the wolf moved closer.

This was it.

This was the end.

A spear of Light shot past Bo and hit the wolf full in the chest. The wolf spiraled through the air and tumbled — *thump!* — to the ground.

Bo spun around and saw a girl his age, her hands held out in front, her eyes bulging, and a sled full of kindling beside her. Her long silver braids were like a bouquet of swords and her skin was a deep golden brown, the color of half-Light in the Burning Season.

The girl hurried toward Bo but pulled up short when the wolf climbed to his feet and snarled.

He pawed at the ground as if to charge, but the girl flung out her hands again and icy sparks shot from each of her fingers, piercing Ranik's fur like knives. The giant wolf whimpered and backed away. The girl looked at her hands as though they didn't belong to her.

But Bo understood. He had seen it before.

Magic.

"What. Are. You?" said the wolf. His lips curled back as he tore his hate-filled gaze from the girl to Bo. "Soon," he promised. "You will. Tell me. Answers. Soon." He turned and raced down the hill, out of sight.

Bo's heart banged against his ribs, like desperate knocks at a locked door seconds before the Dark descended. He had so many questions for the girl but his eyes were drawn to Tam, bloodied and inert.

"Help me," he said to the girl before crawling to Tam's side. He grabbed the Korahku's hand and called her name — no response.

"Don't tell anyone," said the girl as she collapsed to her knees beside Bo, breathing heavily.

"What?"

She blinked at Bo. "About the . . . *magic*."

Bo looked at her: her eyes were large and wide-set, her fore-head high, her chin pointed. "If you promise to help me get Tam to safety, then okay."

She nodded. "Deal."

THE TRUE HISTORIES OF ULV, VOL. IV

HOW THE SILENT SISTERS LOST THEIR VOICES

ou are no doubt aware that the province of Nev'en is ruled by a religious order known as the Silent Sisters. (If you are *not* aware, then what on Ulv have you been doing instead of reading each volume of this illustrious collection with rapt attention? *Tsk!* Go back and see *The True Histories of Ulv,* Vol. III, "How a Lovesick King Lost His Throne.") But do you know how this order came to be?

Of course you don't. Let me enlighten you.

There once were three sisters. They were the kind of beautiful that made young men gather their cheese and jellied pig's trotters and lindberry beer and hop to the highest ground. But wishes had no effect on the hearts of the sisters, and each time they refused offers of marriage, the men grew angry.

One man decided to cast a spell to steal their voices. And when he came to ask for the eldest sister's hand in marriage, she could not say no. She was dragged to church and forced to marry him.

But on their wedding night she cut out his tongue and ran back to her sisters. The village men came for them with knives and fire and pitchforks, but the women of the village had formed a circle around the sisters' hut and would not let them through.

So the men left. And when the three sisters marched up Lunaris Mountain and carved a temple into the rockface, the women of the village followed them, devoting their lives to healing and prayer and philosophy.

And so was born the Temple of the Silent Sisters. Each Sister takes a vow of silence and an oath to protect all citizens of Ulv in times of trouble. So, if you have an ailment — of the body or mind — the temple is the place for you.

CHAPTER THIRTEEN

A SHEEN OF SWEAT GLISTENED on the girl's forehead as they hauled Tam in the sled over the craggy, windswept landscape. She was lankier than Bo, with limbs that dangled as if the screws that kept her together needed tightening.

Nix trotted beside them, licking Tam's limp hand that hung over the side and whimpering at the trail of blood behind them. *My fault,* thought Bo, hugging the Korahku's blue robe to his chest. *It's all my fault.*

Tam had woken briefly, enough for the two children to help her into the sled, but had quickly slipped back into unconsciousness, despite Bo's pleas. The girl had wrapped Tam's wounds in an unfamiliar leaf before handing Bo a rope and ordering him to pull.

Soon, they crested a rocky hill and Bo stumbled at the impossible sight looming ahead of him.

There was a castle.

There was a castle carved *into* the mountainside.

There were other buildings too, clusters of villages circling the castle, all carved into the steep vertical rockface, their windows illuminated with flickering candle-Light.

Bo's mouth fell open. "What on Ulv?"

"Temple City, capital of Nev'en," explained the girl, cheeks puffed as she breathed in short, sharp, spluttering bursts. "The Sisters will help your friend, even though she's a Korahku. We take an oath to help *all* peoples of Ulv, regardless of which province they're from, and Sister Magrid is —"

"Did you say *Sisters?*"

"Of course! The castle you see there is the Temple of the Silent Sisters. Don't you know *anything?*"

Before Bo could respond, two tall women approached them, shimmering in orange robes patterned with golden teardrops. The girl bowed her head reverently but Bo stared up at them in awe — skin in shades of mellow brown and ochre and limbs that moved, soft and delicate, as though conducting great symphonies. Their gazes brushed over Bo and Nix and then Tam, and without a word, they scooped up the Korahku as if she weighed no more than a single feather and carried her away.

"Wait!" cried Bo. "Where are you taking her?"

"To see Sister Magrid, of course," said the girl, dropping the sled rope at her feet. "Follow me."

They climbed the stone-carved stairs that zigzagged up the mountainside to the temple entrance, leaving the now-empty sled at the base. Already the two women were far ahead of them.

"Do you know the Scribe?" Bo asked.

The girl glanced over her shoulder at him, a frown troubling her brow. "No. There's no Scribe here," she said, and then doubled her pace. "Keep up, Irin boy!"

Bo was breathless by the time they reached the stone entranceway, hands on knees and gasping for air. The two women had vanished.

Was there really no Scribe? Had the Un-King lied? Bo's disappointment knotted with his guilt and his fear for Tam and he felt sick. He would have to look elsewhere. But where?

"Remember you promised," said the girl. She tugged on his sleeve. "Say nothing about *magic*." She screwed up her face, as though the word tasted bitter. "And don't tell them I said a *word*. Sister Agnethe will have my tongue for a hat if she discovers I've been chitter-chatting when it's not the Time of Speaking."

Though he didn't understand a word she said, Bo nodded. He didn't have the breath to speak anyway.

"Well, I'm Selene," she said.

"Bo." Bo nodded at Nix. "And Nix."

Selene's answering grin was wonky. "Brace yourself, Bo."

Before Bo could ask, *What for?* Selene had shoved open the heavy stone door and he was hit with a wave of angry voices.

"And now they bring a Korahku here. A *Korahku!*"

"We'll be murdered in our beds!"

"We'll be sacrificed to the Shadow Creatures!"

Selene dragged Bo into a cavernous hall, so large it could fit a forest and the treetops would barely tickle the ceiling. It was overflowing with shouting, sneering, arm-waving Irin.

Hundreds of makeshift tents were crammed into every nook and cranny as far as Bo could see — tatty blankets slung over washing lines, underneath them miserable-looking people huddled close for warmth. They were dressed in dirty rags, cheeks hollow with hunger.

More women in orange robes drifted among them, offering food and water in silence.

Selene bent close to his ear. "Shadow Creatures have run everyone out of their villages. The displaced Nev'en are being housed in the city, so the Irin are coming to the temple for safety but—"

Selene jumped as a sour-faced Sister appeared in front of them — wide-set eyes, small mouth, reddish-brown skin like river rock. "Bring him, Selene." Her voice was sharp enough to draw blood. "The Time of Speaking has started and he must explain himself to the High Sisters. After all, what sort of Irin consorts with a Korahku?"

The crowd scattered, clearing a path as she marched away.

"That's Sister Agnethe," whispered Selene, dragging Bo after the haughty woman. "Nastier than a grimboil on a pungpong, but she's second in charge after the High Sisters, so you'd better listen to what she says."

Hundreds of eyes burned into Bo's back as he was led through the crowd, their angry whispers chasing him: He *brought the Korahku? Is he a witch? Will he kill us in our beds?* It felt like being home again, having stale bread tossed at his head and hearing children told to "keep away from that boy — he's cursed." Nix growled but even that did not stop the chatter.

They turned a corner into a room with a high ceiling and open arches. It was filled with orange-robed women sweeping back and forth like a flock of birds. They held scrolls and read aloud as they walked, their robes swooshing and arms sweeping in grand, graceful gestures.

"What is happiness?" said a woman as she wafted past. "Is it the absence of sadness or something more?"

"And if we add *three* drops of essence of trolldung to the mixture, then I am certain it will make an excellent tincture for the removal of boils," said another.

Sister Agnethe weaved through the sea of orange, marching toward the far side of the room, where Bo spied three women in elegant ruby-red robes perched on thrones carved from stone.

Selene followed, dragging Bo with her.

"What are your thoughts on the migration patterns of the yellow-breasted titter?" said a plump woman with glasses as

Bo passed. A woman with bony fingers and a hawkish nose grabbed his arm — he almost dropped Tam's robe. "Never mind that — how can you tell the difference between *something* and *nothing?*"

Bo shook his head. "I don't . . . I mean . . . I'm not . . ."

Selene pulled him away, rolling her eyes. "It's the Time of Speaking," she explained. "We only get one hour a day and it's hard to get it all out at once, you know?"

When they reached the far side of the room, Sister Agnethe was waiting, flapping her hand. "Come here. Quickly. We haven't got all day, child." From their thrones, the three women in ruby-red robes watched him carefully. Bo's eyes skittered over them and then behind to where several large tapestries depicted scenes of mountains and trees and people — was one woman holding a *tongue?* — and wolves and, *oh,* what were those tiny dots of bright Light all over the thick, black night sky?

"The High Sisters," whispered Selene, nudging him forward. "Sister Noora, Sister Ffion, and Sister Vela. Good luck!" She bowed and scurried away, instantly lost in the throng of babbling orange-robed women. Nix brushed against Bo's calf with a low growl.

Sister Noora and Sister Ffion watched him with cool interest but Sister Vela smiled warmly. Her hair was a wild tangle of gold, bronze, and silver, her skin a bluish black.

"The Irin child who brought us the Korahku," announced

Sister Agnethe. She scowled at Bo as if he were a colossal spit-mouth slug that had just spat steaming sludge all over her shoes.

Sister Vela stepped down from the dais, opening her arms wide. "Welcome," she said. Her voice tinkled like wind chimes and Bo felt soothed by the warmth in her gaze.

"Is my friend going to be okay?" he asked. "Tam? The Korahku?"

"*Tsk, tsk, tsk,*" said Sister Vela. "Never you worry. We have the best healers in the land tending to her. Now come, you must tell us why you are here. Where is your family?"

"I ... I don't have one," he said, lowering his head. "My guardian was killed and my mother abandoned me when I was a baby. My father died before I was born."

Sister Vela laid a hand on Bo's shoulder, sympathy twisting her mouth downward. "I am sorry to hear that, my child. But rest assured, you may stay here for as long as you need."

Bo thought back to the villagers in the cavernous hall, their mouths pressed thin and their eyes narrowed. But he nodded, thankful — he was unused to such kindness and it made his skin prickle. He would stay until Tam was better, of course, but then he would have to leave again. Where was the Scribe if she wasn't here?

Sister Vela smiled brightly at him, her perfectly white teeth like the little dots of Light on the tapestry behind her. He looked over her shoulder and frowned. There was something about them . . .

"Excuse me, but what is that?" He pointed at the tapestry. Sister Vela turned to look.

"Oh, don't you know about the Stars? Not many people do, I suppose." She guided him to the wall hanging despite Sister Agnethe's cluck of disapproval. Up close the woven wool was thick and fuzzy and soft, and Bo longed to reach out and pluck the Stars from the sky before the leaping wolf could eat them. They were not at all like he had imagined — they were *better*.

"You see, long ago there were thousands of Stars, but three shone brightest of all." Sister Vela pointed to three Stars that were indeed bigger and brighter than the others. "And there was a Moon who was the mother of all Stars. She ruled the heavens, see?" She pointed to a large orb in the center of the tapestry. "The three bright Stars were named Elena the Protector, Mathias the Gift-Giver, and Freja the Magic-Maker. The people of Ulv prayed to them — to Elena for protection, to Mathias for wishes, and to Freja for magic. The more the people prayed, the brighter the three Stars shone. But that made the Moon angry — she wanted the people to pray to *her*. She wanted to shine brightest of *all*."

Bo leaned closer, practically squishing his nose against the fuzzy wool. He wondered which one was Mathias the Gift-Giver. Which one would have granted his wishes?

"In a jealous rage the Moon cast the three Stars from the heavens. They fell to Ulv and into bodies — people like you and me. Freja was angry and wanted revenge but Elena refused to help; a war in the heavens would be catastrophic for the people of Ulv and it was her duty to protect us. So Freja used her Star-magic and turned Elena into a statue that is still in Aud to this day! But Mathias agreed to help, so together they bewitched two wolves, tricking them into believing that if they ate the Sun, Stars, and Moon, they would become all-powerful."

"*Two* wolves?"

"Indeed. The Sun was saved — her powerful rays of Light burned one of the wolves, and he fell back to Ulv and disappeared forever, cursing all wolves to never walk in full Light again — but the remaining wolf managed to eat all the Stars in the sky before he became so sick he fell. The Moon was frightened, so she fled — no one knows where to.

"But when Mathias saw that Freja had no intention of returning to the heavens, he knew he had to stop her — she had become the Shadow Witch, a hateful creature consumed by a desire to destroy the Stars and let Darkness rule. So, he locked away the wolf who ate the Stars and defeated the witch in battle."

"That's ..." Bo frowned at the tiny flecks of Light. "That's a sad story." Bo was a tangle of relief — *Finally! Some answers! Some clarity!* — and niggling confusion. Why didn't Mads tell him the full story? Why did Tam refuse to talk about the Stars *at all?*

The High Sister smiled. "It is. Most Ulvians have come to see the Stars as a myth, a bedtime story for children. But we here at the temple are different. We like truth and we love to ask questions." She winked. "I think you might too."

Was that why? Did Mads and Tam not know the truth?

A commotion behind them turned Bo's head. A man was pushing against the flow of the muttering Sisters, elbowing his way through with red-faced anger.

Bo gasped when he recognized the man's face.

It was the Innkeeper.

"That's him!" spat the Innkeeper, jabbing a stubby finger at Bo. His chest heaved as he came to a halt. More villagers followed him, pushing past the Sisters. They pointed their fingers too. "That's the Devil-child who set the Shadow Creatures on us," one of them said.

Since Bo had last seen the Innkeeper, his cheeks had hollowed and there was a large gash above his right eye, but he had lost none of his arrogance, none of his puffed-up anger. "You have no idea the trouble he caused our village. As a baby he survived a night in the Forest of Long Shadows — not a scratch on him! He leads the Shadow Creatures, you see?" The Innkeeper folded his arms across his chest and glared. Bo bit back his retort; it stung, sour and rotting in his belly.

"I lost my daughter because of him!" shouted a member of the crowd.

"He ate all my chickens!" yelled another.

"He led the Shadow Creatures right to us!"

A ripple of frightened gasps echoed through the room. Bo wanted to fold up into himself and hide forever. He gripped Tam's robe with tight fists to stop his hands from shaking and tried to think of good things: running through the forest with Nix, splashing in the river in the Burning Season, stuffing his face with apple crackling, catching Mads smile as he made shadow puppets with his hands in the candle-Light.

"Kick him out!" yelled someone from the crowd.

"Nonsense," said Sister Vela, but Bo saw how the other Sisters were looking at him now, how Sisters Noora and Ffion frowned deeply. "The child stays with us."

"This is a travesty!" shouted the Innkeeper.

Sister Vela's eyes narrowed as she rounded on him. "If you disagree, then you are welcome to leave the temple and seek shelter elsewhere," she said.

The Innkeeper lowered his head.

"Thank you," murmured Bo as Sister Vela's fingers squeezed his shoulder gently.

"The Time of Speaking is almost at an end," announced Sister Noora as she stood. "Sisters, retreat to the prayer room for quiet reflection. The rest of you, return to the Great Hall and we'll hear no more on this matter."

Sister Vela gave Bo a nod and a smile before she exited behind her fellow High Sisters.

Every woman in orange filed out of the room quietly, but the villagers stood their ground, scowling and murmuring their dissatisfaction. Bo gasped as hands grabbed him from behind; Sister Agnethe had taken hold of him, fingers pinching his arm as she dragged him out of the room. She sneered as Nix barked at her. "You will make yourself useful while you are here, boy," she said. "You will stay out of trouble and you will work hard. Every eye will be on you. Do you hear me? Every eye."

Bo nodded. He wanted to duck his head and hide but he couldn't help looking at the people he passed. At the scowling Innkeeper and the grimy, muck-stained faces that sneered and frowned and narrowed their eyes at him.

"Just wait until I find you alone, boy," said the Innkeeper.

Bo looked away; he wouldn't give the Innkeeper the satisfaction of seeing him tremble.

Sister Agnethe dragged him through the Great Hall and through winding, empty corridors before she shoved him into a small windowless closet with Nix.

"What about Tam?" said Bo. "I want to see her."

But Sister Agnethe had already closed the door and there was nothing but cold silence.

Later, as shadows dripped like candle wax down the closet walls, Bo sat in a pool of Light on the stone floor, brushing one hand through Nix's fur, and in his other hand he held the mysterious key. He turned it over and over.

"It's no use," he told Nix. "Can't figure out what these carved squiggles are supposed to be. And what are all those dots?"

His troubles weighed heavy on his shoulders — he felt as if he were carrying an invisible giant on his back. If he couldn't figure out where to find the next key, he would never be able to release the Stars. Then there wouldn't be enough magic to bring Mads back, and Bo could never make a wish to find his mother.

And then there was Tam . . .

Bo pulled his knees to his chest and hugged them. He glanced nervously at the shadows around him. "If the Scribe isn't here, then where is she?" he asked Nix. He tried to blink his tears away, but they were stubborn and slid down his cheeks regardless. "At least we've got each other," said Bo in a small voice. "Let's just sleep, okay?"

There wasn't a bed or blankets, but Bo and Nix curled up beside each other on the stone floor, Bo resting his head on his new rucksack, Tam's robe spread across them both. "Maybe things will be better in the morning," he whispered. "Tam will be well again and we can keep searching for the Scribe. Maybe Tam will come with us. Do you think that's why she came back and saved us? Do you think she's not angry at me?"

He drifted to sleep with tear-stained cheeks and a heart that ached with homesickness.

CHAPTER FOURTEEN

EARLY NEXT MORNING the door to Bo's closet opened and Selene came running in, dropping the basket she carried. *Splat!* Noxious liquids and powders smashed all over the floor. "Hogsbeard!" she cursed.

Nix barked.

Bo sprang to standing. "How's Tam?" he demanded.

Selene glowered at the spill. "I'm in so much trouble," she moaned. She bent and gathered everything that wasn't broken into her basket.

"I asked you a question," said Bo. "How's Tam? Where is she? Why can't I see her?"

Selene looked up, narrowing her eyes. "Don't get your tongue in knots," she snapped. "She's in the hospital wing and Sister Magrid is seeing to her *personally*." When Bo's face remained unimpressed, Selene screwed up her nose. "You know who Sister Magrid is, don't you?"

Bo shrugged. She could be the troll queen for all he cared.

"Only the best healer in the entire land," said Selene. She tapped a fist to her chest, raising her chin. "And I'm her apprentice, so that makes me the second-best healer in the land. Sort of. If you think about it. Anyway, I'm here to fix you."

"You've got green gunk on your foot," said Bo.

Selene rubbed her foot clean and then stared at Bo for a long time. "You're short," she concluded.

"And you've got magic," said Bo.

"No, I don't! It was a mistake. And it doesn't make you any less short. But you're short because you're an Irin." She grinned, big and wonky. "It's an honor to meet you." She leaned forward and waited. When Bo just stared she rolled her eyes. "You're supposed to press your forehead to mine. It's how you say hello, don't you know?"

"Oh." Bo stood on his tiptoes to press his forehead against hers. "Nice to meet you," he said, then flinched as her nose brushed his, their foreheads bumping.

Selene rubbed her brow. "Is that how Irin greet each other? I like our way better."

"Your way?"

"The Nev'en way. You're an Irin and I'm a Nev'en, but we've got common ancestors — we're basically cousins. Don't you know *anything*?"

Bo blushed furiously. Nix yapped.

"I suppose I ought to fix you." Selene pulled some potions

from her basket and scraped together a handful of powder that had been spilled on the floor.

"I'm not hurt."

"I've got just the thing," she said, ignoring him.

Selene was clumsy as she slapped sticky potions and powders on Bo's cuts and grazes. Each time he winced, Selene clicked her tongue and told him not to be such a baby. "I know what I'm doing. I mean, I *did* use sneezewort instead of freezewort, but that was only one time, I swear. Well, maybe twice but the second time was not my fault. Who stores sneezewort next to freezewort? That's just asking for trouble if you ask me, but nobody ever does."

Bo sniffed the blue powder Selene had just daubed on a gash on his arm. "So, you're an apprentice healer?"

"To the *best* healer in the *entire* land," said Selene, her nose lifted and her voice haughty. "I don't get to go to the school with the children in the city, but it's far better to be here, where it's . . . it's . . . quiet."

"Well, for a Silent Sister you've got an awful lot to say. *Ouch*."

Selene slapped a broad purple leaf over Bo's arm. "I told you we're not *supposed* to talk. The Time of Speaking is for Deep and Profound philosophical discussions, but I've got more than an hour's worth of things to say. I'm *very* deep and profound." She stood back and appraised Bo. "Let's be friends," she said. "I've never had a friend, so you can be my first."

Bo's cheeks flushed. "I—"

"Brilliant." Selene flashed him her wonky grin. "And because you're my friend, you're going to help me harvest the corpse weed."

"I am?"

"Oh yes! It's what friends do." She turned on her heel and marched away. "It only eats you if you touch the flowers. Or is it if you *don't* touch the flowers? I'm sure we'll work it out. Come on!"

Bo frowned down at Nix. "I'm not sure I like her idea of friends," he said. But he donned his cloak and followed anyway.

∽

Bo and Nix were roused at first Light by pounding on the closet door. It swung open to reveal a sour-faced Sister Agnethe, who grabbed Bo's arm and yanked him down corridor after corridor without a word, Nix trotting behind them.

Bo had been with the Silent Sisters for five days. Five long days filled with chopping wood, fetching water, washing dishes, scrubbing floors, "do this" and "do that." Five days of trying to avoid the Innkeeper; of begging every Sister he passed for news of Tam, only to be met with silence; of being shooed away every time he tried to get near Sister Vela.

Five nights of barely seeing Selene, and sleeping on the floor of a cold, damp closet.

Sister Agnethe led them to the kitchens and Bo's heart sank;

he had spent all yesterday scrubbing the gunk off pots and pans, and it appeared today would be no different.

The kitchen hands turned to stare as Bo entered; they wore rags and the same sad, hollow-eyed expression as the people in the main hall. Thankfully, the Innkeeper was not among them.

Yesterday, Bo had been carrying firewood through the Great Hall, his eyes lowered. "There he is," someone hissed. "The boy who rules the Shadow Creatures." Bo had hunched his shoulders and quickened his step, knowing that anything he said back would be twisted and used against him. But he wasn't fast enough.

Bo had just enough time to register the feeling of someone's boot knocking his feet out from under him and Nix yapping madly before — *splat, crack, thump!* — he landed on the stone floor, firewood tumbling everywhere and pain shooting from his wrist to his shoulder.

For a moment everything was quiet — a stunned hush as Nix nuzzled the side of Bo's face. But then the laughter started. The sneers and the hoots and the backslaps. Bo's anger tore through his insides like a firecracker. He wanted to stand and swing his fists. But instead, he pushed himself onto his knees and looked up at the hate-filled stares surrounding him. His throat was tight with the pain of refusing to cry.

Suddenly the Innkeeper was beside him; he recognized him

by his boots, rabbit-fur boots full of holes and covered in dust and perfect for tripping people with.

"You might have those simpering Sisters fooled," hissed the Innkeeper, "but I know what you are and I've got my eye on you. You'll never escape me, do you hear?"

Bo had run from the hall, Nix at his heels; he didn't even bother to pick up the spilled firewood. He was glad the tears hadn't fallen until he was out of sight.

Now Bo looked at the kitchen hands and wondered whether any of them had witnessed his humiliation. Had they called him names and whispered about his "curse" and how they would be better off without him here?

Sister Agnethe snapped her fingers at Bo, scowling as Nix growled at her. Her robes *swish-swoosh*ed as she hurried down the central aisle, headed for a small room in the back. Bo chased the Sister's echoing footsteps, avoiding the accusing eyes that followed him. In the back room she pointed to a mountain of dishes that looked as if a colossal spit-mouth slug had vomited all over them.

Down and down Bo's heart sank.

Bo took the dishcloth Sister Agnethe offered him, scrunching it into his fist. "You haven't told me about Tam. Can I visit her?"

Sister Agnethe snorted, giving him one more pinched-mouthed scowl before swishing away.

"I guess that's a no," he said.

As Nix curled into a ball by his feet, shivering from the cold air, Bo set to work on the dishes — he didn't have a choice. He would not leave this temple until he was certain Tam was better. He owed her that at least.

An hour later and Bo was sure the mountain of dishes had grown twice its size. "Where do they even come from? Is it magic? How am I supposed to find the next two keys and set the Stars free if I can't even clear a pile of dishes?"

He didn't realize there were tears in his eyes until the mound of dishes became a hazy blur. He rubbed the backs of his hands across his damp cheeks and muttered angrily about Sister Agnethe and dishes and wolves and innkeepers and Stars.

"Stars?" asked a voice behind him before it was swallowed up in a loud crash. Bo spun around in time to see an avalanche of pots and pans rolling onto the floor.

"Hogsbeard!" cursed Selene, glancing down at the mess. "Oh dear."

Bo had hardly seen his new friend over the last five days — she rushed about the temple, chasing an errand or slogging away at her chores. But she always shot Bo her wonky smile and made sure to whisper reassurances about Tam. "I'm not allowed in the hospital wing until I'm a red-level apprentice," she told him regretfully, "but I do know Sister Magrid is the very, very *best*. I'm sure your friend is fine."

Selene quickly gathered the pots and pans and dumped them on the counter. She ran up to Bo, breathless. "What were you saying about Stars? They're a cure for sadness, are they not? Yes, that's right. You grind them up with fonkeling seeds and keep them in a pouch under your pillow for three days. Or is that majars?"

Bo shook his head, rubbing his eyes clear of any remaining dampness. "I was only talking nonsense because I'm angry. Sister Agnethe keeps making me clean dishes. She's nastier than a boil on a troll's bum."

Selene's high-pitched laugh was muffled behind her hand. Bo smiled until he remembered the mountain of dishes in front of him, that Tam was hidden somewhere in this enormous castle, that Ranik was waiting to harm him. Until he remembered Stars and witches and keys and Scribes.

"I'm stuck here," he said. "Maybe forever."

"I know what you mean," muttered Selene, lowering her gaze to stare at her bare feet.

Bo frowned as he watched her. "How come you live here?" he asked. It was a question that had tickled the tip of his tongue every day he had been at the temple. Bo thought this place — the silence and the scowls and the rules — was a cage for her. She was like a young sapling struggling to find enough Light to grow under the thick canopy of much bigger trees. Bo thought he understood what that felt like better than anyone.

Selene rolled back her shoulders, stabbing a thumb at her chest. "Because I'm an apprentice," she said, "and Sister Magrid is the *best* healer in all of Ulv and my parents are very important people. They're *so* important that they live in the Sovereign State with the Queen of Ulv — the *actual* queen — and they don't have time to raise me because my mother is head of the Queen's Guard and my father is . . . He's, um, he's the Queen's *personal* advisor and if I want to be as successful as them, then I have to train here and . . . and . . . and . . . they left me here to be an apprentice when I was just a baby even though they really didn't want to because they loved me *so* much but they write to me *every* day and tell me how much they miss me and . . ." She frowned as her blustering speech ran out of puff. Bo couldn't help but feel a pang of sadness at the little crease of worry between Selene's brows. "And they'll come back for me one day," she said in a quiet voice. "I know they will." Her frown deepened; her lips pursed in annoyance. "Do you want to know something?" she said, looking up at Bo. "Something I've never told anyone?"

"What?"

"I don't even want to be a healer. I hate Sister Magrid's boring lessons and learning about sneezewort and freezewort and skrimsl pong and blue nightshade. I want to be in the Queen's Guard."

Bo smiled so big his cheeks ached. "You'd make a brilliant guard. Just look what you did to that wolf, Ranik."

Selene clamped a hand over her mouth, eyes wide. "But that was . . ." She leaned forward and whispered, "That was *magic*. And magic is bad. Very bad."

Bo shrugged. "I don't understand why."

Selene rolled her eyes. "Of course you don't. They never taught you *anything* in Irin. I know magic is bad because everyone says so. Sister Magrid told me all about it — how there used to be magic and that's how the Shadow Creatures were created and everyone who had magic was evil and tried to rule over the non-magic folk. But then it vanished and it was supposed to *stay* vanished. Something terrible must have happened."

"But there is good magic," said Bo. "Not *all* magic is bad."

Perhaps it was her honesty in telling him her true feelings about being an apprentice, or perhaps it was that *she* had trusted *him* to keep her secret about magic. Either way, Bo realized he could trust Selene. She was, after all, just as trapped in this place as he was. And did he have any other choice but to trust her? No — not unless he wanted five more days of chores and being bullied by the Innkeeper and worrying about Tam.

From his pocket, Bo produced the first key and showed it to Selene. "Can you keep a secret?" he asked. When she nodded, he told her everything that had happened since the wolf attacked Mads.

"Mads said magic was returning but it *can* be good," he

added when he had finished telling Selene his story. "If we find the Stars we can make wishes — anything we want!"

"I could wish to become an apprentice guard!" She chewed on her lip.

"I just need to figure out where the second key is, but I don't know what these scribbles are . . ."

Selene grabbed the key and held it almost to her nose as she inspected the engravings carefully. A grin spread across her face. "It's writing!" she said. "Can't you see?"

Bo chewed on the inside of his cheek as he shook his head. His face grew hot.

"Oh. It's in Ancient Ulvish, so maybe you can't read that," offered Selene, and Bo nodded.

"Yeah," he said. "That must be it."

Selene cleared her throat. "It says: 'To speak of me is to break me.'" She turned to Bo with a satisfied smile, head tilted as though waiting for praise. But all Bo could do was frown: the words meant as much to him now as when he hadn't even known they were words. It must be another riddle.

"What does it mean?"

"How should I know?" said Selene, nose in the air. "Even though I know *heaps* and of course I really *did* know what Stars were all along. I didn't really think they were a cure for sadness. It's just that Sister Magrid does go *on* and *on* and how can I be expected to listen to *everything* she says?"

Bo's shoulders sagged. What was the point of knowing what the key said if it was just a load of gibberish?

"I'm never going to figure this out," he murmured. At his feet, Nix whimpered. Bo glanced over his shoulder at the dishes that hadn't washed themselves while his back had been turned. If only he had magic too.

Selene handed the key back, a thoughtful look on her face. "I don't know what it means," she said, "but . . ."

"But what?"

"I know who might." Selene looked up and met Bo's frown with a glint in her eyes.

"Who?" said Bo.

Selene grinned. "The Scribe."

CHAPTER FIFTEEN

T HE SCRIBE?" BO CRIED. "But you said she wasn't here!"

Selene shrugged, still grinning. "The Scribe is a *secret*. We're not supposed to tell strangers she's here."

"I'm not a stranger," said Bo. He wrung the dishcloth in his hands.

"Not *now*. You were when you first asked. But now you're my friend, and friends tell each other secrets." Selene charged from the room. "What are you waiting for, Irin?" she called over her shoulder. "You're slower than a slugskild swimming through a bogmarsh!"

Bo rolled his eyes and threw the dishcloth to the counter. "The dishes can wait, right, Nix?"

Nix barked.

They chased after Selene, excitement thrumming through Bo's veins. This time, the hollow-eyed kitchen workers ignored him as he passed, engrossed in their conversations: ". . . and charged me twenty Raha for a ghost charm that didn't work!"

Bo caught up to Selene in the corridor. The young Nev'en was tapping her foot and scowling. "Honestly, if I had to spend my life waiting for you I'd be as bored as a rurer on a flodhestopomus's nose."

"Don't know what a flodhestopomus is, but I'm sure its nose is a perfectly nice place to be," said Bo. Nix yapped in agreement.

Selene rolled her eyes before hurrying away with a snort of laughter. "Keep up, Irin. You and your dog."

Bo looked down at Nix. "Why does no one know what a fox is? Come on, then. Before we lose her."

Down steps, around corners, and over smooth stone floors they hurried until Selene gently opened a door to a room overflowing with books and scrolls and torn paper and feather pens and chairs and empty teacups and dust motes floating in the air in a silent, mournful waltz. In the center of the room was a wooden desk and sprawled across the desk's smooth surface was a scroll, unraveled and dotted with lines of small, spidery black marks.

Sitting at the desk with her back to them was a woman hunched over her work, a feather pen in her hand. She was fine-boned and small, with glowing, wrinkled, golden-brown skin. Her gray hair was coiled on top of her head.

But the woman was not alone in the room.

There were owls: two on the windowsill, three perched on the desk, one atop a bookcase, and two little ones hopping along the back of the chair. *Hoot, hoot, hoot,* said the owls, tilting their heads at Bo.

But the woman didn't turn. Bo watched her rock back and forth as she scribbled on the parchment.

"Won't do, won't do," she muttered. "Wrong, wrong, wrong!"

Selene leaned against the doorframe and sighed loudly. "Hogsbeard! She's in the middle of writing. She won't want to be disturbed."

Bo wondered why the old woman didn't turn at the sound of Selene's voice, but all she did was mutter and scribble and continue to rock back and forth. How could she not have noticed that two kids and a fox had wandered into her room? The owls had certainly noticed.

"*This* is the Scribe?" whispered Bo.

Selene nodded. "She's a bit . . . eccentric. She's the one who records *The True Histories of Ulv.* Everything that has ever happened in the entire land and she writes it all down. Can you imagine? Everything that has *ever* happened! No one knows how she does it, but the last person who dared ask ended up with a boil on her tongue so big she couldn't speak for a year!"

One of the owls—russet feathers and a broad oval face —hopped along the edge of the desk and bobbed its head, hooting loudly at the Scribe. The Scribe's hand shot up. "Ha! That's it! Yes, yes, that will do! That will do nicely. Thanks ever so much for that tidbit, Abnus. You're ever so wise," she said before returning to her furious scribbling. A tawny owl fluttered through the window and landed, with a shiver of feathers, on top of a teetering pile of scrolls. It looked familiar somehow.

"What do we do if we want her attention?" whispered Bo.

"Well, that's the thing, see. She's a Qirachi — same ancestors as Irin and Nev'en except there was something about a shape-shifter or an Elfvor princess. I'm not sure — Sister Magrid does tend to go on and I don't always listen. But the point is Qirachi don't take lightly to interruptions. In fact, one time she called Sister Agnethe a rotting wratweezle for breathing too loudly three rooms away. Ha!"

Bo frowned. "A Qirachi? What's —"

"A Qirachi," said a surprisingly deep voice from the center of the room, "is one of the Seven Great Kin of Ulv, and what your friend tells you is true. We do *not* take kindly to interruptions."

Bo spun around to find the Scribe had turned to face them and was peering over wire-rimmed spectacles at him. The owls stared at him too.

Mumbling his apologies, Bo shuffled backwards until he brushed against the wall. "We didn't mean to disturb you . . . or . . . I mean . . . we *did* wish to disturb you but . . . we thought . . ."

"*The True Histories of Ulv,* Volume Three, 'The Qirachi,'" said the Scribe. She tilted her head upward, squinting as if trying to remember something. "'The Qirachi live mainly in the northwest, south of the Lost Lands of Sneeskove,'" she said in her rumbling voice. "'They have shockingly good hearing—in tests conducted by the Royal Ulvish Academy of the Extraordinary, it was proven that an adult Qirachi could hear the beating of a butterfly's wings from a distance of ten miles away! Of course this makes the world a rather loud place for the Qirachi, so you will find they are none too fond of jabbering fools.'"

Bo stared at the woman. She blinked at him with eyes that were large, round, and gray.

"Did you like that?" she asked. "*I* wrote it, so think very carefully before you answer."

Bo's mouth opened and closed but no words came out.

"Irin," she said. She had a way of stretching her words, rounding the sounds until they were bloated and puffy. "*The True Histories of Ulv,* Volume Three. 'The Irin are a primitive, pale-skinned, and short piglike people who find great comfort in persecuting others, whether for actual or invented differences. Show an Irin the sweetest baby fluefenhare and he will find fifty or more reasons to be afraid of it.'" She tapped the side of her head and grinned. "See? Memory like an elkefant."

"Piglike?" gasped Bo.

"Ever met the Un-King? Fool of a man. Can't abide my owls."

"We're *nothing* like pigs, thank you very much. Selene says I've got the same ancestors as her. And Tam said we didn't come from pigs."

The Scribe looked him up and down and grinned. "True enough. And I dare say you've got a bit more Nev'en in you than you think, judging by those lanky limbs and that tawny skin. Still, how do you feel about fluefenhare?" The Scribe narrowed her large eyes at him.

Bo looked to Selene for help. She shrugged.

"I'm more afraid of wolves," said Bo.

"Well, right you'd be," said the Scribe. "And I dare say our lovely Sister Agnethe curdles your blood too. Just between you and me, I can't bear the officious toad either. Have you read *The True Histories of Ulv,* Volume Twenty-One, 'The Surslang Dragon of Sur'? No? Pity! One of my favorite entries — ugly beast of a thing that prowls the swamps in Sur. Very poisonous and, oh! Quite a temper! Spits on you, you see. Instead of fire, as you might well expect from a dragon, it spits a sour-smelling poison all over you and if the stench of it doesn't kill you, then don't worry, you'll be dissolved by the acid in mere seconds — distant cousin of the colossal spit-mouth slug, but try telling your Un-King that. Ha! He'd have a fit! But such a horrible way to go, dissolving in the dragon's poison. Such a good entry. You should read it. Managed to work in a comparison to our dear Sister Agnethe. It's the sour stench, you see." The Scribe threw back her head and laughed, honking cries of *hoo, hoo, hoo!* The owls joined in: *Hoot, hoot, hoot!*

Selene and Bo shared a look.

"Never heard her talk so much in my life," whispered Selene.

"Because I relish the quiet," said the Scribe. Of *course* she had heard Selene. "When you hear as well as I do, you come to value the quiet. And here it is mostly so very, *very* quiet. Don't have people shouting at me all day long. And I hardly ever receive visitors who aren't owls, see. Too much work to do and people think I'm half-mad and who wants to talk to a half-mad Qirachi? I'm certain they're worried I'll compare them to the Surslang Dragon of Sur if they interrupt me. *Hoo! Hoo! Hoo!*"

Selene nudged Bo in the ribs. "Get on with it, then," she whispered.

Bo fished the key out of his pocket and took several tentative steps into the room. When he spoke, his voice sounded achingly small.

"I was hoping you could tell me what this means, Scribe. It's terribly important. And my guardian, Mads, thought you could help me."

Bo chewed his lip with worry. Perhaps this strange woman would turn out like Galvin — not to be trusted, eager to steal the Stars for herself. He took a deep breath and dropped the key into the Scribe's waiting palm.

The Scribe snapped her fingers shut, enclosing the key in a fist. She settled a cold, hard stare at Bo. "*The True Histories of Ulv*, Volume Three, 'The Wolf's Prison,'" she began to recite. "'Though not a soul could tell you *where* the wolf who ate the Stars is imprisoned — only Mathias the Gift-Giver knows — what *is* known is that three keys are needed to unlock the chains that bind the wolf to this earth. Mathias scattered the keys throughout the land but ensured that each key led to the next . . .'" The Scribe tapped her temple again. "See? Elkefant. I remember every entry I ever wrote. Pity nobody seems to read them . . ."

Bo felt the heat in his cheeks. "But what does —"

"Silence!" shouted the Scribe. She opened her fist and looked at the key, though not a second passed before she snapped her fingers shut again. "I *write* history — I do not make it."

"But you barely —"

"Don't you know how busy I am?" Her voice rose with indignation. "I'm responsible for recording *everything* that happens in this land. Every teeny tiny little thing." She waved her hand at the scroll in front of her. It waterfalled off the edge of the desk, pooling in a great heap on the floor. "And with the spell holding back magic having been broken, well, I have my work cut out for me, don't I? The owls have been nonstop, reporting this and that and everything."

Bo nodded stiffly. He had pinned all his hopes on the Scribe — how would he find the second key now? "I'm sorry to have bothered you," he said before his head snapped up. "Hang on — do you know *how* magic returned?" Bo was certain the Shadow Witch had released magic and was responsible for the rise in

Shadow Creatures—Galvin had said as much. But he didn't know how she had done it.

The Scribe nodded slowly, a smile prickling the edges of her small mouth. She leaned in to whisper. "Just a draft at this stage. Not my best writing." The Scribe pointed to the scroll on her desk with a flourish of long, knobby fingers.

"I'm . . . ah . . . I'm sure it's . . . wonderful," stammered Bo. He forced a polite smile, but his cheeks burned with embarrassment. All he could see when he looked at the scroll were meaningless dots and squiggles.

The Scribe waved his compliment away with a "Pish, pish" and a bashful smile. "Shall I tell you what happened? What I *believe* happened?"

Bo nodded quickly.

The Scribe cleared her throat—*agghem hem urrrrgh*. "Listen. I believe magic was locked away somewhere natural—no artificial prison would do. Magic is a naturally occurring phenomenon, so only nature can contain it, see? It would have been something like, say . . . oh, I don't know, how about a . . . a tree? Yes! Sounds wonderful! A tree in a forest. In a small, Dark forest that hardly anyone ever enters. Some insignificant place that no one would think twice about."

A gasp caught in Bo's throat; his heart thrummed in his chest. A tree? He looked down at Nix; the little fox whimpered in the back of his throat.

"But for a tree to contain magic for over seven hundred years! Oh, it would have required a *very* special spell. A spell that would need to be maintained with special powders — ground valarius root, for instance, lovely gold-red color — otherwise the spell would fade, the lock would break, and magic would seep back into the world. So Mathias would have left a guardian in place. Someone who would stay close to the tree, someone who would tend to the lock. But it would become hard for the guardian, you see. Magic is so strong! And a spell trying to contain it, to keep it hidden, well, it would grow weaker and weaker and after seven hundred years the guardian would need more strength to hold it back, see? More than the ground valarius root on its own could offer. He might even need someone to help him. An innocent. Yes! What an idea! That would work — an innocent child, for there is nothing stronger against the most sinister of magic than a child with no ill will, no guile, no malice, no impurity. That's old magic, don't you know? The strongest spells always called for a child to cast them — every Ulvian knows that!"

The Scribe shifted closer to Bo, her eyes never leaving his. Sweat gathered on his upper lip but he was frozen to the spot. He could hardly process what she was saying but he felt her words crawl into his mind, where they grew like vines — tangled, prickly vines that curled around his every thought, pulling tight until he couldn't think, couldn't breathe.

"So the guardian would use a child," continued the Scribe.

"Any child would do, but an abandoned child is best, since longing amplifies magic and there's no one in this world who longs for more than a child who isn't wanted, is there? And that child would tend to the lock — perhaps he might not even realize he is doing it! Could you imagine such a thing? And perhaps he might become forgetful or perhaps he might be lazy or perhaps he might just be tired of being told what to do without explanation, but whatever the reason, one day he doesn't tend to the lock and that's all it takes, see, one loose link in the chain and *CRACK!*"

Bo jerked back as the Scribe's sudden cry rang through the room. His heart hammered loudly, a ringing chorus of *guilty, guilty, guilty!* Could the others hear it? Nix pressed close to his side, a warm comfort. But even that was not enough.

The Scribe snapped her fingers. "Just like that, the lock breaks and the worst of magic seeps through and the Shadow Creatures draw on it, growing stronger, growing in number, growing bold and hungry and desperate. And when there's enough magic in the air, enough Shadow Creatures to draw strength from, enough fear in the land, then the witch Freja will find a way to piece herself together and she will rise. She *is* rising . . . There have been unconfirmed sightings in the Valley of One Thousand Deaths, the Broken Plains, the Forest of Tid, in every corner of the land. But why has she returned? Will she try to find and destroy the Stars? Will she attempt to claim the sky and the land for her rule yet again? No one knows, not even I, not even the owls. The only thing one can know for sure when it comes to Freja and her return to our land is that nothing good can come of it." The Scribe paused; her large gray eyes wandered Bo's full height, up and down, up and down. "Well, now, what do you say to my theory, young Irin?"

Bo's mouth was too dry to speak. Somewhere in the room was a clock — he could hear it ticking softly. But that was the only sound save for Bo's heart breaking.

It was me.

It wasn't the Shadow Witch.

It was me.

I released magic.

I gave the witch the strength to rise again.

The Shadow Creature attacks really are my fault.

I am a curse.

Tears threatened to spill, but Bo held them back. Somehow, he held them back.

Selene's mouth gaped. "But magic returning is horrible!" She looked down at her hands.

The Scribe ran her fingers slowly over the parchment, tracing the lettering that Bo couldn't understand. Did it say his name? Would everyone know that he had cursed the land? The tawny owl hooted softly, blinking its large eyes at Bo. *That* was where he had seen the owl before. In the Forest of Long Shadows.

When he had been too late with the gold-red dust. All the owls were staring at him; they knew.

"In some ways, yes," said the Scribe, her knowing eyes still locked on Bo. "But magic is not all bad. In fact, much of it is good, so long as it is in good hands. And, of course, should anyone find and release the Stars, then we would have Star-magic —the strongest of all—and with that, we would be able to rid the land of Shadow Creatures and the Dark, and we would have wishes again! Wouldn't that be a thing? I'm certain we'd all be prepared to move mountains to make such a thing happen, wouldn't we?"

Bo could no longer meet her gaze. Instead, he looked down at his hands. "Yes," he murmured. The guilt of what he had done weighed heavy inside him. *Guilty, guilty, guilty!* "I think I'd do just about anything."

"Good," said the Scribe cheerfully. "I say, isn't that a lovely painting?"

Bo followed where the Scribe was pointing. On the opposite wall was a painting of a large mountain with a wolf atop its very peak, howling. "Oh, y-yes," Bo stuttered, frowning in confusion. "I suppose it is."

"Wonderful! Now you can leave me alone. I have work to do. In *silence*. I absolutely must have *silence*. It is my favorite thing in the world, *silence*. And Sister Agnethe will be angrier than the Surslang Dragon of Sur if you don't wash those dishes like you're supposed to. *Hoo! Hoo! Hoo!*"

Hoot, hoot, hoot, said the owls.

Bo nodded, his head still lowered as he turned to leave. Truthfully, he couldn't wait to be alone. He almost craved being stuck in that small room in the back of the kitchens, scrubbing a never-ending mountain of dishes. It seemed a fitting punishment for all he had done. Perhaps he could hide there forever.

"One last thing!" cried the Scribe just as Bo had reached the door. She held out her hand; in it was the key. Bo had almost forgotten it.

"Thank you," he said, blushing as he returned to her side and took the key from her. Bo gasped as the Scribe grabbed hold of his hand and tugged him close.

"It really is a very lovely painting," she whispered, deep and raspy.

"S-sorry?" Bo stammered. Up close he could see the silver flecks in her large gray eyes. They were magical. The Scribe released Bo's hand as suddenly as she had taken hold of it. He stumbled away from her. She grinned. "Have a good day, child," she said before turning her back on him.

CHAPTER SIXTEEN

B O WAS ON HIS HANDS AND KNEES, scrubbing the stone
floor in the Great Nev'en Library until his knuckles ached.
Nix nudged the bucket along with his snout, keeping it
always within Bo's reach.

Earlier, Selene had helped Bo clear the mountain of dishes
before sneaking him into the library, despite his protests. She
had pulled him into the stacks, far away from prying Sisters,
and removed an armful of scrolls about Freja. All Bo wanted
was to wallow in his misery — Shadow Creature attacks and an
evil witch rising to destroy the land and it was all his fault; Ranik's return was probably his fault too — but Selene had been
determined to learn everything she could.

"I feel a bit sorry for her," she'd said with a shrug, keeping
her voice low so as not to be overheard breaking the rules. She
read everything out loud and Bo had found himself listening in-
tently despite his suffocating guilt. He learned more about Stars
and wolves and witches and even about wish-mines. And Bo

found he agreed with Selene: he did feel sorry for Freja. Why had the Moon thrown the three Stars from the sky? Because she was jealous? That wasn't fair.

Just like it wasn't fair that Mads lied, said a small but persistent voice in the back of his head. It wasn't fair that Mads had used him to maintain a spell without telling him what or why or how, leaving Bo to break the lock and pay the consequences on his own. And it wasn't fair that his mother had left him in the forest, either. She was just like the Moon.

Underneath his guilt, Bo was angry, too, a small spark of anger in the deepest corner of his heart, which grew hotter and hotter the more he thought about Mads and lies and Moons. Nix had pawed at Bo's leg, whimpering in sympathy.

"I know Freja caused the Dark but the Moon wasn't very nice, was she?" Selene had whispered. "Parents shouldn't do that. They shouldn't abandon their children like that." Selene had chewed on her lip. "If the witch really *is* returning, what do you think she wants?"

Bo had not known how to answer her. But his anger had fed a new certainty. That, more than ever, it was vital for him to find the wolf and release the Stars so he could destroy the Dark and prevent the Shadow Witch from taking over — he would prove that Mads should have trusted him all along, that he could do this. But he didn't even know what to do with the riddle: *To speak of me is to break me.*

Just at that moment, Selene had dropped the scroll she'd been reading, breaking the silence in the cavernous room.

Breaking . . .

Silence . . .

Bo had slapped the heel of his palm to his forehead and groaned. "Of course! The Scribe was telling us the answer all along: silence! When you say 'silence,' you break silence. Of course! The answer to the riddle is silence!" Selene had cheered but Bo had shushed her.

"But what does it mean?" he'd whispered.

Nix yapped.

"And you can hush too," Bo had said. "If you knew the answer was 'silence' all along, then why didn't you say so?"

Selene had rolled her eyes. "*More* importantly, why was the Scribe going on about that painting of Lindorm Mountain? It wasn't *that* good."

Before Bo had been able to answer, Sister Agnethe had come for him; they hadn't done a very good job hiding, after all. The Sister had scowled, beckoning him with a curled finger. Bo had never met the Surslang Dragon of Sur but he thought the Scribe had been spot-on. He could picture the beast perfectly — it looked just like Sister Agnethe, with her pinched mouth, her furrowed brow, and her cold eyes. It even smelled like her.

The Sister had said nothing, of course, but had pointed at a bucket of suds and a scrubbing brush and then at the expanse of dusty library floor. Bo bubbled over with frustration: How would he ever find the second key and prove everyone wrong when he was stuck here scrubbing floors?

Sister Agnethe had then turned her scowl on Selene, pressing her lips into a thin sash. She'd pointed at the messy pile of scrolls. Selene had paled, lowering her head before rushing to return them to their rightful places, then scurrying out of the room. Sister Agnethe had followed her and that was that. Bo and Nix had been left alone for a long afternoon of scrubbing floors.

"We need to get out of this place and find the second key," said Bo.

Nix barked.

"Of *course* I won't leave without Tam but — ouch!"

Bo sat up, quickly grabbing beneath his shirt for the crystal pendant, which was growing unbearably hot against his chest. He pulled the pendant off and tossed it to the floor. It was glowing, a haze of heat all around it.

Nix began to bark at the space in front of them. Bo looked up and saw a small orb of Light dancing in the air. He blinked rapidly as the Light transformed into a floating blob of liquid silver, exactly as it had done in the Myling Mist, before once again pouring itself into a familiar shape.

Bo stumbled back, his head full of guilt and lies and flames and sparks. "Mads?"

Last time, the ghost had been a mere shell, a wobbly silvery see-through thing that looked a little like his old guardian and a lot like a wisp of smoke. This time, the ghost took on a more solid appearance and there was color, too, smudges of blue and gray and brown. Familiar and yet . . . Bo couldn't help but see everything so differently now.

Bo lowered his gaze, an uneasy tug in his stomach. "You're back," he said. "I wasn't sure if —"

"The keys," snapped ghost-Mads. "Have you found the keys?"

Nix sniffed the air around Mads as Bo shook his head. "Just the first one but I've worked out the next riddle and the answer is 'silence.' I don't know what that means but —"

"All this time and you only have one key?" Irritation clipped Mads's voice. His silvery body shimmered, like a dropped pebble in a river, before settling into the shape Bo recognized once again. "You need to hurry. The Stars *must* be released. Silence, did you say?" Ghost-Mads paced, frowning deeply. "Then it is here! Surely! The *Silent* Sisters. That must be it! Search the temple. Turn it upside down if you must. Find that key."

The angry fire in Bo's heart flared. Would he ever please the old man? Would he ever be enough? He tried — he tried *so* hard — and look at what he got in return.

"Why did you lie to me?" he blurted.

"Lie?"

Bo twisted the hem of his tatty shirt. "You never told me about the lock. About the tree and magic and . . . you never told me you only took me in because I could help you with the spell." Saying the words out loud brought an ache to Bo's chest. He hated that Mads had used him. That Bo had meant nothing to the old man. All those years trying to prove himself worthy, trying to earn love, and for what? His arms and legs felt heavy, as though his sadness was pulling him down, down, down. But the flames would not fade and they rose up, up, up.

Mads laughed ruefully and turned away from Bo. "And clearly I was wrong to rely on you for such a task because look what happened. Is it any wonder I didn't trust you with the truth?"

Bo flinched, as if each of Mads's words had been a fist.

"Listen, child," said Mads, moving closer. "This is not a time to be weak. You must find and release the Stars before they end up in the wrong hands."

"Wrong hands? You mean Freja?"

Mads gripped Bo's shoulder so tightly his nails pierced the tender skin. "Forget about her," he said as Bo winced. "Focus on what is important: the keys, the riddles, the Stars. Can't you obey one simple order? Must you mess up everything?"

Mads let go and Bo stumbled back, wiping unshed tears from his eyes. His throat was tight — *Please don't cry,* he begged himself. *Not in front of Mads.*

"Just find the next key and be quick about it. It is *your* fault the Shadow Creatures are attacking the villagers, *your* fault the land is flooding with malignant magic. This is *your* mess to fix. I tried to shield you from the truth so you wouldn't know this was all your doing, but you had to stick your nose where it doesn't belong. But you won't let me down again, will you?"

Bo shook his head as words clamored on the tip of his tongue. *It wasn't my fault!* he wanted to shout. *You should have told me the truth!* But he couldn't say anything.

Through a mist of angry tears, Bo watched the apparition fade. The edges blurred as Mads shrank back into that little ball of Light until there was nothing more than dust and air and silence. Bo stared at the space where Mads had been. *I will find the Stars,* he told himself. *I will prove you wrong, Mads. I'll prove everyone wrong.*

Nix barked.

"I know," said Bo. He bent to retrieve the pendant from the floor and gasped when he saw that it had singed the stone, leaving a jagged black mark behind. "Why does it grow so hot?"

"Perhaps it's a charm," said a low, purring voice from the shadows of the stacks.

Bo whipped his head around, looking for the owner of the voice. "Wh-who's there?" he stuttered.

"I saw a charm like that once," said the voice, louder this time. "A traveling saleswoman from the Broken Plains showed it to me. Grew hot every time a ghost was nearby. I stole — I mean, she *gave* it to me as a gift and I sold it on the Dark Market for three hundred Raha."

Nix growled, shifting in front of Bo as the familiar gold-toothed smile of Galvin appeared at the end of the stacks. He folded his arms across his chest and leaned against a shelf. A mishmash of feelings whooshed through Bo as he found himself face-to-face with the Irin who had left him for dead in the quagmires. He didn't know if he should fling himself at Galvin or run from the room screaming for help.

Galvin smiled crookedly and pointed to his face; his left eye was cloudy white and a long scab ran from the corner of the eye to his chin. "Quite a trick you pulled, sending me to the Myling Mist. Those ghost-children aren't all that friendly as it turns out and not a single Star or wolf to be found."

Bo swallowed around his fear, edging backwards. Nix held his ground.

"But now I know all about the keys, thanks to your illuminating conversation with that ghost. So I'll be having the first key, thank you very much." The Irin pushed off from the shelf and slowly stepped toward Bo, his grin stretching his face. "Either you hand it over or I take it. Perhaps I'll take an eye, too — an eye for an eye, you know."

Bo's gaze flicked about, searching for the quickest way out. Behind him? To the left? Right? But where would he run to?

Would he get lost in this maze of a temple? How quickly would Galvin corner him, all alone in a dead-end corridor, with no one to help, to witness, to save him . . . ?

Before Galvin could act, however, thumping footsteps neared them, the cries of a bloodthirsty crowd filling Bo's ears. It sounded as if every villager in the Great Hall was running toward them. Either that or a herd of elkefants was stampeding through the temple.

"Oh dear," said Galvin. "Looks like you might be in trouble. Guess I'll just pry the key out of your hands once the villagers are done with you." In the blink of an eye Galvin was gone, slipping into the shadows again.

Selene came running into the room first, silver braids dancing wildly, almost as wild as her eyes.

"Bo," she said, panting, doubling over. "You have to. Leave. Great Hall. Gone. Shadows. Scream. Terrified. Coming for you!"

"I don't —" he started, but Selene interrupted him, grabbing him.

"No time! Hurry, Bo!"

She tugged on his arm and turned, crashing into a wall of villagers surging toward them.

"There he is!" cried one.

Selene and Bo stumbled back; Nix bared his teeth and growled, keeping close to Bo.

A woman was pushed to the front. She was wailing, clutching a small child to her chest, rocking it back and forth.

"Gone!" cried the woman. "Taken right before my eyes!"

A sharp-faced man stepped forward to jab Bo in the chest. "This woman's husband went to fetch firewood in the cellars with his kid, and a Shadow Creature came out of nowhere and grabbed him. Dragged him into the shadows and now he's gone. And it's all your fault."

Bo staggered back. "But that's inside the temple! It's Light! There are candles *everywhere*. How could . . . ?"

"All your fault!" cried the crowd.

Nix barked loudly until a woman waved her walking stick at him; the threat was clear. Bo felt his blood boil.

"Don't imagine the High Sisters will let you out of this one," said the Innkeeper, appearing beside Bo to grab hold of his arm, fingers digging in roughly. He pulled Bo against his side and grinned with teeth stained black from chewing tar-bark. "I'll see you punished for this, Devil-child. It'll be the end of you."

The crowd parted, making room for the Innkeeper to drag Bo to the High Sisters.

CHAPTER SEVENTEEN

ELENE SLID DOWN THE WALL of the cell and sat, hugging her knees to her chest while Bo paced furiously, Nix on his heels. Tear tracks stained her cheeks. "That was *horrible,*" she said.

She was right; it had been *awful.* The villagers jeering, shoving them at the feet of the High Sisters and demanding retribution.

"Is it proof enough that Shadow Creatures attack inside our safe haven after *he* is allowed to stay?" the Innkeeper had spat, waving his hand at Bo before turning on Selene: "And *she's* a magic-user, caught practicing the evil art in the stables. Singed the hair off Lucky Karl's dog. Lucky Karl *saw* her do it!" Selene had stomped on the Innkeeper's foot and called him a dimwitted slothendung, but it did her no good. Sister Magrid — small and bony and brittle — was called upon to give testimony. "Thirteen years I've known her," said the Sister, "and it doesn't surprise me one smiggitty-wit to discover that she is a witch. We should have thrown her to the Shadow Creatures years ago."

And that was that.

"Lock them up," Sister Noora had shouted. "They will be punished by death!"

Although Sister Vela had frowned deep with remorse, her lips had remained locked and Bo's heart had broken. He'd been certain she would be on his side, but . . . but perhaps the Scribe had shown her the scroll; perhaps they'd *all* seen it and knew the truth.

He ground his teeth so hard his jaw ached.

Bo stopped his pacing and knelt in front of Selene, reaching out to pat her knee. "I'm sorry about Sister Magrid," he said. "If Sister Agnethe is the Surslang Dragon of Sur, then Sister Magrid is nothing but a smear of Skugs fud on the Surslang Dragon of Sur's little toe."

Selene spluttered a laugh but there was no heart in the sound. "Whoever Lucky Karl is, he won't be feeling so lucky once I'm through with him." She grimaced, lowering her head. "Why are people so cruel?" she asked, heartbreak shimmering in her eyes as she looked up at Bo. "Why do the people who are supposed to love and protect you hurt you the most?"

Bo searched for the right words but couldn't find them. He had a suspicion that, even if he found them somewhere deep within his belly, the right words would be too big, too heavy for him to drag out of their hiding place.

"I can't believe she would . . ." Selene's voice was small, her lip trembling. "I can't believe it happened again."

"Again?"

"I . . ." Selene shook her head slowly. "It doesn't matter," she said, her whole body rising and falling with a heavy sigh. Nix pressed his nose to the back of her hand with a gentle whine until Selene smiled sadly. "We're stuck here and we're going to die and it doesn't matter," she said.

"It *does* matter," said Bo, squaring his shoulders despite Selene's groan of protest. "We're going to get out of here. We *have* to."

Bo stood and began pacing again, Nix chasing him back and forth.

The Nev'en didn't have a Fuglebur. Instead, Bo, Selene, and Nix had been locked in a cell with four stone walls, a floor, and a ceiling — no candles anywhere. High up, there was a window open to the elements, the wind hissing angrily as it slid inside the cell and wrapped cold, sharp claws around Bo's skin.

It was Light now but when the Dark came . . .

Perhaps they wouldn't even last until Dark. *Shadow Creatures moving through the Light! It should be impossible but . . .*

"You're making me dizzy," said Selene. She slapped her hands against her cheeks and shook her head. "Sit down."

But Bo was not listening. He didn't have his rucksack or his cloak or Tam's robe — what could he use to escape?

Nix rammed snout-first into Bo's ankle as he came to a sudden halt. "If there was a tree right here," said Bo, waving his hands at the center of the room, "I could climb it, and then we'd be through that window quicker than a piquee bird will steal your dinner."

"But there's no tree, Bo."

"Then we could magic one! *You've* got magic. Go on, make a tree. Right here." Bo waved his hands at the empty space.

Selene clenched her jaw. "I'm *not* going to use magic. It's evil." She folded her arms across her chest and pouted. "And I don't even know how it works."

"It's easy," said Bo. "You just . . ." He held up both hands, palms out toward the wall. "Like this," he said, and pushed the air. "And then sparks shoot out and magic happens. Simple."

Selene narrowed her eyes. "Until a few days ago there was no such thing as magic," she said, standing up. "You think they teach us how to use it? I'm not even supposed to have it. No one is!"

Bo felt his frustration bubbling in his stomach, bubbling up and up until he couldn't hold the words in. "Well, then it's wasted on you if you can't even use it properly. If you won't even *try*."

Selene's eyes sparked as she stepped up to Bo. "I'm in this cell because of you. It's your fault I'm going to die!"

Bo watched flashes of lightning in Selene's pupils. The hairs on the back of his neck stood on end, his whole body tingling. Nix whimpered, hiding behind Bo's legs. "Selene, I think you should—"

"You're nothing but a short, ignorant pig-child!" she screeched, but her eyes grew wide as white sparks suddenly spat from her palms. "Oh no!" she cried. "I think—"

Bo ducked; his whole body thrummed with heat as magic shot from Selene's hands above him.

A burnt, sickly smell filled Bo's nostrils. He waited for the smoke to clear before he straightened slowly—the front wall of the cell had melted away!

Selene stared at her hands, dumbstruck. "I didn't ... I can't ... I—"

"I see I am not needed after all," said a voice from outside the cell, a voice that tinkled like wind chimes.

Sister Vela stood in the smoldering ruins, a small V in the space between her brows.

"I'm—" started Selene, but Sister Vela shook her head.

"Oh, I know what you are, child," she said. "And it is *nothing* for you to fear. Magic can be good if it is in the right hands." Her lips curved into a wry smile as she surveyed the still-smoking ruins. "Despite appearances."

Selene bit her lip and looked away.

"Now, come quickly," said Sister Vela, gesturing them closer.

Bo, Nix, and Selene edged out of the cell, Bo's stomach tense with uncertainty.

"The Sisters are in Evensong," explained Sister Vela. "They are locked in the chapel for an hour of deep, silent prayer. They will assume that the Shadow Creatures will take you at Dark — I volunteered to be the one to confirm your deaths. Your Korahku friend should be well enough to travel, but you cannot escape tonight. I will hide you until dawn, then when the villagers are in the Great Hall for breakfast and the Sisters are in Morning Prayer, you can —"

Bo blinked furiously. "You're letting us go?"

Sister Vela knelt before him, her features soft and understanding. "I made an oath to protect *all* Ulvians, Bo. Irin, Nev'en, Korahku — it doesn't matter."

Nix sat and raised a paw. Sister Vela held it, smiling. "And little Ulvian dogs, of course."

Nix yapped.

Sister Vela returned her gaze to Bo. Her smile faded, replaced with a look of grim determination. "I will not let baseless fear-mongering destroy that oath," she said. "You seek the key, yes?"

Bo jerked back. "How did —"

Sister Vela chuckled. "The Scribe and I are old friends. I am quite fond of her owls."

"Do you know where it is?" asked Selene.

Sister Vela nodded once, firmly. "Rumored to be in the Golden Hall."

Selene elbowed Bo's side. "That's a museum where we keep Ulv's greatest treasures," she said in her haughty voice. "It's shaped like a teardrop to honor the widow whose tears formed the sea at the foot of this mountain and —"

"A teardrop? That explains the shape of the key — it was a clue too!" Bo reached down to give Nix a head scratch. Bo could hardly contain himself; his body hummed with hope.

"Come," said Sister Vela, eyes once again sweeping the damaged cell. She smiled wryly. "Let us find you more suitable sleeping quarters."

~

Early next morning, Sister Vela roused them from sleep after a long night hiding in the servants' quarters. She handed Bo his belongings with a smile.

"I put a little extra food in there," she said. "And your friend's robe, of course."

Bo was speechless with gratitude. The Sister had let them sleep in a snug, firelit room with a bed that felt as though it had been sewn together from clouds. She surely knew what Bo had done — she was good friends with the Scribe and her owls, after all — but Sister Vela was still going to let them go.

Selene flung her arms around the Sister's waist. "Thank you," she said. "For everything."

"You had better be going," said Sister Vela. "You don't have much time."

Selene let the Sister go, wiping her eyes with the backs of her hands.

Bo nodded. "First we need to find Tam, *then* we go to the Golden Hall for the key, and *then* we leave," he said.

Sister Vela stood back. "Selene can lead you to the hospital wing. I will make sure the Sisters stay in Morning Prayer, and remember to avoid the Great Hall. The Irin villagers will be there. Go. Quickly." She cupped Selene's cheeks, pressing a light kiss to the top of her head. When she pulled back, Sister Vela gave Bo a smile and winked at Nix. "And good luck."

Bo watched her walk away, his emotions a complicated swirl. In many ways her kindness hurt him — how could a near-stranger treat him better than his own flesh and blood, his own guardian?

Selene dragged them down corridor after corridor until they reached a long, narrow hall. The hall was a spine with small alcoves poking out on either side like ribs, each recess separated by whisper-thin curtains.

The three of them crept down the hall, barely making a sound, until they came to an alcove where a large feathered body slumbered.

"Tam!"

Bo rushed to Tam's side and tugged at her hand, but the Korahku didn't stir. "What's wrong with her?"

Selene frowned at the vials of crushed herbs and colorful liquids on the bedside table. "She should be better. Sister Vela said so and Sister Magrid is the *best* and she's been . . . ha!" Selene pointed to a bowl of yellow powder. "They're keeping her in deep sleep with drewsberry powder. It helps with recovery."

"Do something," Bo urged.

Selene swallowed. "I . . . I guess we could . . ." She lifted each vial, inspecting them while her tongue poked out the side of her mouth. "I think this one . . . no, this one . . . yes. Definitely this . . . oh, no, *this* one! We'll give her a dose of opperhullim. That will wake her." She waved a vial of blue liquid triumphantly.

"Are you sure—"

Selene jutted out her chin. "Who's the apprentice healer? You or me?"

"Who's the apprentice healer who once mistook sneezewort for freezewort?" said Bo.

Selene gave him a stern look. "I *know* what I'm doing." She leaned over Tam, opening her beak and pouring the blue liquid down her throat.

Bo held his breath. Not a movement. And then . . . Tam bolted upright, spitting blue liquid down the front of her orange hospital tunic.

"You've killed her!" cried Bo.

Tam pounded a fist against her chest until her coughing subsided. Finally, she looked down at Bo, ruffling her feathers. "Little Irin?"

Forgetting himself, Bo threw his arms around the Korahku's waist and squeezed.

Nix joined in too, trying to push his snout between them.

"Ah well," said Tam, patting Bo lightly between his shoulder blades.

"I thought you were dead," said Bo, voice muffled in Tam's robe. He pulled back to wipe the traitorous tears pooling in his eyes. "I ran away but you . . . and then you . . . Ranik could have killed you and that would have been my fault too!"

Tam threw her legs over the side of the bed and almost fell off. The Korahku waved away Bo's offers of help as she pushed herself to standing, wobbling like a norfir in the strong winds of the Howling Season. Once steady, she fixed Bo with a wary gaze and seemed about to speak before she snapped her beak and tilted her head at Selene. "And who is this?"

"The one who saved you," said Selene with a proud smirk. "Twice."

Bo huffed. "Her name is Selene. And she's got magic."

"Hush!" said Selene. "I do not."

Nix barked.

Tam gathered her things, swapping her hospital tunic for the pile of mended clothes on the table beside her. Bo handed over the blue robe with a shaking hand. "Whatever the case," said Tam, "I am in your debt, Selene." She bowed as well as she could.

Selene poked her tongue out at Bo. "As much as I'd love to talk more about how brilliant I am, we *are* sort of in a rush," she said, turning on her heel and marching away. "Keep up, you three!"

Before Tam could answer, Bo steered her after Selene, rushing to explain everything that had happened while the Korahku had been sleeping, making sure to leave no room for her to interject with the tongue-lashing Bo knew he deserved. *Perhaps if I keep talking forever she'll have no choice but to forgive me and help me find the Stars,* thought Bo ruefully.

"And now we're headed to the Golden Hall for the second key," he said as Selene guided them through the maze of deserted hallways, Nix trotting beside Bo. "Then we'll escape and find the third key and then the Stars . . ."

Bo was still babbling as they slipped into the large, teardrop-shaped room covered from floor to ceiling in gold-edged mirrors. Sprinkled throughout the room were stone plinths on which sat glass cases filled with treasures. He stumbled to a halt just inside the door as Tam grabbed hold of his arm. "Wait," said the Korahku.

Bo turned reluctantly, curling in on himself. He had stalled for as long as possible but her anger was inevitable now. He could picture it perfectly: *You ran away and I risked my life to save you and now you expect me to play along with this superstitious cluckity muck? Nonsense!*

But the Korahku simply cocked her head to one side and appraised him wearily. "You will not give up this fool's errand, will you?" she said.

Bo met her gaze, feeling the determination in him sing. He rolled back his shoulders and shook his head. "No. I . . . I have to do it."

The Korahku sighed with her whole body as she looked away. "I do not pretend to understand why you persist, little Irin, but I made a blood bind and I will keep it. Even if it means . . ." The Korahku trailed off, frowning. "But that is Redfist!" she cried, pushing past Bo, marching toward a fearsome-looking weapon that hung from one of the mirrored walls. It was a long shaft of deep-red wood with a blade shaped like a feather at one end and a spiked ball at the other. Where the shaft met the blade was a ring of black feathers woven together with vines. "This is a Korahku weapon!" She ripped it free from the wires. "It is the weapon of our ruler, passed down from generation to generation. It should not be here!"

Tam weighed the weapon in her hand, looking it up and down with awe, before she hooked it on a loop in her leather belt. "It comes with me," she said, setting a stern eye on Selene.

"They tried to kill me," said Selene. "Take what you want."

Bo did not understand Tam's lack of anger at him — if it had been Mads, well, Bo shuddered to think of *his* reaction — but he wasn't about to question it. He didn't have time to dwell. "Look for a key," he said instead.

Bo, Selene, and Nix searched every glass case while Tam continued to look for stolen Korahku treasures. "This is Firewand! And Ironclaw! Have the Nev'en stolen *all* of our precious objects?"

"What's this?" asked Bo. He had searched all the glass cases and spied nothing at all like a key. Now he was pointing at a tiny silver teardrop stuck to the base of a plinth tucked away in the corner of the room — the teardrop symbol was shaped just like the end of the first key. Bo knelt before the plinth. "I wonder . . ." he said, and pressed the teardrop with his finger. It sank into the plinth — it was a button! Out popped a hidden drawer and in it sat a small wooden box carved with yet more teardrops. Bo pulled it out of the drawer and stood, shaking the box — it rattled! Something was inside. "Open it," said Bo, nodding at Selene.

Selene's lips puckered with disapproval. "With what?" she asked. "And how? There's no keyhole."

"Magic," said Bo.

Selene stomped her foot. "I *told* you. I don't know how to control it. I could easily melt this entire room trying."

"I think it helps if you get angry," muttered Bo. "That's what happened last time."

Selene folded her arms across her chest. "Well, keep talking, Irin, and I'm sure I'll get angry."

A feathered hand reached between them, grabbed hold of the box, and threw it to the floor — *crack!* It splintered against the stone, breaking into three parts.

Nix yelped as the box's contents spilled free — a silver key with a spiral on one end.

"Or you could just do that," said Selene, biting back her smile.

"The key!" cried Bo, bending to retrieve it. The spiral turned out to be a snake, coiled around and around itself. Selene peered over Bo's shoulder to inspect it.

"It's got a message carved on it too," she said. "'I run but do not walk. I have a mouth but do not talk. I have a head but never weep. I have a bed but never sleep.' What on Ulv does *that* mean?"

"We can work it out later," Bo said. "All that matters is we have two keys. So let's —"

"Thank you ever so kindly for finding the second key for me," said a voice behind them.

They all spun around and saw Galvin blocking the doorway, a vial of smoking green liquid in his hand. "Give both those keys to me now," he said. "If you don't I'll have to use this charm." He gestured to the vial. "I'll throw it at your feet and the four of you will become statues, locked in stone for all eternity. Just like Elena—ha!"

"Ha yourself," said Bo. "I know your charms don't work."

Galvin sneered. "Perhaps. But this isn't one of mine, is it? I stole—eh, *borrowed* it from Sister Magrid's personal stock. She's got quite the collection of nasty things, doesn't she?"

Selene's startled gasp was answer enough. Bo's eyes flicked between Tam and Selene. Could they run? Fight?

"*Tsk, tsk, tsk!* Don't try anything tricky," said Galvin. "Do you think you could reach me before I throw the vial? Do you think I am lying? Will you take that chance?" His gold teeth glistened. "Not even your magic girl would be quick enough!"

"Give him the keys, Bo," said Tam with an angry sigh. "We cannot take the chance."

Bo turned a pleading stare toward Selene. *Use your magic!* his eyes begged, but she shook her head: *I don't know how.*

"You're a worm, Galvin," said Bo, but the Irin simply laughed.

"Oh dear, no! Not at all! I am simply a man with expensive tastes. When I sell the Stars on the Dark Market, I will live in such luxury. Ha!" He nodded at the floor. "Set the keys just there between us."

Bo stepped forward and placed the two keys on the floor as Nix barked wildly.

"I don't have a choice," said Bo, and backed away again. "You want to be a statue forever?"

Galvin snapped up the keys and waved them above his head in triumph. "You have made a wise decision, young Irin. It has been a pleasure. Now, if you will excuse me, I am off to find the third key. And to be sure you don't follow me, I'm afraid I'll have to use this charm on you anyway. Thank you kindly once again!"

Before they could react, Galvin had flung the vial at their feet. A cloud of noxious green smoke erupted, making them wheeze and bend double. It took forever for the smoke to clear but when it did, Bo was surprised to find that he could still move and was not, as far as he could tell, a statue. There were a few lingering wisps of green smoke and a foul, rotting stench, but no statues.

"It was a trick!" cried Bo. "That no-good, lying slangrot!"

Nix barked, turning in circles.

"Come," said Tam, already running to the door. "We can catch him if we hurry."

They raced through the temple, chasing Galvin's wild, gleeful cackle echoing through the stone hallways. They were too busy in their pursuit to notice where they were being led until they rounded a corner and found themselves face-to-face with a wall of angry villagers.

Galvin had lured them to the Great Hall.

Bo caught sight of Galvin's grinning face as he disappeared into the teeming mass of angry people before a familiar man pushed to the front of the crowd, wearing a nasty, tar-stained smile. "I should have known a Devil like you would escape yet another night with the Shadow Creatures," said the Innkeeper, gripping a sharpened club in his hand. "Looks like it's time we took matters into our own hands."

CHAPTER EIGHTEEN

THE VILLAGERS CROWDED THEM, circling, pressing, menacing — not even the sight of a Korahku halted them. They had armed themselves with knives and forks, broken pipes, pickaxes, anything close at hand.

Bo backed up, a whimper caught in his throat.

"Stop!" Tam pushed to the front, brandishing Ironclaw — a thick, black mallet. "Let the children go. If you want someone to fight, fight me."

The Innkeeper faltered, his eyes narrowing at the Korahku's weapon. "You can't fight all of us," he said, but his voice trembled with uncertainty.

"I will be happy to teach just you a lesson," said Tam before swinging Ironclaw in a wide arc. The end of the weapon burst open and out shot a mass of metal whips, which snaked around the Innkeeper's arms and legs and belly and neck.

The Innkeeper fell to the floor, writhing. "Get it off me!" But the metal whips squeezed tighter the more he struggled. "Help me!"

The crowd backed away with gasps and wild eyes.

"Truly the weapon of a Devil!"

"Such evil!"

"Let them go before they kill us all!"

But as the terrified crowd parted, something unexpected filled the gap.

Out of the shadows emerged a creature. It was all claws and teeth and spikes and Darkness, like a deadly shadow come to life. It prowled into the Light, gnashing its teeth, growling and dragging its claws along the flagstones of the hall.

Bo had never seen anything like it. But he had heard those scratching, scraping sounds before.

"A Shadow Creature," he gasped. All the blood rushed from his face. He felt as if Ironclaw's metallic tendrils had wrapped around his throat, squeezing tightly.

Screams filled the air as the crowd fled, pushing and trampling one another, fighting to escape. But the creature only had eyes for Bo and his friends.

"Stay behind me," said Tam. She pushed Bo, Selene, and Nix back.

As the Shadow Creature reached the Innkeeper, writhing on the floor, tangled in the metallic whips, it opened a cavernous mouth and swallowed the screaming Irin whole, yanking Iron-claw out of Tam's hand and swallowing the weapon, too.

Bo turned away, sick to his stomach. How was this even possible? A Shadow Creature moving through the Light?

With a bone-shattering roar, the creature pounced, its mouth gaping, its claws slashing. Tam ducked and kicked out her talons. A forked tail slashed at Selene and Bo. Selene screamed, flinging out both hands in defense.

Light exploded from her palms, lightning bolts that sizzled against the Shadow Creature's skin. The creature howled as it fell back — *thump!* — onto the stone floor.

Selene looked to Bo. "I didn't . . . I don't . . ."

The creature pounced again, this time breathing fire — only it wasn't like any fire Bo had ever seen. It was pitch-black and noxious, and it sucked up all the surrounding Light. Selene screamed and threw her hands up; a shower of icy shards rained from her palms, shooting through the air. They cut the black flames into pieces, into small sparks that smoked and fizzled and floated to the floor as ash.

The creature breathed more noxious black fire, but — *boom!* — Selene pushed out her hands and a wall of ice shot forward, knocking the creature backwards. Before it could stand again, Selene thrust out her hands, one after the other, and knives of ice hurtled across the room, piercing the creature again and again and again until it collapsed on the floor, shrinking until all that was left was a wisp of smoke and a dusting of ashes.

Bo rushed to her side. "Are you okay?"

"I can't believe I did that," said Selene, eyes wide, breathing hard.

"You're going to make a brilliant Queen's guard," said Bo.

Selene frowned at her hands, biting her lip in worry.

"Certainly she will," said Tam, a hand on each of their shoulders. "But perhaps it is best we do not linger while more Shadow Creatures arrive."

They sprinted through the Great Hall and onto the landing outside the temple. Bo gasped — he could see for miles and . . . his stomach lurched.

The tree sickness had spread, like a giant black claw stretching from west to east. The forests were crumbling to ash and dying. It had reached below the Temple City: the trees surrounding the mountain and the vast inland sea were blackened and decaying.

"Quickly," urged Tam. "Galvin is at the water's edge, readying a boat. See?"

Tam pointed and Bo saw a tiny speck pushing a boat out to sea.

Bo let himself be dragged down the zigzagging stairs, his head tangled up with worry.

He understood what was killing the trees now.

It was magic — wild, malignant, unbalanced magic — spreading through the land. If he didn't find the Stars soon, it wouldn't matter. There would be no Ulv for him to save. They had to reach Galvin; they had to get those keys back.

At the base of the mountain, Selene led them along a rocky path and into the forest of inky, clawlike trees. Ash was so thick in the air, Bo could not stop coughing. Nix sneezed, too.

When they emerged on the other side of the forest, there was an endless gray-green sea before them. A scattering of stone huts littered the sea's edge, all abandoned, weather-worn and crumbling. They hurried through the empty village, Selene leading them to a small beach where a rickety old boat was tethered.

"We'll take this," she said, grabbing the rope to untie the boat.

In the distance, Bo could see Galvin heading south. Bo shrank back as the water lapped at his toes; it felt strangely thick and syrupy.

"There is a Nev'en village on the other side," said Selene. "It is abandoned but it will be a place to stay for the Dark. It will take us most of the day to cross the sea."

A low mist curled atop the rippling water like tendrils. Behind Bo, an owl hooted mournfully. It made Bo shudder.

"This place," he said, "is creepy."

Nix whined, scratching the sand nervously with his paws.

Selene's gaze flicked toward the decaying trees. "It never used to be," she said.

She untied the rope. Bo picked up Nix and they climbed in, Selene behind them. Tam sloshed into the water and pushed the boat out a short way, then jumped in too. She tried to take the oars but Selene snapped them out of reach. "What does a Korahku know about water?"

"Ah," said Tam, with a wry click of her beak. "Right you are."

Bo glanced back at the shore and saw a tawny owl on the roof of a crumbling hut. The owl blinked at him, tilted its head, and took flight, swooping into the air toward the mountain. Bo turned away, tugging his cloak tightly around him.

Soon they were surrounded by the sea. In the mist it felt as though there was nothing behind them and nothing in front; Bo couldn't see Galvin anymore. The only sound was the gentle *slip-slosh* of the oars gliding through the water.

Bo looked down at his hands clasped in his lap, fingers so tightly laced his knuckles were white. Galvin had stolen the keys, and the Shadow Creatures were so powerful they could attack at any moment. Even during the Light.

"It's not fair," Bo snapped. The small spark of anger in his heart had grown into wild flames that lashed the back of his throat. "I lost both keys and —"

"It's not your fault Galvin is a no-good, dishonest gilly-wacker," said Selene.

Bo shook his head. "No, but it *is* my fault that magic is returning and the Shadow Creatures are growing so powerful."

Tam clicked her beak. "Nonsense."

"It's true," Bo insisted. "It was just like the Scribe said. Magic was locked in a tree — great ugly ancient thing — and I was supposed to tend to it only I didn't because I was too busy wishing I could play with the village children and the lock broke and magic returned and . . ." He unclasped his hands and banged his fist on the side of the boat. "Mads never told me it was a spell. He should have told me! I know what I did was wrong but I never would have done it if I'd known. Why didn't he trust me? Why did he lie to me?" His chest was heaving. He didn't think it possible that he would ever stop feeling guilty, but the anger was all-consuming. "He *needed* me for his spell but he never *wanted* me. He never . . ."

Why does no one ever want me?

Nix crawled into his lap, as if reading Bo's mind and wanting to prove him wrong. Bo hugged him.

"Do you know why I was locked in the Fuglebur in your village?" said Tam suddenly.

Confused by her change of subject, Bo met her eyes and shook his head.

Tam hesitated, caught halfway between turning to face Bo

and looking out across the sea. She gripped the side of the boat tightly.

"I was second in line to the Korak throne, behind my sister, Runa. Runa was fierce, loyal, smart, and commanded great respect. But that did not prevent me from resenting her, from wishing it was me who was heir, me who our father, King Saros, loved most." She bowed her head, shoulders curled forward. "My sister adored me; she looked up to me and would do anything I said. But I was her personal bodyguard, too. 'Protect the future queen,' my father would tell me. 'Her life is worth more than yours.' I would perch awake at night with those words haunting me. Why was Runa's life worth more than mine? Why was I not enough? But I still took a blood oath to protect her; I promised to always protect her life above my own."

For a long moment the Korahku did not speak—the only sound was the hitch of her breath. The mist swirled, rising up to run cold tendrils along Bo's forearm. Were these ghosts too? Bo hugged Nix even tighter.

"There had been talk of Irin soldiers gathering on our western border. I wanted to fight them but my father told me to stay away; he did not say why. 'You do not need to know these things, Tamira,' he told me, 'for you are merely a soldier.' I was so angry at his words. I was always looking for ways to prove myself, to prove how strong I was and what a better queen I would make.

So I disobeyed my father and convinced my sister to come with me — I did not tell her it was against our father's wishes.

"When we reached the western border, I learned why my father had wished us to stay away. When we first attacked, there was a handful of soldiers but we were quickly ambushed by hundreds more — it had been a trap. My father had seen this coming, but I had not."

Bo wondered if Tam had finished — the Korahku stayed silent for so long, head bent and breath rasping. Finally, Tam drew herself together and sat up straight; she did not meet anyone's eye.

"They killed my sister, but I escaped," she said. "I could never return to my flock for the shame, so I roamed the land looking for revenge. I thought: If I am angry at others, then I will not be angry at myself. But I was reckless and was captured near your village and strung up in the Fuglebur.

"And then you came along and I realized I did not need revenge for my sister — I needed to make amends for myself. I could *save* you. Perhaps I could forgive myself if I could save one life."

Tam finally looked at Bo. "I understand guilt and I understand wanting to make amends for your actions. So, I will protect you, little Irin, and I will help you fix this. That will be *my* amends. Finding the Stars, that will be yours."

Bo didn't realize he had been crying until Nix sniffed at his damp cheeks, his pink tongue darting out to lick the tears. Bo pushed him away gently. "That's disgusting, Nix," he mumbled, and then wiped his face clear with the sleeves of his shirt. He wanted more than anything to hug the Korahku and tell her everything would be all right, that it wasn't her fault — her father should have told her, should have trusted her. But Bo knew words would never be enough, not when it came to this.

"And I'll help," said Selene, breathless and eager. "I'll help you get the keys back and find the Stars and then I'm going to find my mother and father in the capital and I'll join the Queen's Guard. My parents will be *so* happy to see me — they'll wish they never left me with the Sisters. You could come too, Bo. You'll join the Guard and together we'll be the Queen's favorites."

"Don't think I'd make much of a guard," said Bo. In truth, he didn't know what he would do after they found the Stars — *if* they found them. Now that he knew Mads had lied to him, he wasn't sure if he'd fit into his old life anymore. Or maybe it didn't fit him — did he even have an old life to return to? The forest was destroyed, the village empty and . . . Just thinking about it made his skin prickle.

He took a deep breath. "So how do we find Galvin and get the keys back?" he said. "We've lost sight of him."

"The easiest way," said Selene, "is to work out the answer to the riddle and make for the third key — that's where he'll be headed, won't he? What was it again? 'I run but do not walk. I have a mouth but do not talk. I have a head but never weep. I have a bed but never sleep.' What does that *mean?*"

As Tam and Selene struggled to untangle the riddle, Bo frowned to himself, staring into the gray-green depths of the sea. If only he hadn't lost the keys to Galvin, if only he had been smarter, braver, quicker.

"A hurdigkat is the fastest animal in Ulv," said Selene. "They're always dashing about, so you could say they run but never walk. And I don't think they talk much."

Tam shook her head. "It is unlikely to be an animal. It will be a place like the first two keys: the Un-King's palace and the Temple of the Silent Sisters."

"But what kind of place has a mouth? And can *run?*"

Bo swallowed the lump in his throat and hugged Nix tightly to his chest. He tried to listen to the conversation around him but his mind was swirling with too many warring thoughts.

What if I can't do it? he asked himself. *What if I can't release the Stars?*

The thought was like tree sap. Tacky, syrupy, sticky, stuck to the roof of his mouth, where no tongue prodding and picking was ever going to set it free. He shook his head and looked up, scowling at the Dark cloud that had gathered on the horizon.

I have to find the Stars. I have to prove everyone wrong about me. The villagers, Mads, even my mother.

All of them had treated him like a mud-myg in their pom-papple juice. And he was tired of it. Tired of being tossed aside, blamed, ignored, teased, lied to.

He let the angry flames warm him, let them chase back his fears, his worries, his lingering guilt. In a strange way, the anger was a comfort. It made his resolve to find the Stars stronger. So he let it grow.

And grow and grow and grow.

CHAPTER NINETEEN

A S THEY NEARED THE SHORE, Tam jumped out, the water
lapping up to her knees. She pulled the boat through the
shallows and onto a beach with large gray pebbles.

A tangle of trees grew close to the water's edge — knobby
olive-green trees with bulbous trunks and thick crowns. Bo
heaved a sigh of relief at how alive they looked; thankfully, the
sickness hadn't reached them yet. But they were completely still
— not a leaf fluttered. Perhaps they were holding their breath,
waiting for the sickness to come.

Bo scooped up Nix and plonked him on the shore, where the
little fox ran in circles, barking loudly.

"It was my first time in a boat too, but you don't hear me
complaining," said Bo. He did feel sick but he was certain it had
little to do with the choppy water.

While Tam and Selene were bickering about which way Galvin might have gone, Bo wandered toward one of the trees and
pressed his palm against the bark. It was cool and rough and

thrumming with life. Late-afternoon Light flickered through the canopy and cast mottled shadows against the back of his hand. The Light, the air, the trees, all of it reminded him so much of home.

He traced patterns against the bark and closed his eyes, trying to picture himself back in the Forest of Long Shadows. The image sat uncomfortably in his mind, like a troll trying to balance on the head of a needle.

"You're not listening to me!" Selene poked Bo in the arm.

He opened his eyes to Selene scowling at him. "Sorry, I was . . . What did you say?"

She rolled her eyes. "Come on, the village where we'll stay is this way," she said, turning to where Tam was waiting for them. "Honestly, what sort of manners do they teach in Irin?" she muttered. "Didn't your mother tell you it was rude to ignore people? I was calling you for *ages*."

Her words were a punch to his gut. She didn't mean it that way but it didn't stop the pain. "My mother abandoned me in the forest when I was a baby," said Bo with nonchalance he didn't feel. "So, she didn't teach me any manners."

Selene's eyes grew wide, her footsteps stuttering to a halt. "Abandoned you?"

Bo looked away and shrugged. "It doesn't matter. She left a note. She didn't . . . she didn't want me and . . . it's fine. I don't even care." The lie tasted bitter. He *did* care. He cared more than he'd ever realized. He didn't know why his mother had abandoned him — was she as fickle as the Moon or was it something else? — but it hurt nonetheless. It was the kind of hurt that blanketed him like the Myling Mist, until it was impossible to see anything else, to feel anything else.

Perhaps that was why he was so angry with Mads. It wasn't just the lie about the spell; it was the realization that the old man had never wanted him, which had forced Bo to acknowledge that his mother hadn't wanted him either. She wasn't waiting for him to run into her arms like Mads had shown him in the vision. That felt like a silly dream now. It felt like another lie.

And even if he wished for a mother who wanted him, it would always feel like a lie.

Selene brushed her hand against his forearm. "That's horrible. That's *really* mean."

Bo cleared his throat, picking at a nearby leaf, relishing how supple it felt between his fingertips. "When your mother —"

"*My* mother is the captain of the Queen's Guard," snapped Selene with her chin lifted. "She is too busy and important to leave her post. The Queen simply cannot live without her. That's the *only* reason she left me with the Sisters. But when I help you release the Stars, she'll see that I can be a guard too and then we'll never have to be apart again."

Selene spun on her heel and stormed off, head held high.

Nix barked.

"I know," said Bo. "She's as unpredictable as the Scribe, but are *you* going to tell her and risk being blasted with magic?"

Nix scooted off after the others in a hurry.

"Thought so," said Bo, and followed.

They weaved through the tightly packed trees until they came upon a small village of abandoned stone huts, many of them little more than rubble. They searched for signs of Galvin but he was long gone or had never been there. When Tam motioned to the tracks leading from the village to the forest, Bo's blood turned to ice. Neither of them said a word but Bo knew they both had heads full of gleaming bones and straw dolls.

They didn't follow the tracks. Instead, they chose the strongest-looking hut and locked themselves inside, then lit as many candles as they could find. They ate a meager meal of dried meat and bread, all of it scrounged from the bottom of Bo's rucksack. *Thank you, Sister Vela,* thought Bo.

"We sleep in shifts," announced Tam. She did not say why but Bo understood — candles did not keep Shadow Creatures away anymore. "I will take the first shift — you sleep. We will decide our next move in the morning."

Bo's body ached with exhaustion. It felt like an age since he had last slept. Rolling his cloak into a pillow, he curled up beside Nix and closed his eyes. *I'll only nap for a bit,* he told himself. *Make sure I wake up for my shift.* But when he next opened his eyes, pale morning Light streamed through the window.

He sat up, groggy and confused. Nix snuffled in his sleep, lying across Bo's shins and refusing to budge. Bo rubbed his eyes and spied Tam sitting in the same spot he had last seen her. She was wide awake.

"We were supposed to share the lookout," he grumbled.

Tam was cross-legged on the floor, the weapon she had called Redfist in her lap. She was running her fingers in slow circles along the feather-shaped blade. "I did not feel like sleep," she answered. "I have slept for too long."

Bo prodded Selene awake; the Nev'en was curled up on a pile of blankets beside him, snoring loudly enough to frighten away any Shadow Creature.

"Careful," she said, voice syrupy with sleep, "if you jolt me awake I might accidentally zap you with magic." Despite her grumbling, she sat up, scooping her long silver braids into a pile on top of her head, securing them with twine. "How come no one woke me for lookout?"

"I have been thinking," said Tam. "All night. About the riddle. I think, perhaps, it is a river."

Bo knotted his brow in thought. *I run but do not walk. I have a mouth but do not talk. I have a head but never weep. I have a bed but never sleep.* His eyes lit up. "That's it! You're a genius, Tam. A river fits."

Tam chuckled quietly. "Ah well."

Selene stood and dusted off the back of her trousers. "But

how do we know which river? There have to be hundreds in Ulv. Maybe more."

Bo rubbed the back of his stiff neck and sighed; he hadn't thought of that. Searching every river in Ulv would take forever!

"Ah, but there is only one called the Serpent River," said Tam. "Remember the shape of the key? A snake. So."

Selene broke into her wonky smile. "Oh, you really *are* a genius, Tam. Where is it? Is it far? Maybe we can beat Galvin to it. Do you think he's worked it out too?"

Bo leapt up, dislodging Nix with a yelp. He was so busy gathering his things, eager to get started on their journey, he did not notice Tam had remained silent. Finally, he looked up and saw the Korahku with her head lowered, eyes trained on her lap. She ran her finger along the edge of the blade until it reached the tip. She drew her finger up to her face and calmly inspected the slither of blood she found there.

"The Serpent River runs through the Valley of Eyes," said Tam.

An uneasy feeling squirmed in Bo's stomach. "Where is that?" The place sounded familiar but Bo couldn't think why.

Tam stood, dusting off her tunic, refusing to meet Bo's eye. "It is close to where you will find my flock. In Korak."

❧

"Keep moving," said Tam, voice tight. "Quickly."

"We don't have to do this," said Bo for what felt like the

hundredth time. He had been arguing with Tam ever since they'd left the hut. If Tam set foot in Korak, then her flock would surely capture her and sentence her to death. There was no way on Ulv Bo was letting that happen — he *owed* her. "You should stay here. Selene and I will collect the key and return to you."

"Do you know what a blood bind is, little Irin?" said Tam. She had asked this question at least five times already.

"I understood it the first time you explained it to me and it still doesn't make a difference," said Bo. "I'm not letting you —"

"Hush, little Irin. We will sneak into Korak and beat Galvin to the key. We leave before my flock realizes I have returned. It is no worry. Now, hurry, we have much land to cover before Dark."

It was no good. There was simply no arguing with Tam.

"I could try and magic her, tie her to a tree," whispered Selene as she passed. "Can't promise I won't turn her into a mud-myg, though. Or a togre." She shivered.

Bo told Nix to come along and quit barking at nothing. They were weaving among the trunks of a thick forest — still no sign of the sickness, thank the Light.

The trees were so densely packed that both Tam and Selene kept disappearing from view, obscured by the massive trunks. Nix stuck close to Bo's feet. Bo tried to keep his distance from the shadows but did it matter? Now that Shadow Creatures could attack in the Light . . .

"Tam?"

"Keep up," called the Korahku, though Bo couldn't see her.

He caught a glimpse of movement to his right. Was that Selene flicking in and out of view between the trees? "Selene?"

Bo jumped as Selene suddenly appeared at his left. He grabbed her hand in fright. "Did you see that? There was . . . something."

"Don't worry, I'll blast any Shadow Creatures with my magic. I'm getting the hang of it. Sister Magrid always said I was a slow learner but she was wrong. You just think about what you want to happen and it happens. Sort of. I have to really want it. And *feel* it. Something like that, anyway. And I guess magic can't be bad if it saves people. Right?"

But Bo wasn't listening. He stared hard at the gaps between the trees. Were the shadows moving?

"I'll have my hand back now, please," said Selene. Bo looked down and found he was still gripping it tightly. He dropped it, blood rushing to his cheeks.

Selene smiled at him, a dangerous twinkle in her eyes. "It's not just Shadow Creatures you have to worry about here, though," she said. "We're in the Labyrinth of Liars, after all."

"The labyrinth of what?"

"The Labyrinth of Liars. It's a forest that stretches for miles and miles and it's haunted."

Nix barked.

"I know," muttered Bo. "Maybe one day we'll stumble upon a forest that *isn't* haunted."

"It's because of the Elfvor," said Selene. "There used to be two kinds of people: the Elfvor and the Ulvians. You and me, we come from the Ulvians but some people, like the Korahku and the Qirachi, come from both. But here's the thing." She leaned in close, lowering her voice to a husky whisper. "Elfvor are monsters. You best not catch sight of one. Keep your eyes on the ground — you don't want to step on their tails."

Tails?

Bo kept his eyes on his feet as he hurried after Selene. He skipped over exposed roots and rocks and mulch and leaves but no tails. *Do trees have tails?*

"And they have hooves," said Selene. "And wooden horns that grow out of their foreheads and if you look them in the eye, you turn to stone. Some of them can shape-shift into animals and instead of skin they have bark and flowers and vines growing all over them and they live *forever*. So, really, any one of these trees could be an Elfvor in disguise," she said as she hurried away.

"I'm not sure what you read about being friends in those scrolls, Selene, but this isn't it," Bo called after her, but she only answered with a hoot of laughter. "I think she's making a fool out of me," Bo told Nix.

"Of course she is," said Tam, suddenly appearing in the gap between two trees on Bo's left. "There is no such thing as Elfvor anymore. They left these lands long ago."

"But what are Elfvor? And why did they leave? And how come they're your ancestors and not mine?"

Tam clicked her beak. "I see you have not lost your appetite for questions."

"I see you still refuse to give me answers," Bo grumbled. He sidestepped a shadow nervously.

"The point is, there are no Elfvor here anymore," said Tam. "No more monsters, okay?"

Bo let out a shaky breath.

"See?" he told Nix. "Nothing to worry about." *Except Shadow Creatures and wolves and witches,* he thought wryly.

"Oh, I would not say *nothing* to worry about," said Tam. "She is right about one thing: this *is* the Labyrinth of Liars. With magic returning, this might be a dangerous place to be for dishonest folk." Without further explanation, Tam strode off, disappearing among the thick trunks.

Bo frowned at Nix. Nix barked.

"I am *not* dishonest," he said. "I wasn't the one who stole a second helping of rabbit this morning, was I?"

Nix nipped at Bo's ankles before charging away.

As they trampled through the forest, the trees grew closer

together and the ground became harder to navigate — rocks and exposed tree roots and holes and dense scrub but still no tails. Shadows loomed ominously around them.

Bo's foot caught in a tree root and he fell forward, landing on his hands and knees. "Skugs fud," he said, and felt a cold nose press against his arm. "I'm fine, Nix," he said, dusting off his palms and knees. Bo tried to stand but his foot became tangled in the root again; down he tumbled.

"I think this forest hates me," he told Nix.

"Better hope that wasn't a tail," said Selene.

"Better hope I don't set Shadow Creatures on you," said Bo. Unlike the village children, who would have run away screaming, Selene merely rolled her eyes and skipped ahead. She didn't fear him at all. *Maybe she does know a thing or two about being a good friend,* he conceded.

Bo looked up and saw a flash of blue robe: Tam appeared between two trees, frowning at him.

"No time to rest," said the Korahku.

Bo opened his mouth to protest but was shocked into silence when the vines crisscrossing the ground suddenly rose up and charged toward Tam.

She hacked at the vines with one of the small swords she'd claimed from the temple, but each time a vine was cut, two more replaced it.

"What is this?" Bo yelled. He looked left and saw Selene with her eyes wide in shock as the vines sprang up off the forest floor and walled her in too.

She was trapped.

THE TRUE HISTORIES OF ULV, VOL. XVII

ON THE PECULIAR RELATIONSHIP between TREES AND MAGIC

D id you know trees are particularly susceptible to the whims of magic? Don't believe me?

Then you will find yourself in trouble should you stumble upon a certain forest in the easternmost corner of Ulv, called Ov Carn Flik in the local dialect, which translates to "evil magical trees that rip off your face and eat it."

And let us not forget the Great Future-Telling Birch of Ny, which, should you place your hand on its trunk, will offer three glimpses into your future. Which is splendid! Astonishing! Fabulous! Except that the Great Future-Telling Birch of Ny has a wicked sense of humor and takes great joy in making misleading predictions to drive you mad.

One particularly fascinating — and by "fascinating" I mean "ghastly" — case of magical trees is the Labyrinth of Liars, a forest on the southern banks of the Sea of Widow's Tears. Should you enter the forest with a lie in your heart, the tree roots will rise up and entomb you, squeezing the life from you slowly but surely. Cut a vine and it doubles, triples, quadruples! So take a big breath before you're all wrapped up because it might well be your last for a while!

Of course, since magic vanished, the Labyrinth of Liars is a perfectly ordinary forest and is a lovely destination for day walks and picnics, even for liars.

Edit: Magic has returned. Be wary of the Labyrinth of Liars.

CHAPTER TWENTY

NIX BARKED AT THE TANGLED VINES that had wound around Selene — there wasn't even a gap Bo could see through.

"Selene?"

"Bo?" Her voice was muffled and faint.

"Keep back," said Tam, unsheathing Redfist. She slashed at the vines but more kept coming, tangling around her feet. Bo danced on the spot to keep the vines from curling around his ankles, but they slithered right by him, drawn only to Tam and Selene. "It is no good," said Tam, panting heavily after several minutes of fruitless slashing and chopping. Another vine slithered up her calf.

"I'm going to try something," came Selene's muffled voice. "You lot might want to get out of the way."

"Are you sure that's —" Bo ducked as a flash of blue Light zapped through the air; the hair on the back of his neck stood at attention. More Light zoomed by him as he huddled on the ground, arms wrapped around Nix: *zap, zap, zoom!*

Bo coughed on smoke as the *zap*s finally stopped. He looked up, and through the hazy blue smoke, he saw Selene's long limbs tearing at the singed vines.

"How about *that?*" said Selene, ripping off the final charred vine. She grinned in triumph, then sent a blast of magic to free Tam, too. "Take that, creepy vines! Ha!"

Bo rolled his eyes but couldn't help the fond smile that curled his mouth. "Magic isn't so bad, is it?"

Selene bit her lip, trying to contain her own smile. "Perhaps."

But their relief was short-lived as new shoots suddenly sprang up from the ground and began weaving toward Selene and Tam.

"Hogsbeard! Why do they keep coming for *us?* Why not go for Bo and Nix?"

"Hey!"

"Quickly," said Tam, taking Selene's hand and pulling. "Run!"

They dashed through the forest, weaving between the trees with vines slithering after them like rabid snakes. Though they brushed past Bo and nipped at Nix's tail, their focus was Selene and Tam. *Zap, zap, zap!* Selene shot sparks of fire at the vines as she ran. Soon, they reached a large clearing.

With a startled cry, Selene tripped on a tree root and fell. As she hit the ground, a luminous green vine roped around her ankle. A dozen more sprang from all directions and wrapped her up tight, arms pinned to her sides.

"Hogsbeard! How am I supposed to magic these vines now?"

In a frenzy, Tam attacked the creepers trying to capture her — *chop, chop, chop* with her sword. Bo looked for a rock, a fallen branch, a bone, but there was nothing.

He kicked them. "Get back, vines. Leave them alone!"

The vines coiled tighter around Selene, squeezing the air from her lungs. She gasped. "Help me!"

Bo tore the vines with his bare hands until an unmistakable sound froze him to the spot: a wolf's howl.

"No." He shook his head. *"No."* He tore at the vines until his fingers bled. "Not now! He can't come now!"

Tam crouched into her battle pose, head tilting as she listened for the approaching wolf. The vines continued to claw at her but she chopped them one by one. "Use this." Tam handed a small sword to Bo — it was Firewand. "Free Selene and then run," she said. "Whatever happens, do not stop."

The sword shook in Bo's grip. No matter how much air he gulped, it was never enough to fill his lungs.

"My arms," Selene wheezed, struggling against the tightening vines. They were up to her neck. "Free my arms."

Bo hacked at Selene's sides where the vines were thickest, wincing with every wild slash, afraid of hurting her. He was swimming in sweat. So hot!

The wolf howled again, closer this time.

Selene squirmed against the shredded vines as they wrapped around her. "Just a few more," she groaned.

"Hurry, Bo," said Tam as the *thump-ta-thump-ta-THUMP* of Ranik's approach drummed through Bo's body.

At the cracking of a branch, Bo looked over his shoulder and saw the wolf bounding toward them, weaving through the densely packed trees with mystifying grace. He reached the clearing and pulled up in front of Tam.

"Is you. Again," sneered Ranik, baring his teeth at the Korahku. "Thought I. Killed you."

"Not as strong as you think, wolf," said Tam. She deftly slashed the vines curling up her calves, all the while keeping a steady eye on Ranik.

"Will be glad. To finish you. This time," said Ranik, pawing at the earth, readying himself to attack. "Best you. Stay out of. My way. I just. Need to speak. With boy. He has. Answers."

"And if he does not give you the answers you are after?" said Tam.

The wolf grinned. "Then he. Is of no use. And I am. Hungry."

Bo attacked the vines with a roar, but each cut only increased the number of vines constricting Selene. Sweat was dripping from his chin, down his chest. So hot! He was burning up! It took Bo a moment to realize it was the crystal pendant around his neck, burning hot and throbbing, making him sweat.

But that meant . . .

Bo turned in time to see the air rippling before a familiar ball of Light bobbed and expanded and poured into the shape of Mads. Instead of joy or relief, Bo felt queasy.

The apparition maneuvered between Tam and Ranik. "No, you don't, wolf," Mads growled. "Why must you always spoil my plans?"

The wolf backed up, confusion twisting his snarl. "Not possible," he said. "Killed you."

Mads was almost completely solid this time. Save for blurry edges, he looked whole and so alive. Bo's mouth was suddenly dry; he slashed at the vines around Selene but it was hard to focus.

"What . . . what is this?" said Tam, turning to Bo. The vines curled around her ankles but she was too stunned to react. "Who is this?"

Bo's mouth opened and closed but he could not find the words.

Ranik pawed at the ground, tilting his head and sniffing the air. "You are. Familiar. But you. Are not."

Mads chuckled. "Smart wolf," he said. "But are you smart enough to realize when you are already beaten?"

The wolf growled, his hackles rising. His milky white eyes snapped from Bo to Mads and back again. "What can. You do. In this state?"

Mads echoed the wolf's growl, louder and deeper. "Let's find out, shall we?" Mads drew both arms into the air, and with a spray of colorful sparks suddenly three tendrils of smoke rose from the shadows, morphing into Shadow Creatures.

Bo almost fell over trying to back away, Nix right beside him. Bo couldn't breathe, as if the vines had wrapped around his lungs and squeezed tight. How was it possible to create Shadow Creatures out of thin air? What kind of magic was that?

Bo gasped as the Shadow Creatures flung themselves at Ranik, twisting and turning, obeying every one of Mads's commands. With talons and teeth like knives, the creatures attacked; they moved like liquid Darkness as they slashed and clawed at the wolf. Bo knew that Mads had magic—he'd seen it himself the last time Mads had faced the wolf—but this was . . . Bo still didn't have the words.

Ranik shrank back with a whimper, batting at the Shadow Creatures and snapping with his powerful jaws. At full strength he might have fought off one creature, but he was so frail his ribs were showing and his sunburnt skin wept with sores from traveling in the Light, so he was no match for three of the magical beasts. Soon, several deep gashes adorned his chest and his sides and he was cowering, whimpering as the creatures dived for him again and again.

Finally, with a strangled howl, the wolf leapt to his feet and ran away, whimpering until the sound faded completely.

Despite the wolf's leaving, Bo was still paralyzed by fear. The Shadow Creatures loomed above them, snarling and scratching at the air. But with a wave of his hands, Mads turned the creatures into puffs of smoke that floated away on the breeze.

The old man turned, knocking Tam out of the way as he strode toward Bo.

"How did —" Bo was shoved to the side too; he stumbled on a tree root and fell to the ground. "Oof!" Anger shot through him in blistering waves. He squeezed his hands into fists in his lap, biting his bottom lip to stop it from trembling. Why did the old man always treat him like dirt?

Mads held out his hands and puffs of fire shot from each fingertip, burning the vines that had engulfed Selene. When the smoke cleared, Selene ripped the blackened vines off her, gasping for breath.

"About time!" she snapped. "How come it took you —" Her eyes grew large as she noticed the tall stranger who had rescued her. "Oh. Sorry. I didn't —"

Next, Mads shot magic at Tam's legs; the vines that weren't singed retreated quickly, hiding from the magical fire. Mads whirled around and leveled a gruff look at Bo. His eyes, normally a pale, watery gray, shone bright, as though a fire lit them from within. "Did you find the second key?" he demanded.

Bo accepted the hand Tam held out for him. He stood,

dusting off his pants and shirt. He nodded because he *had* found it; Mads just didn't need to know Bo had also *lost* it.

"Then hurry up and find the third key," said Mads. "You have no excuse. Do *not* let me down."

Without sparing another look, Mads strode away. But he stopped when Tam's voice cut through the shocked silence. "How did you do that? Command Shadow Creatures?"

Mads's shoulders tightened as he turned to face them. Bo expected a growl or a glare, but he shuddered with surprise when he saw Mads was smiling.

"Magic," said Mads, and laughed. "Just like this." And then he was gone, vanishing in a flash of blinding Light.

Bo puffed out a shaky breath. Nix barked at the now-empty space where Mads had been.

"Well," said Selene, "*that* was something. Anyone going to tell me who that was?"

Bo grabbed the crystal pendant through his shirt, the delicate skin on his chest still smarting from the burning heat. "My guardian."

Selene arched a brow. "The ghost?"

Bo nodded, chewing on his lip.

"Well, he's not very nice," said Selene. "Quite rude, if you ask me. Keys, keys, keys! He didn't even stop to ask if you were okay! Was he always that awful?"

Bo shrugged — he didn't know what to say. Unease crept up

his spine like icy fingertips when he thought of Mads using magic in such a horrible way — it wasn't the kind of magic that Selene used; it was the kind that turned the trees to ashes. The chill only grew stronger when he thought of the cold-blooded look in Mads's eyes when he had demanded to know about the keys. A feeling of dread settled deep in Bo's bones from where it could never truly be pried free. And something else. Something worse.

It was doubt.

Mads had lied to him, bullied him, said cruel things, but . . . was he *evil?* Bo had every reason to be angry with Mads but did he need to be afraid of him too?

"We must go," said Tam. She would not look at Bo. Instead, she stared, troubled, at the sword Bo was still holding. "Quickly. Before the vines return for us." She grabbed the sword from Bo's hand and hurried away.

Bo turned to find Selene glaring at the charred vines at her feet. "Listen here, forest. If you try to tangle me up again I'll zap you faster than a humminzinger in a snurre rundt."

She kicked the vines with a huff and strode away.

Bo shared a worried look with Nix before he chased after Selene, shaking all thoughts of Mads from his head as best he could. "But how come they attacked you and Tam?" he asked Selene.

"They're evil, magical vines, Bo," she said. "It's what they do."

He panted as he jogged to keep up. "But they didn't come for Nix and me. Tam mentioned something about this place being dangerous for dishonest folk. It *is* called the Labyrinth of Liars, like you said, and I just thought —"

Selene spun around. "Are you calling me a liar?" She balled her hands into fists by her sides.

Bo shook his head, backing up. He could see the telltale sparks raging in Selene's pupils.

"No," he said. "Not at all. Definitely not." His words tumbled over one another.

"It's because I have magic," she said, lifting her chin. "That has to be it. Nothing more."

Selene didn't wait for Bo to answer; she stalked after Tam with her head held high, her arms crossed.

Nix rubbed against Bo's legs, quietly growling.

"I know," Bo said. "If they came for magical people, then why did they come for Tam, too?"

Bo didn't have an answer, so he pushed all thoughts of liars deep, deep down with his feelings about Mads and magic and wolves and keys and Galvin.

"Come on, Nix," said Bo. "We don't want to lose them."

CHAPTER TWENTY-ONE

A TRICKLING STREAM separated the forest from a luscious tree-lined valley beyond. Bo collapsed on a rock and mopped his brow with his sleeve while Nix dived into the stream and splashed about, barking. Bo took a swig of water from his canteen, then passed it to Selene.

Tam stood with her back to them, gazing into the valley. Bo attempted to read her feelings in the way she held herself, but the Korahku gave nothing away; what must it be like to see her home again? Could it ever be the same after so much had changed?

"There are nests scattered across these lands," she said, "refuge for Korahku caught too far from home by the Dark." Instinctively, Bo glanced up; the Light had fallen low and the half-Light was fast approaching. "We make for one and set off for the Serpent River in the morning, yes?"

Selene slouched by the edge of the forest, kicking the fallen leaves. She shrugged but didn't say a word as she handed back

Bo's canteen. She had been uncharacteristically quiet since the vines had attacked her.

"This is Korak?" asked Bo. It looked much the same as Irin: lush green grass, thick forests, rolling hills.

Tam pointed to the babbling stream. "Northern border," she said, a smile in her voice.

Bo frowned. "There's a wall big enough for giants to have built it between Nev'en and Irin. How come —"

"We protect our borders in . . . other ways," said Tam, her posture stiff; there was no smile in her voice now.

"Other ways?"

Tam cleared her throat but did not answer.

Bo shifted uncomfortably on the rock. "You promise we can find the key and leave before they know we're here?" he said.

Tam kept her gaze on the quiet valley. "Yes."

Bo chewed on the inside of his cheek and frowned. His stomach felt strange, as though rocks had been his breakfast rather than rabbit. But all he could do was trust Tam. Surely she knew better than him?

He stood. "Get out, Nix. We're going."

The little fox jumped and kicked his feet, soaking Bo in water.

Selene clapped a hand over her mouth to hold back a laugh. "You should see your face," she said before giving in to the laughter, slapping her knee. "It's redder than a boil on a witch's nose!"

"Well, at least she's not in a huff anymore," muttered Bo, wringing out his shirt. Nix leapt out of the water and nipped at Bo's calf on his way past.

Something black floating downstream caught Bo's eye: a charred leaf. The rocks in Bo's stomach churned as he looked over his shoulder at the forest behind him.

It was not noticeable at first but when he peered closely, Bo saw a handful of leaves were curled and charred. They fell to the ground and Bo quickly turned away.

"Come on, Nix," whispered Bo. The water was freezing as he stepped into the stream and crossed to the other side.

Tam led them into the valley, where the grass was soft underfoot and a cool breeze tickled Bo's hair and skin.

The tree trunks were wider than a hut and stretched high enough to breach the clouds. In their branches perched strange raven-like birds — hundreds of them. *Thousands.* Their feathers shimmered in the Light and their beaks were short and hooked to a razor-sharp point. They squawked — deep, throaty, rasping — the sound echoing throughout the valley.

Bo shivered.

"Do you think we'll meet anyone on the road?" he asked. He thought back to Irin, to the villagers pushing their carts, fleeing for safety.

Tam pointed overhead. "Korak roads are that way," she said. "Down here we are safe."

Bo guessed that made sense. He looked up and saw one of the black birds flying above: *Squawk, squawk, squawk.* That was when Bo realized the birds had *three* eyes. One in the center of their head and one on the underside of each wing.

After they had walked for a short while, Bo began to notice something strange.

On a low-hanging branch, one black bird stretched out its wings so all three eyes could watch Bo and his companions pass. Other birds did the same. It happened over and over.

"Is it my imagination or—" Bo peered closely at a tree and jumped back when he saw an eye in a trunk knot—it winked at him! "We're being watched!"

"Why do you think it's called the Valley of Eyes?" whispered Selene. "The birds are cryven and the trees are knot-eyes. Have you noticed the butterflies?" One had just landed on the bud of a small yellow flower. Bo leaned down as the fluttering wings stilled; there was a colorful pattern on each wing that, when Bo peered closer, looked like a pair of amber eyes. The eyes blinked and Bo jerked back. "There are Korahku spies *everywhere,*" said Selene as the butterfly took off, fluttering away.

"Spies? Tam, you said—"

"It is fine, little Irin. The spies will not report you because you are with me. As far as they can see I am a Korahku and have every right to be on this land. They will assume you are my prisoners and leave us be. All is good."

At least Bo knew what "other ways" meant now — there wasn't a giant wall because there were spies to guard the border.

But Bo could not shake his unease; no matter where he turned, he felt eyes burning into his back. *Squawk, squawk, squawk.* A canopy of leaves rustled above them as several cryven took flight.

Tam whistled a cheery tune as she walked.

"But what if the spies recognize you?" said Bo, jogging to catch her. "You were second in line to the throne, so —"

"There." Tam pointed to a thick trunk, the bark deeply ridged like a crinkled shirt left to dry all scrunched up. "There are nests in this tree. We stay for the Dark."

Because Tam's wings were clipped, they had to climb. Bo didn't mind — he had been climbing trees since before he could walk — but Selene gave the trunk a weary look.

With whispered reassurances, Bo strapped a whimpering Nix to Tam's back and the three of them took off; Selene waved away Bo's offer of help, gritting her teeth as she jumped for the closest branch and pulled herself up. It was a long climb but for once, Bo felt at home.

Tam pointed them to the lowest-hanging nest, an oval, straw-woven thing with a round hatch for a door.

Once inside, Selene slumped to the floor, putting her head between her knees. "I'm okay. I'm okay. I'm okay."

As soon as Bo freed a squirming Nix from Tam's back, the fox nipped Bo's heel and barked.

"Well, you couldn't climb on your own, could you, Nix?" said Bo.

Nix yapped and turned his back on everyone.

Tam poked about the candlelit space and discovered plenty of supplies. The nest was a single round room with thick mud-and-straw walls, and no beds, only wooden perches.

Bo sat down and soon found himself munching on some kind of pickled worm — he was too hungry to refuse the slimy critters and was pleasantly surprised by the nutty taste.

Bo took the first shift on lookout so Tam would have to sleep at least some of the night. He was glad to be helping, but he didn't like being alone with his thoughts and the sounds of Shadow Creatures howling in the distance.

Nix whimpered, skulking over to Bo and pressing close to his thigh.

"Friends again, are we?" said Bo with a hollow chuckle. He dropped a hand to the fox's back, tangled his fingers into the soft fur, and blocked out his worries as best as he could.

∽

"How much farther?"

The day was hot, the air sticky and close. Bo could hardly hear himself think for all the cryven squawking and flapping.

He was tired of the way his skin prickled from being constantly looked at, watched, followed.

"A hair's width less than the last time you asked," answered Selene at the same time Tam said, "Not far."

After too few hours of restless, nightmare-filled sleep, Bo had been grumpy all morning. His head pounded, his belly ached, and his thoughts were twisted. Walking for hours on end was not improving his mood.

They walked for miles before Bo heard the dull roar of the Serpent River ahead of them.

"How big is it?" Bo asked, his worry weighing heavily in his heart. If the river was as big as it sounded, then how would they ever find the key in it? He had been hoping for something more like the trickling stream.

Tam seemed to read Bo's thoughts. "There is an island in the river called the Snake's Eye. If I was going to hide a key, I would choose there, don't you think?"

Bo nodded, but when they rounded a bend in the valley and finally saw the Serpent River in all its glory, he sucked in a quick breath and swore.

"What's 'Skugs fud'?" asked Selene.

"Do not ask," said Tam.

The river was wide, the other side a hazy, bluish-green blur. Bo wondered where the water went and why it seemed to be in such a hurry to get there; the current was strong, the choppy, foamy waves roaring as they charged downstream.

They walked along the river's edge with the flow of the current until Bo saw a rickety wooden bridge that connected the riverbank to a small island in the middle of the water.

An island covered in cryven.

"Oh," said Bo, and Nix barked.

"That's a lot of birds," said Selene.

Tam said nothing.

The island was bare of trees, so the cryven covered the ground like a blanket; the only gap in all the black was the occasional wink of gold from their eyes. The raspy *squawk, squawk, squawk* of the hundred or more cryven was loud enough to cut through the roar of the river.

"How do we search *that?*" said Bo. He kept a nervous eye on the birds. He didn't like the way they moved — sharp, purposeful, lingering. If a flock of piquee birds tried to steal his lunch, he would stomp his foot and shout until they flapped away in a tizzy. He doubted that would work on cryven.

"Slowly," said Tam. "No sudden movements. No loud noises."

"Or I could blast them with magic," said Selene.

Tam clicked her beak. "Thank you. But that will not be necessary. The cryven mean us no harm. They are safe so long as we do not spook them."

Tam stepped on the bridge; it creaked under her weight.

"What happens if they're spooked?" said Bo.

"Then they will mean us harm," she said, and started across the bridge in slow, purposeful steps.

Selene shrugged and followed.

Bo turned back to Nix. "Sorry, but I think you should stay behind."

Nix barked.

"I know that, but they're still birds, and if they see a fox trotting among them they'll get spooked."

Nix whimpered, turning nervous circles.

"You and me both," said Bo. He stepped onto the bridge.

The wood was fragile under his feet — how old was this thing? He glanced over his shoulder, glad to see that for once the fox had listened to him.

"First time for everything," he muttered under his breath.

The muscles in his legs shook as he inched slowly across the bridge. He had to stop himself from running the last few steps, desperate as he was to be off the rickety old bridge before it collapsed. But as he finally set foot on the island, he remembered there were more urgent things to worry about than rotted wood.

Cryven.

Lots and lots of cryven, their unblinking eyes pinning the three intruders to the spot.

"This isn't creepy at all," whispered Bo.

"Give me a haunted forest any day," agreed Selene.

Tam hushed them and took a step into the flock. Bo held his breath, waiting for the birds' reactions.

Those closest to Tam scuttled out of the way with a disgruntled *squawk, squawk, squawk* but nothing more. Bo let out his breath.

They crept through the cryven; each step Bo took felt like being in the quagmires again, taking long, careful strides from tuft to tuft to avoid the mud. *Which would be a better way to die?* he wondered bitterly. *Drowned in mud or pecked to death?*

"There's nothing here," whispered Selene. "Where are we supposed to look?"

A bird next to Bo's foot opened its wings, and three eyes stared at him. Bo fought back a shiver of revulsion as he quickly looked away. The last key had been in a box, hidden inside a secret drawer. The first . . . perhaps it had been in a box once, discarded by the careless Un-King. But there was nothing on this island to hide a box in, on, or under. Unless the cryven were hiding it? Another bird opened its wings and watched Bo with three golden eyes. *Squawk, squawk, squawk.*

"What if—" Tam started to say, but a bark cut her off.

Bo whirled around to find that Nix had followed him after all and was turning excited circles at the final step of the bridge, barking loudly.

"Nix! No!"

It was a chain reaction. The cryven closest to Nix flapped

their wings in a frenzy, screeching until all the birds around them had joined in, and then the whole island was in turmoil. Bo covered his ears as the screeching grew, the sound ringing in his ears until he was certain they would bleed.

And then the cryven attacked.

They took flight but only high enough to dive-bomb Bo and his friends — again and again they swooped, pecking every piece of exposed flesh they could reach, pounding with their wings.

The air was filled with screeching, wings beating, and his friends' screaming as they tried to protect their faces from the birds. Bo heard Nix bark, and looked over to see him jumping and weaving, trying to nip at the chaos of feathers and claws and beaks.

With a cry, Selene threw out her hands, and a shimmering blue shield pushed the cryven back, halting the onslaught. Bo was breathing hard, bleeding from so many pecks to his hands, his neck, his face.

"I don't know how long I can hold them off," she said through gritted teeth. The birds were attacking the shield, their sharp beaks tearing holes in it. "Find the key."

Tam began searching, bent low.

The island was covered in molted feathers and blotches of white bird droppings and grass — uneven, scraggy grass that seemed to form some kind of pattern, a spiral pattern . . .

"That's it!" cried Bo. "I bet anything that from above, that pattern looks like a spiraled snake, just like the second key." He ran to the center of the island, where the spiral ended. He dropped to his knees and began to dig, dry-retching as he shoveled through the bird-dropping-stained dirt with both hands. Nix ran to him and dug with his paws too.

"Don't know why you can't follow a simple instruction, Nix," said Bo.

Nix barked.

"What do you mean 'warn me'? Warn about what?" But Bo didn't hear the answer because his fingers had hit something smooth and hard—a wooden box! He dug around it until he could pry it free and then smashed it against the hard earth, exactly as he had seen Tam do. It took several attempts before the box cracked open and a small copper key tumbled out.

"I've got it!" shouted Bo. He held the key aloft, jumping up and down. "I've got it!"

"Great!" called Selene. "Do you think we could get out of here now?"

Bo pocketed the key without examining it—there was no time.

As if at the bidding of some secret signal, all the cryven flew away at once, leaving an eerie silence behind them.

Selene dropped her shield, panting.

"We must go," said Tam.

"Why did—" started Bo, but his words were drowned out by

the violent beating of wings, like a bird caught in a trap, fighting to be free. Bo glanced up and saw four shadowy shapes overhead, much, *much* larger than the cryven.

"No!" hissed Tam, unhooking Redfist from her belt. "Scouts!"

Selene threw another shield up but some kind of dust rained down on it from above. The shield lit up orange before it fizzled out with an acrid stench.

Bo realized the shadowy shapes were birds too, but they were *ten times* as big as the cryven — large, red-feathered birds with the same three eyes.

All four scouts swooped at once.

"No!" shouted Tam, swishing Redfist back and forth. "Take me — leave the children. They mean no harm. Take me!"

Selene screamed as one of the giant birds swept her up in its claws and lifted her into the air, arms pinned to her sides.

Bo reached for her, but large claws clamped around his waist and suddenly his feet were pedaling air. He heard Nix yelp and looked across to see his friend nipping at the clawed feet of the bird that had grabbed him. He was too high up to see what happened to Tam.

The giant birds swept up through the air, so fast the wind cut against Bo's skin. When he glanced down, the breath was knocked out of him — they were so high!

When they broke through the cloud cover, Bo's mouth fell open.

In the sky was a city.

A scattering of trees reached high above the clouds, and in the canopy was a whole city of interlocking nests, hundreds of them. *Thousands.* Like giant, bulbous sacks, the nests hung from the branches, connected by narrow suspended walkways. Each nest was woven out of gold-red straw; the fading Light rippled across the surface of each of them, shimmering like fire. Bo spied small black dots zipping between the nests, like mud-mygs dancing in the humid air of the swamps. When he got closer, however, Bo realized the dots were Korahku, flying through their city.

"The Golden Aerie!" shouted Selene. "Korahku royal city."

The giant birds dropped everyone except Tam onto a deck hugging the middle of an enormous egg-shaped nest on the outskirts of the city. Bo rolled to a halt, knocking heads with Selene before nearly tumbling over the edge of the deck.

Bo scrambled back and jumped to his feet, finding himself face-to-thigh with a sour-looking Korahku, his black robe billowing in the wind. "Who are you? And what have you done with Tam? Where is she? Is she okay?"

Nix barked.

Ignoring them, the Korahku lurched forward and grabbed both of Selene's arms.

"Hey!" she cried as he wrapped a translucent, silvery cuff around her wrists. "Stop that! It burns!"

A sharp pecking in his back sent Bo hurtling forward. He turned and saw that the giant scout birds were behind them, pressing in. Bo, Selene, and Nix were herded into the nest. Inside was a honeycomb of what looked like prison cells. *Great. Another prison,* thought Bo. His stomach wobbled as he peered over the edge of the hanging walkway that ran through the middle of the nest; he couldn't even see the bottom, it was such a long way down.

At the end of the walkway, the guard threw them into a cell, sending them tumbling to the floor. "You trespass on Korahku land and consort with a known traitor," he boomed, seizing Bo's rucksack. "Once the Dark has passed, you will stand before the King. He will decide your fate."

Bo scrambled to his feet. "Quick! Blast him, Selene!"

She raised her bound hands but nothing happened. Her face fell. "I think the cuff is suppressing my magic," she said.

Nix barked.

With his hand on the cell door, the Korahku paused. His beady black eyes shone with malice. "The punishment for trespass is death, in case you were wondering," he said.

He slammed the door shut.

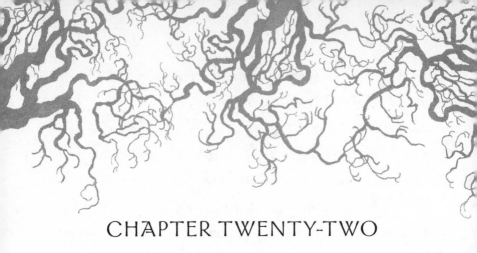

CHAPTER TWENTY-TWO

B O PICKED AT THE DRIED BLOOD on his hands and arms from the cryven's frenzied pecks. His face was scabbed and bruised from the attack. Nix licked his paw, then rubbed it across his bloodied ears and snout, trying to clean them.

When a small tray of food and water was pushed through a steel flap in the cell door, Bo divided it into three. After every last crumb was gone, his stomach still rumbled and his body ached and his mind was bursting with worries. He hugged a whimpering Nix close; the fox's scar was weeping.

"At least we got the third key," said Selene.

Bo pulled it out and examined it by flickering candle-Light.

Like the others, it had a strange shape at one end — this time, a wolf's head. There were carvings, too: another riddle.

Selene leaned over his shoulder and read it out: "'I have a foot but no legs. I have a peak, but I am not a hat. You can climb me, but I am not a tree. I am tall, and yet I never grow. I am the largest of them all.'"

"It must be a clue telling us where the wolf's cage is," Bo guessed. "What can you climb that isn't a tree?"

Selene shrugged. "How can you be tall but never grow?"

Bo argued back and forth about the riddle with Selene for hours. "It's a pity we don't have the Scribe here to give us her cryptic clues," he said in the end.

Selene snorted. "Or blither-blather about a silly painting of a — oh no, wait!" She sat up straight. "That's it! A mountain! The answer to the riddle is a mountain. And the tallest of them all is Lindorm. We're not far from there!" She pumped her bound fists in the air.

Too bad we're locked up for trespass and the first two keys are missing, thought Bo.

"Let's get a good night's sleep," he said out loud. He folded his cloak into a pillow and lay down on his side, Nix curling into a ball next to him. "We can figure out what to do tomorrow."

He wanted to be excited about having figured out the third and final clue, but he was too filled with worry and fear and doubt and anger — lots of bubbling, growing anger.

He closed his eyes and willed himself to sleep.

∽

Outside the cell, the wind churned, battering the curved wall, howling like a wounded wolf. Inside, candles flickered in their iron sconces, casting long shadows.

Bo huddled against the wall made from itchy woven straw,

knees hugged to his chest, keeping a careful eye on the jittery shadows. At his feet, Nix dozed, and across the cell, Selene was splayed on the floor, snoring softly.

He hadn't slept a wink; his mind was too clogged with worries.

What would the Korahku do to them? Where was Tam? What happened to Galvin and the first two keys? Was Mads evil? When would the Shadow Creatures attack next?

With a metallic, high-pitched *squawk,* the cell door swung open and the black-robed guard barged in.

Selene shot up, startled from sleep. "Is it Shadow Creatures? Is it —" She looked around wildly, blinking.

"Where's Tam?" Bo scrambled to his feet, eyes on the impassive guard. Nix leapt up beside him and growled. "You tell me *now!*"

The guard grabbed Selene and Bo by their collars and dragged them out of the nest. Three giant scouts were perched on the railing that bordered the walkway outside. Soft early-morning Light cast a fiery sheen on their feathers. They cawed, stretching their wings wide to stare with all their eyes.

Nix barked, snapping at the Korahku's feet.

"If you wish for me not to kick your dog over the ledge," said the Korahku, "perhaps you will tell it to be quiet."

Bo did as he was told, and reluctantly Nix grew silent.

The scouts took to the air, swooping to clasp each of the

prisoners in their claws. Selene screamed as she was lifted up, beating her cuffed hands against the sharp talons. "Get off me, you feathery lump! Let me go!"

The scouts sailed toward the center of the city, sweeping low to zip among the bulbous nests, glistening as though woven from pure gold. The air crackled with Korahku birdcalls —a deep, raw *caw, caw, caw* that turned Bo's blood to ice as he dangled from the scout's grip.

City life streaked by them —open nests filled with bustling markets, clusters of homes, towering nests filled with unknown industry. The nests grew in size the deeper into the city they flew, needing thicker and longer web-like ropes to tie them safely to the branches.

The scouts finally zoomed into the center of the city, revealing the most incredible sight.

A colossal nest hung from a branch, the straw shimmering gold and red and orange. It was a palace —that much was clear —with a collection of smaller, rounded nests clumped on the outside like boils. A wide perch jutted from the palace's front entry and it was here that the scouts dumped the three prisoners, who rolled until they landed at the feet of waiting guards.

"Take the trespassers to the roost until the King is ready for them," instructed the black-robed guard, landing smoothly beside them.

Bo was pulled to his feet and shoved through a hatch, and

he stumbled into a cavernous entry hall. The walls were straw, stretching far above, farther than Bo could see. Beams of carved wood crisscrossed haphazardly overhead and the curved walls were adorned with ornate tapestries depicting gory battle scenes.

As Bo was pushed through the long hall, he couldn't help but gawk at the tapestries — most seemed to show Irin slaughtered in battle and, *oh*. Was that the Irin royal family being beheaded?

"Keep moving, pig-child," snapped the guard behind him. He shoved Bo between his shoulder blades.

A dead end in front of them was covered with the biggest tapestry of all: a snow-tipped mountain that looked like a monstrous worm curled around and around itself. Lindorm Mountain, Bo guessed with a fluttering of hope. Selene had said it was close by. Perhaps if . . .

But as they were quickly herded past the tapestry and shoved into a small wood-lined room, Bo's fluttering hope vanished. It didn't matter how close they were — they were still prisoners.

"You will wait here for the King to see you," said a guard before slamming the door, the lock rattling into place a second later.

Selene banged on the door with her bound fists. "You can't boss me around! My mother is the captain of the Queen's Guard and she'll have you all arrested!"

"Arrested?" said a voice from the corner of the room. Bo turned to find a familiar set of gold teeth glimmering at him.

Nix growled. Bo squeezed his hands into fists as Galvin advanced on them — *that lying, cheating, no-good trollhead!*

Galvin's right eye slid over Selene. "Did I hear correctly, child? Your mother is the captain of the Queen's Guard?"

"Yes," snapped Selene in her haughtiest voice. "You did. And if you think you can hurt us, then you'd best be prepared for her to arrest you, too."

Galvin laughed. "Are you sure? Because I happen to know that the captain of the Queen's Guard is part Qirachi, part giantess." He looked her up and down. "You're rather short for a girl with giant blood in you."

Selene's eyes grew wide as she swung around to Bo. "He's . . . he's lying," she spluttered. "I . . ." All the fight left her at once. She fell back against the door and slid to the floor, head in her hands. "Oh, hogsbeard!" she snapped. "He's right. I lied."

Bo sucked in a sharp breath as Galvin cackled. *More lies?* He sat beside his friend, his chest tight with confusion. And hurt.

"The vines came after me, remember?" she said, lifting her head to peek sidelong at Bo. "Because I said my mother and father sent me to be an apprentice with the Sisters. I said they were important people, my mother the captain of the Guard and my father the Queen's chief advisor." She took a deep, shaky breath. "The truth is my mother died giving birth to me, and my father didn't want me. He only wanted sons. So he dumped me on the Silent Sisters." Selene sniffed, rubbing her eyes with the backs of her hands. She shifted around to face Bo. "I'm sorry I lied to you, truly I am. I don't like admitting that my father didn't want me and that my mother is . . . is . . ."

She's just like me, Bo realized. *Angry because nobody wanted her.* He slid his hand into hers.

"It's not your fault. What your father did has *nothing* to do with you," he said. He was certain he ought to be mad at Selene for lying, but instead he felt a twisty, sticky kind of anger at her father; it clung to every inch of him and wouldn't let go. Her story reminded him too much of his own mother and father. Of the Moon. Of Mads.

"Do you think he misses me?" asked Selene, eyes wide with hope.

"He'd be a trollhead if he didn't," said Bo.

"Yes, yes, very touching." Galvin clapped his hands together. "But I have more pressing matters to discuss. Such as: Where is the third key? You have it, don't you? Those blasted Korahku scouts grabbed me before I could reach the river, but I'd wager you're tricky enough to have gotten that far. Give me, give me, give me!"

Bo scoffed, folding his arms across his chest. "I don't have it. And even if I did, I wouldn't give it to *you*. Why don't you hand me back *my* two keys?"

"*Tsk, tsk, tsk.* My, how rude you've become! Such a polite boy when I first met you and now look at you." Galvin dusted off his ripped and mud-stained trousers. In fact, all his clothes were torn and stained.

"What happened to you?" said Bo.

"Labyrinth of Liars," mumbled Galvin, picking at a healing sore on his arm. "Never ran so fast in all my life."

Bo laughed. "Of course the vines would attack *you*."

Galvin shook his finger at Bo. "Now, listen here, boy. You give me the third key, the one I know is tucked in your pocket. Now!"

He made to lunge at Bo, but Nix rushed at him, barking wildly, baring his teeth. Galvin jerked back, teetering on his tiptoes. "Argh! Control your dog!"

Selene scrambled to her feet, Bo with her. "No, *you* listen to *us*, thief," she snapped. "If you don't give Bo back the keys, then I'll turn you into a pongslug." There was so much venom in her voice Bo almost forgot she couldn't use her magic because of the cuff. "Don't test me," she warned. "Or I'll conjure a Shadow Creature to gobble you up. You know what happened in the temple, don't you? I fought one off! All by myself!" She raised her hands as if preparing to blast him with magic.

Galvin laughed at her again. "You can't stop lying, can you, girl? I see that cuff. These Korahku know a thing or two about magic. They know how to stop people like you." He shot Bo his golden smile. "Listen, if you give me the key, I'll tell you how to escape this place."

Bo huffed. "If you know how to escape, then why are you still here?"

"Because I have to wait for the right moment. If you give me the key, I'll even take you with me." He scowled at Nix. "All of you."

Nix barked.

"Exactly," said Bo. "As if we'd trust you."

Galvin threw his hands up. "Lug-headed dumdedongs! These are *Korahku,* don't you know? They'll have our limbs for drumsticks!"

"We're not leaving without Tam," added Selene.

Bo nodded.

"Nit-witted slomplugnongs!" yelled Galvin, stomping his feet. "You'll have us all killed!"

A door on the opposite side of the room opened and the black-robed guard barged in. "King Saros will see the prisoners now," he announced. More guards followed and the four of them were dragged from the room and into another grand hall.

"I'm a victim here!" cried Galvin, voice echoing in the cavernous space. "These children kidnapped me and forced me to trespass on Korahku land! You must set me free immediately!"

The hall was decorated with more gory tapestries — Korahku warriors standing triumphantly on piles of dead Irin. Bo shuddered.

Up spiraling stairs and down long, tall hallways they trudged until they were led into the biggest and grandest room of all and dumped in front of a golden straw throne high up on a dais.

"Oof!" cried Bo as he landed, but he felt worse when he looked up and saw a fearsome Korahku sitting stiffly on the throne.

He wore lush robes of purple and black and a crown of twisted golden thorns. He had a plume of red feathers, and painted copper-colored rings adorned the length of his curved, sharp beak. As Bo watched, horrified, the Korahku plucked a plump worm from a bowl at his side and dangled it over his beak before gulping the poor creature down whole.

This must be the King.

Tam's father.

The King stood and stepped down from the dais, Redfist in his hand. Bo's blood ran cold — if the King had Redfist, did that mean Tam was . . . *No*. Bo couldn't bear to even *think* the words. It *couldn't* be true.

The King peered at Bo, Selene, Nix, and Galvin as though they were yellow-bellied tree slugs. Galvin immediately flung himself to the floor and kissed the King's talons.

"I'm not with them!" he cried. "Spare me!"

"Your plan for escape is to beg?" said Bo.

"You have a better plan?" snarled Galvin. The King kicked him; he flew back and landed with a thud and a cry of pain.

"They were caught trespassing on Korahku land," announced

the black-robed guard. "By their own admission they are in league with the traitor."

"Tam's no traitor," said Bo, standing. "She's fierce and loyal and she saved me *twice*. She's my friend."

Bo was knocked face-first to the floor by a boot to his back. "Kneel before King Saros!" snapped a guard.

The King clicked his beak, running a careful eye over each of the prisoners. "I can see the boy and man are filthy Irin, but the girl? Perhaps Lahesi?"

"Nev'en," said Selene, chin raised.

The King chuckled, though there was little kindness in the sound. "Ah yes. Nev'en. Just as filthy as Irin." He held Redfist aloft. "They have a nasty habit of stealing Korahku belongings. All in the name of preserving the land's history, they say, but we know the truth. Nev'en are greedy liars."

Selene held her tongue.

"What are two Irin, a Nev'en, and their dog doing in Korak? With a traitor?" asked the King.

Bo shook his head and said nothing.

"They kidnapped me," said Galvin, "and — argh!"

The black-robed guard clipped him around the head. "No lies," he snapped.

Galvin grumbled but didn't say another word.

The King trailed his beady eyes up and down Bo with

contempt. "Let us hear what the traitor has to say, shall we?" He made a small sign with one hand, and a heavy set of doors opened at the back of the grand hall. Two guards barged in, dragging a limp body between them.

"Tam!" Bo made to run toward his friend, but a guard grabbed his collar and forced him to his knees again.

Tam was shoved to the floor at the King's feet. While Bo was overjoyed to see her still alive, a wave of nausea gripped him as he took in her appearance: battered and bruised and swollen and weak. Her own flock had broken her.

The King stared impassively at the limp form at his feet, his own daughter.

"She who was once known as Tamira Mura is a traitor," he announced to the room. There was a chorus of agreement among the guards. "And a murderer. She killed my daughter. Our future queen."

Bo shrank as the guards all raised their weapons and jeered.

"Kill the traitor!"

"Kill them all!"

"But not me!" pleaded Galvin. "It was them that set magic free! All these Shadow Creature attacks are the Irin child's fault. I've been trying to *stop* them. You must believe me!"

The King turned his gaze on Bo.

"This is *your* doing?" he asked, eyes glistening with rage.

"Though we have long prepared for the return of magic, we have lost many of our best soldiers to the growing Shadow Creature attacks."

Bo's mouth was raw and dry as the flames of his anger burned brighter than ever. "It wasn't my fault!" he shouted, shocking the room into silence. "Mads should have told me and . . . it doesn't matter because I'm trying to fix it and *you*" — he stabbed a finger at Galvin — "keep getting in my way and stealing my keys and *you*" — he stabbed a finger at the King — "should forgive your daughter because she's brave and loyal and good and she's trying to help me save the land, too."

Bo's chest heaved as though he had run for miles. Everyone in the room stared at him, this Irin child who had *dared* raise his voice in front of King Saros. Bo knew he should feel afraid, but the flames of his anger were so fierce they had filled his entire body, controlling him like a puppet, moving him, speaking for him.

"See! There's your traitor right there!" cried Galvin, pointing wildly. "But I've got charms that ward off Shadow Creatures. If you'll kindly give me back my bundle of goods, I can sell them to you for ten, eh, *eleven* Raha each."

There was a loud groan as Tam pushed herself up off the floor and swayed on her knees.

"Tam? Are you all right?" Bo struggled in the guard's grip.

"Ah well," she croaked. She met Bo's eye with wry amusement. "I have been better, Irin child. I have been better."

Bo blinked back tears as he watched his friend proudly turn and bow before King Saros.

"Father," she said, "I have a deal for you."

The King laughed bitterly. "You are in no position to bargain. In this flock, you do not even possess a name; you are not worthy of the name Tamira, so it has been stripped from you. We only know you as traitor." He spat at his daughter's feet.

Tam did not flinch. "You will free my friends in exchange for my life."

"Tam, no!" Bo made to lunge for her, but the guard's fingers dug deep into the tender flesh of his arms to hold him back. The only pain Bo felt was the aching of his heart.

The King pointed Redfist at Tam, using the blade to forcibly lift her chin to meet his eye. "I already have your life," he said. "When you murdered my child—heir to the Korahku throne and *your sister*—you gave up your life. There is nothing more than your death that I could want from you." As the King withdrew Redfist, the tip of the blade nicked the soft skin under Tam's chin. She winced but did not cry out as three drops of her blood fell to the floor: *drip, drip, drip.*

The King turned away with a grunt of displeasure and made for his throne. But Tam's next words froze him in place.

"But you do not have the Stars," said Tam. King Saros slowly turned back, eyes narrowed. "The Irin child can claim them for Korak," continued Tam. "With them, you can rule all of Ulv —that is your greatest wish, is it not? That is why you refuse to acknowledge the Queen's rule? If you set him and his companions free, he will bring them to you. You may do with me as you wish."

Bo felt as though he might throw up as he listened to Tam bargain for Bo's life in exchange for her own.

It wasn't right.

He could *not* let this happen.

"I can bring you the Stars," said Bo. The King turned his steely gaze on him. "Only *I* know where they are and how to release them. No one else." Bo willed his voice to be steady, not to betray him. "But I won't do it if you hurt Tam. You have to set us *all* free and only then will I find the Stars for you. If you don't, then bad magic will grow, the witch will return, and there'll be no stopping the Shadow Creatures."

The room grew suddenly quiet and there was a long, agonizing pause as the King appeared to consider Bo's bargain. Bo's heart fluttered like a butterfly moments before takeoff.

Then the King threw back his head and laughed. "You think the Korahku fear the rise of magic? You see what we do to magic-users." He nodded at Selene's bound hands. "We are not superstitious like Irin—we never forgot about magic, never stopped telling our children about the power of the Stars! We have been preparing for magic's return for centuries. We already have our weapons master working on powerful magical swords that can defeat Shadow Creatures, and as for Freja . . . I fear no witch. Let her come for us. We are waiting."

Tam's shoulders dropped, and with that small movement Bo's own body felt suddenly limp and lifeless.

There was no way out.

CHAPTER TWENTY-THREE

THE KING'S CRY of "Guilty!" rang in Bo's ears, blowing out the final embers of his hope.

The guards stomped their feet. "Dragon-worm, dragon-worm, dragon-worm, dragon-worm!" they chanted.

"For the crimes of trespass and treason," continued the King, "you will be taken to the home of the mighty kroklops —"

"Dragon-worm, dragon-worm, dragon-worm!"

"— where you will liquefy in the stomach acid of the ancient dragon-worm."

The guards clicked their beaks in a frenzy as the King turned away with a flick of his hand as dismissal. "It is an honorable death," he added. "More honorable than you deserve."

Galvin lunged for him, desperately clawing at the King's feet. "Forgive me! Pardon me! I was kidnapped and dragged onto your land against my will! I have charms I can sell you! I can get you the Stars! Let me serve you, my lord!" It took two guards to drag him away, his face twisted and red like a bawling child's.

The black-robed guard grabbed Bo by his arm and hauled him to his feet. "Come, child. Time to die." Bo struggled against the Korahku's grip but he was too weak. Selene grappled with two guards, trying to stomp on their feet and kick their shins. The guards only laughed at her, gripping her tightly.

"Father," called Tam. The King paused with stiff shoulders but he did not turn. He tilted his head, though. Listening. The guards listened too, frozen in place. Bo held his breath.

Tam wobbled on her knees. "I am sorry for Runa," she said. "More than you will ever know. More than I can bear. But do not punish the children for my mistakes. Set them free. It is what Runa would want."

The King lowered his head, shoulders curling forward. Bo was certain his mask of cool indifference would crumble, revealing something pained, something raw, something broken underneath. For a long moment the King said nothing; the silence in the room was suffocating. Then, at last, he raised his head and squared his shoulders.

"The only thing I am sorry for," he said, "is that I ever knew you as my child." With those words, the King of Korak walked away, leaving his last remaining daughter to die.

They were flown for miles in the claws of the scout birds — high enough for Bo to glance back and gasp at how much more land the sickness had claimed.

Finally, they were dumped in a shallow crater at the base of a snow-tipped mountain.

Lindorm.

If only we were free, thought Bo.

The scouts circled above them, their haunting cries of *caw, caw, caw* piercing the air. Bo scrambled to his feet and rushed at Tam. "You lied," he said, helping her up. "That's why the vines went for you in the Labyrinth. You lied about how safe it was for you to enter the Valley of Eyes. You knew all along they would capture and kill you."

Tam hung her head, features twisted with shame. "I hoped we would find the key and escape before they found us, but in my heart, I think I knew it was a false hope. I was protecting you by keeping my plans hidden. But to keep the truth from you leaves you vulnerable. I made a blood bind," said Tam, "to protect you, not to keep you ignorant. I am sorry I let you down."

Bo swallowed. "You've saved me more times than I can count, Tam," he said. "But you don't have to sacrifice yourself to make amends. And you *need* to trust me with the truth."

Tam frowned. "I know. I —"

"Very touching," sneered Galvin. "But I'll have the final key and be off now, thank you kindly. Before this dragon-worm shows its ugly face."

Bo glanced up at the swooping scouts. *Caw, caw, caw,* they cried. "And how are you going to manage that?" Their wing-eyes stared down at them, watching their every move.

"I have my ways," said Galvin. "Now, give the key to —"

Nix barked loudly. Bo turned, searching for what had caught the fox's attention. "Is that . . ." He stumbled back.

The scouts screeched with menace as the giant one-eyed dragon-worm slithered toward Bo and his friends from the other side of the crater.

"Kroklops," said Tam.

Bo couldn't hold back his gasp at the hideous creature.

The kroklops was taller than two huts placed one on top of the other and longer than a fallen norfir tree. Its only eye — a large yellow orb with a slit of black at the center — took up most of its head, but it was the dragon-worm's mouth that was the most terrifying sight: a gaping hole filled with razor-sharp teeth, big enough to swallow Tam whole.

Galvin dived to the ground, pressing his hands to his ears and screaming for help.

"What do we do?" Bo shouted over Galvin's screams. His heart raced — *boom, boom, boom!*

Tam grabbed hold of Selene's bound wrists and, with a slash

of her talon, sliced through the translucent cuff. "Magic," said Tam.

Selene raised her free hands and out shot red lightning strikes that zapped through the air and — *crack!* — hit the dragon-worm dead-on. The creature let out a piercing scream but did not slow down. In fact, it sped up. Selene zapped again but the kroklops continued to advance. The scouts began to swoop, screeching and aiming their razor-sharp beaks at Selene.

"The eye!" yelled Tam. "The eye is the weakest part." Though she was still shaky on her feet, Bo watched her bend her knees into that familiar battle pose.

"When I lead the kroklops away, you run. Run to the mountain. I will meet you there."

As Bo watched Tam prepare to go into battle for him again, he felt an eerie calm settle over him. Though the kroklops slithered toward them, though Selene shot thunderous bursts of multicolored magic from her hands, and though Galvin continued to wail, it felt as if everything had stilled, as if Bo had all the time in the world to make his decision.

He would *not* run away while others fought for him. Mads had never trusted him, the villagers hadn't either, not even Tam at times, but Bo knew he was brave and strong enough to help. He was determined to.

But as Bo lunged forward, a pair of hands dragged him back, tackling him to the ground. He was pinned in place by Galvin, the Irin clawing at Bo's shirt and trousers. "The key!" Galvin cried. "Where is the key?"

"I don't have it!"

"Liar!"

Nix lunged at Galvin and clamped his jaws around the Irin's ankle, tearing into the flesh. Galvin screamed in pain, thrusting his head back. "Get this beast off me!" He turned and swung his fists at Nix.

Bo tried to shove Galvin off, gripping the Irin's shirt in his hands. His fingers curled around something cold and hard in the pocket. *Two* cold and hard things. Keys!

Galvin grabbed Bo's wrist, twisting the skin raw, ripping open the scabs from the cryven attack. "Oh no, you don't, Devil-child. Those are mine."

Bo cried out in pain but he didn't let go.

They struggled, tearing into each other with fists and nails. Nix leapt on Galvin again, jaws locking around his bicep. Galvin howled, his grip on Bo's wrist slipping.

The Irin thrashed wildly, trying to dislodge Nix, but the little fox held tight. Bo pulled the keys from Galvin's pocket just before the Irin tumbled, falling backwards off Bo with a *thump*. Nix let go, barking as Galvin curled on the ground, cursing boys and foxes and keys through clenched teeth.

"Come on, Nix," said Bo. He scrambled to his feet and shoved the keys in his trouser pocket. "We don't have much time."

The kroklops was almost upon Tam, unperturbed by Selene's blasts of magic.

"Hey!" he cried, waving his arms above his head. "Hey, you! Big ugly worm! Over here! Come get me!" He waved and jumped and yelled until the dragon-worm's single eye turned on him, and the giant creature veered off its path, headed straight for Bo.

"Bo! Get back!" shouted Tam, Nix barking wildly too.

Bo ran, all the while yelling for the dragon-worm to follow. For a moment he wondered what it would be like in the kroklops's stomach. Would he be swallowed whole or would the razor-sharp teeth slice him in two on the way through?

Selene kept shooting bolts of magic at the dragon-worm, slowing it down. But she couldn't focus all her magic on it — the scouts were still swooping, attacking her with their talons and beaks. With a roar, Tam ran and jumped onto the dragon-worm's side and clawed her way up to the top.

The kroklops shrieked in pain, writhing, trying to shake Tam off, but the Korahku had dug her talons in deep.

"Over here!" yelled Bo. He stooped to pick up a rock and hurled it at the dragon-worm's giant yellow eye. "Come eat me, you big ugly worm."

The kroklops slithered toward him, moving with lightning speed.

All Bo could do was watch in horror as the beast bore down on him, fangs as big as tree trunks. He didn't have time to crouch or fling his arms over his head before the kroklops was right in front of him, knocking him back with a foul stench.

But Tam had reached the dragon-worm's head. She kicked downward, stabbing her talon deep into the beast's eye. The eye exploded and a river of yellow pus gushed everywhere, splattering Bo. The dragon-worm reared back, screaming and thrashing in agony. Tam was flung off and landed with a sickening thud.

The beast writhed and screeched before coming to a juddering halt. It made a final gurgle of pain before . . . silence.

Bo sprang to his feet, dripping in the revolting yellow gunk, and ran for Tam, reaching the Korahku just as Selene and Nix did. He dropped to his knees and shook Tam's arm.

"Tam? Wake up! Tam?"

She sat up, rubbing her head. "Is it dead?" she asked.

"Yes," said Bo, and screwed up his nose as he looked down at the yellow gunk dripping from his cloak. "Very."

An echoing *caw, caw, caw* from above alerted Bo to the swooping scouts. He ducked but Selene shot balls of ice from her hands and clipped the wings of one. *Caw!* it screeched before retreating. The five birds stopped swooping and flew above them, circling much higher than before.

"Will your flock be back?" asked Bo.

Tam nodded as both Selene and Bo helped her to her feet. "They can see through the eyes in the wings. They will already be on their way."

"Then we need to leave," said Bo.

"Wait." Selene grabbed his arm. "What happened to Galvin?"

Bo looked back to where the Irin had attacked him but no one was there. "He's run away!" He slapped his hand over his trouser pocket — the three keys were still there. He heaved a sigh of relief as he pulled them out to show the others. "We've got all three now," he said. "We need to go to Lindorm Mountain."

"Galvin is on his own, then," said Tam. "We must keep moving. My flock will return and —"

It grew Dark all at once, as though someone had hung a giant black cloak over the sky. It couldn't be Dark yet — it was still morning!

"What is it? What's happening?" Bo twisted around. He had visions of a flock of Korahku so thick they could block out the Light. Or scouts. Or cryven.

But it was none of those things.

It was Shadow Creatures.

A horde of them had gathered at the south end of the crater, like a rolling wave of writhing shadows on the ground and in the air, blocking out the Light — teeth and claws and wings and forked tails. A medley of monstrous creatures, every possible nightmare come to life.

"Is th-th-that —" stuttered Selene, pointing.

"Run!" cried Tam.

They ran.

"Head for Lindorm Mountain," shouted Bo, but he doubted they could hear him over the roar of the approaching Shadow Creatures, hooves thundering, wings flapping, claws scraping. He just had to hope his friends knew where to go.

Bo ran, a tangle of limbs and panting breath and rocketing heartbeat. He wasn't sure they could climb up the walls of the crater quickly enough. They were shallow but . . .

"What if we —" yelled Selene, but then she let out a blood-curdling scream, and there was a loud crash. Bo watched in horror as Selene disappeared, swallowed by the earth.

"Selene?" Bo ran to where she had been only moments ago. "She just . . ." There was another cracking, crashing sound and Bo felt the ground give out beneath him as suddenly he was falling, tumbling down, down, down through a hole and into the Dark below.

THE TRUE HISTORIES OF ULV, VOL. IV

THE MYSTERY OF LINDORM MOUNTAIN

⁓

Listen. You might look at that gentleman over there and say, "Gosh! Isn't he a tall fellow?" or you might wander into the forest and say, "Golly! Isn't that tree mighty tall?" but it's not until you stand at the base of Lindorm Mountain that you understand the true meaning of the word "tall." Because it is *gigantuous*.

And do you know how the mountain came to be? According to Korahku legend, it was formed when Kragona, the queen of the kroklops, curled up for a sleep and never woke up.

Inside the mountain is a labyrinth of tunnels, a remnant of when Lindorm was mined for precious minerals and jewels. And if you happen to find yourself wandering these tunnels, you may solve one of Ulv's greatest mysteries.

You see, even on a still day the winds of Lindorm Mountain can be heard howling. But is it *really* the wind or something else?

According to Korahku legend, just before she took her sleep, Queen Kragona had swallowed a wolf, trapping the poor creature in her belly forever.

Alas, none of the adventurous souls brave enough to enter the labyrinth in search of the wolf has returned to answer the mystery. Because as tall as the mountain is — monstrously, outrageously tall — it is nothing compared to how twisty and tricky those tunnels are. You see, once you have entered the belly of the mountain, the chances of finding your way out again are . . .

Zero.

CHAPTER TWENTY-FOUR

B O LANDED HEAVILY on the cold, damp earth.

It was Dark. He sprang up, wobbly on his feet because he couldn't see a thing. The Korahku had confiscated his rucksack filled with candles and matches — what would he do now? He held his hands out in front, the cold, wet air caressing his skin. He couldn't see where the others had landed — *if* they had fallen too.

"Nix!" he called, and the fox whimpered beside him, gently nuzzling his arm, assuring Bo he was okay. There was another crash and Tam groaned somewhere nearby as she landed. At least, Bo hoped it was Tam . . .

"Tam? Where are you? What happened?"

"Fell," said Tam, voice rough. Where was Selene?

"Fell *where*?" Bo looked up, but there was no Light from the surface to show from where they'd fallen. The hole had closed, trapping them inside whatever this place was. His heart thudded in his ears. There could be Shadow Creatures all around them, right this second, waiting to pounce. Now that he had thought it, Bo could *feel* the creatures creeping toward him. He trembled, heart racing.

Bo heard a strange *scritch scratch* nearing him — he held back a cry. Who was it? *What* was it?

All at once a small orb of Light bobbed in the air. Bo's breath hitched — was it Mads? But his crystal pendant wasn't burning. The orb grew bigger and bigger until the whole cave was awash with Light, and Bo finally saw that the orb was attached to Selene's hand as she approached, *scritch scratch, scritch scratch, scritch scratch* over the rocky ground.

She grinned, shoulders jiggling with giddy excitement. "I just thought how great it would be to have a Light and then — *zap!* — there it was," she said. She gazed up at the Light in awe. "I think . . . I think perhaps magic really *is* good sometimes. And maybe I don't mind having it."

"Can your magic tell us where we are?" said Bo.

"We have fallen into the tunnels below Lindorm Mountain," said Tam as she stood and looked around. They were in a large cave, water dripping down slime-covered walls, boulders scattered here and there, and pointed rock formations on the ground and on parts of the ceiling, too.

"Well, that's good," said Selene. "We're right where we needed to be. Sort of."

They each looked around the cave — those pointed rock

formations made it seem as if the cave had teeth. Like the kroklops had been turned to stone. Bo hugged his arms around himself; he was still shaking, despite his warm cloak.

"So how do we find the wolf's cage?" asked Selene. She pointed at the numerous tunnels branching off from the cave. "There's no telling where they lead. This mountain is gigantuous and these tunnels are a maze — we're more likely to wander lost for the rest of our lives than find the wolf. It would be like trying to find a lillepieni in a valvstrompstak!"

Despite Selene's magical orb, Bo felt as though the Dark was pressing in around him. Any of the surrounding shadows could be a Shadow Creature waiting to pounce — they weren't even afraid of the Light anymore! Bo looked to Tam, hoping the Korahku had the answer. But all she had was a shrug.

"The girl might be right," she said.

"The *girl?*" said Selene, rolling her eyes. "You mean the *girl* who has saved your life countless times now?" Her orb of Light was strobing brightly. "Of *course* I'm right. Who out of us four has read the most scrolls in the Great Nev'en Library?"

Tam ducked her head. "Ah well. All we can do is walk and hope to find our way to the wolf. Unless there is a map of the Lindorm Mountain tunnels in the Great Nev'en Library that you have memorized?"

Bo's thigh began to pulse with heat. *What on Ulv?*

Selene poked out her tongue. "All I know is people who

wander beneath this mountain never come out again," she said. And then she grinned. "But maybe that's because they never had a friend with magic."

Tam chuckled. "Perhaps."

Bo shoved his hand into his pocket and rubbed his fingers over the three keys. They were warm! He pulled them out; they were pulsing with heat and Light. It was just like the crystal pendant around his neck, glowing each time Mads's ghost was near. Did that mean the keys were trying to tell him something too?

"Maybe we'll hear the wolf," said Selene. The orb cast an eerie glow across her face. "Or he can hear us." She howled loudly, the sound echoing off the walls.

Bo held his breath, almost expecting to hear a return call. There was nothing but silence save for the steady *drip, drip, drip* of water and their ragged breathing.

"You are a smart girl," said Tam with a click of her beak. "Please tell me you did not think that would work."

Selene puckered her lips sourly. "Well, do *you* have a better idea?"

"I do," said Bo, holding out the three keys for the others to see. The keys were pulsing, warm and glowing in his palm. "I think it's magic," he said as Selene pressed close, almost with her nose in Bo's hand. "I think the closer we get to the cage, the warmer they glow. What do you think?"

"Well, we can't stand here forever, so I think it's as good an idea as any," said Selene. "Which tunnel, Bo?"

He stood in front of the first tunnel, but the keys did not change. He moved to the second; it had no effect on the keys either and Bo's shoulders slumped. Perhaps he had been wrong. He moved to the third, holding his breath. The keys pulsed, bright blue and hot against his palm. He was right! The keys would lead them to the wolf!

"This one! It's this one!"

"Let's go," said Selene.

"Stay close," said Tam. She placed a hand on Bo's shoulder before she made to lead them into the chosen tunnel. She took two steps before Selene cleared her throat loudly. Tam stopped, turning with a furrowed brow. At the sight of Selene's tapping foot and pursed lips, Tam tilted her head.

Selene cleared her throat again and muttered under her breath, "The *most* scrolls in the Great Nev'en Library."

Tam bowed grandly and then motioned for Selene to lead the way. "After you," she said.

With a smile, Selene marched toward the tunnel entrance. "I like you, Tam. You're a quick learner." Light bounced off the walls as she hurried ahead. "Follow me and don't get lost."

"If the Queen of Ulv doesn't make her head guard, then she's not a very smart queen," said Bo.

Tam chuckled as she let Bo walk in front, Nix keeping pace

just ahead of them both. Though the moment felt strangely light, considering all they had been through, the one thought Bo could not untangle from his mind was how Tam must be feeling after seeing her father again — the father who had sentenced her to death. He knew what it was like to be rejected by a parent. He understood the grinding, blazing, pulsing anger.

"I'm sorry your fa — ah, the King of Korak didn't forgive you," he said. "He doesn't know what he's missing. You're the best fighter I know. And the bravest. He's such a trollhead! It must make your blood boil. After we free the Stars, we can go back and you can teach him a lesson."

Bo heard Tam sigh, but the ground was too uneven to risk a glance over his shoulder while trying to keep up with Selene.

Tam didn't answer for a long time, so Bo guessed she didn't want to talk about it; he understood why — Bo didn't even know why his mother had abandoned him, and it still made him so mad he thought he would burst.

But then Tam did speak. "Forgiveness is a tricky thing," she said, and Bo jumped at the sound.

"What do you mean?" he asked.

"Well, do you think we would be here today if the Shadow Witch had been able to forgive the Moon for casting her out of the heavens?"

Bo couldn't help the stirring of anger that bubbled, sour and rotten, in his stomach when he thought of the Moon. "Sister

Vela told me that story," he said. "I thought the Moon was very mean."

"The Moon was powerful, especially when she was full. But she changed her mood as quickly as she changed her shape. So, yes, she could be mean but she could also be gracious."

Bo shook his head. "Wait. *You've* seen the Moon? I thought she vanished with the Stars centuries ago. How old *are* you?"

Tam chuckled. "Korahku do not age like Irin. I am young for Korahku but old for Irin."

"So, fifty?"

"More like seven hundred and fifty."

Bo almost fell face-first into the rocks. "Seven *hundred* and fifty?"

"But I do not look a day older than four hundred," said Tam.

"How long do Korahku live for?"

"Many centuries. They say we were born when an Ulvian prince fell in love with a shape-shifting Elfvor. He was not allowed to love her, of course — the Ancient Ulvians and the Elfvor were enemies — but she would come to his window every day in her bird form and sing to him until one day he asked her to carry him away so they could be together forever. Elfvor are immortal, so that is where we get our long life from."

Bo sucked on the inside of his cheek as he thought. "So really," he said, "you're just as young as me. In Korahku years, I mean. Can I call you 'little Korahku'?"

Tam dug her hand gently into Bo's back. "Keep walking, little Irin."

Bo watched Selene's deft footwork as she bounced lightly over the rocky ground, and he tried to match her graceful gait. He stumbled.

"But you are right: what the Moon did was cold-hearted," said Tam after they had walked in silence for a while, "and Freja could not forgive her for it. Mathias could not either. So they wanted revenge. That is why Freja went to war with the heavens, why she bewitched the wolves to try to eat the Sun, the Stars, and the Moon. And even when the Stars were gone and the Moon had vanished, Freja's angry heart fed on the Dark, and her hatred grew." Tam sighed deeply. "Should she have forgiven the Moon, do you think?"

Bo looked down at his clenched fists: What would *he* do when Mads returned for good? Bo no longer wanted everything back to the way it had been, being lied to, bullied, and taken for granted. Did Mads *deserve* to be forgiven?

And what about his mother? She had abandoned him! Just like the Moon! Bo had learned that no matter what you did, you could never force someone to want you, to love you, if they just didn't have it in them. And it hurt so much to try and try and try and always fail. But did that mean he should hate her, the way Freja hated the Moon? Could he forgive her?

Tam nodded at Bo's troubled expression. "See, little Irin?

That is what I mean: forgiveness is a tricky thing. It is a wonderful gift, to forgive or to be forgiven. But it must be earned and it cannot be forced. Very, very tricky."

Selene paused where the tunnel branched into two. She held out her orb and peered down each possible direction. Bo pulled out his keys; they glowed blue in his palm when he moved toward the tunnel on the left. "Left," he said.

Nix trotted ahead, barking over his shoulder for the others to follow.

"You heard the fox," said Bo.

"What do you think will happen if the Shadow Witch rises?" asked Selene. She was not walking quite as far ahead now. Instead, she kept her pace slow, turning to look over her shoulder every few steps. "Will she come for the Stars? Strange we haven't seen any sign of her yet."

Bo frowned. Selene was right, but maybe they just didn't know what signs to look for.

"There is no doubt she will come for the Stars," said Tam. "Her hatred consumes her; all she can think about is death and destruction. You see, forgiveness is tricky but letting go of anger, once you have allowed it into your heart, is even trickier."

Bo shivered as he turned Tam's words over in his mind. They made sense to him but . . . the anger was so strong! It wrapped him tightly like the vines in the Labyrinth of Liars and he didn't know how to break free.

The magical orb in Selene's hand sparked and hummed. "Keep up, you two," she called over her shoulder.

"Daughter of the King of Korak and here I am taking orders from a child," said Tam under her breath.

They came across several more forks in the tunnel, each time allowing the glowing keys to choose the way. They were getting hotter and hotter.

Bo was breathing heavily as they trudged uphill, a windy tunnel that felt as if it would last forever. They had walked for hours and his mouth was parched; his stomach rumbled with hunger. They had been quiet for some time — the only sounds were their footfalls and labored breathing. They soon entered a large cavern with a handful of tunnels leading off in different directions. Bo held out the keys; they pulsed brighter for the tunnel on the far right. "That way," he said, pointing. He shoved the keys back into his pocket.

"This cave is humongous," said Selene, glancing up at the high rocky walls around them. "You could swing an elkefant by the tail and still have room for a kizamutti." The cave was almost as large as the Great Hall at the Temple of the Silent Sisters. Selene threw back her head and howled at the top of her lungs: *Ah-woooo!* The echo in the cave was earsplitting — the howl bounced back and forth, and Bo wondered if it might bounce all the way to the wolf's cage and he would answer, but there was silence.

Silence.

Silence.

Silence.

And then . . .

"If that's the way you expect to find Hagen's cage, then I am surprised you have made it this far," said a voice from the shadows. It was a voice that reminded Bo of ice crystals dangling from tree branches in the White Season — the gentle *tinkle, tinkle, tinkle* as the wind fluttered through the boughs, clinking the crystals together.

Bo's head jerked up and he saw a figure emerging from the Dark surrounding them. A very tall, very familiar figure.

Mads.

CHAPTER TWENTY-FIVE

N O.

The apparition *looked* like Mads but the voice was not Mads's voice at all. Nix bared his teeth and growled, moving to stand in front of Bo.

Bo clutched at the pendant beneath his shirt; it was burning with a sudden heat. He hissed at the contact. Why did it always do that when Mads appeared? Was it really a charm like Galvin said?

"Poor child," said Mads in a voice like . . . like a *woman's* voice. "You look as though you've seen a ghost."

The apparition shimmered until it no longer looked like Mads, but instead it was a woman in a crown made of lightning, a woman with long silver hair and pale white skin and a cruel smile. Bo held back a cry of fear; the pendant seared his skin until he pulled it out, letting it hang on the outside of his cloak.

"That is because you *have* seen a ghost," said the woman, "just not the one you thought. My name is Freja. Perhaps you have heard of me?"

Bo's mouth fell open. He shook his head wildly, mumbling incoherent noises of disbelief. He didn't understand. Where was Mads? He stumbled back, barely registering Tam's hands on his shoulders. The only way Bo knew Tam was holding him was because he wasn't falling, despite how boneless he suddenly felt.

Freja glided toward them, her silver-white hair billowing like a cape of ice behind her. "How nice to run into you again," she said, raking her nails against the cave wall as she approached. "And so much better that I can visit you in my true form now."

Bo buckled at the knees, his heart in his throat. It was as though every coherent idea had been picked up by a fierce wind and all he could do was jump about, clutching at his thoughts, trying to catch one but failing.

"I don't understand," said Bo, finally finding his voice. "What happened to Mads?"

Freja tilted her head, such hateful mirth in her eyes. "I'm afraid, little one, that there never was a ghost of Mads. Your dear guardian is long dead. I simply needed a form that would catch your attention, one whose advice you would listen to. And it worked, did it not? You have the three keys? I was too weak to find them myself but now that magic has grown stronger — so much destructive energy to draw from! — I am almost complete.

I am almost strong enough to return for good. And I have you to thank for it. You're setting me free!"

The orb was shaking in Selene's hand, throwing unsteady rays of Light throughout the cave. "Is this her?" she whispered. "Is this the Shadow Witch?"

But Bo couldn't wrap his head around *anything* right now. There was only one tangible thought able to push its way to the forefront of his tangled mind. "Mads isn't coming back?" It was all a lie? *Another* lie?

Freja clicked her tongue. "That time has passed. A wish can only be used to bring back a loved one within a single rotation of the Light." For a moment Bo thought he detected genuine sympathy in her eyes. "I'm afraid you'll never see him again."

The bottom dropped out of Bo's stomach. He had been helping the Shadow Witch all this time. He had been fighting to save Mads — even after realizing how badly the old man had treated him — and it was all a lie. He had tried to make amends for his mistake and he had only made it so much worse. Was there any point in *anything* he had been through?

"I am sorry to have given you false hope," she said. "Truly I am. But there was no other way. You would not have helped me otherwise. You have all been corrupted against me. You call me the Shadow Witch. You say I only wanted to destroy the heavens to rule over this land. You say I created the Shadow Creatures. You call me evil."

She tilted her head, silver eyes running the length of Bo's body before returning to meet him square in the eye.

"But I only wanted to make my mother see me again," she said. "She had turned her back on me. You know what that's like, don't you, Bo? You *all* know what that is like."

Bo curled his hands into fists, fingernails cutting into his skin, and he shoved them deep into his pockets, one hand holding the keys, the other empty. He had been manipulated *again*. He had messed up everything *again*.

"I wanted her to see how angry I was with her, and I was so angry, Bo. So angry. Aren't you angry, Bo?"

Bo shook his head, but the fire inside him raged with such a force now that he knew — without a doubt he knew — that if he opened his mouth it would blast out of him and he would never be able to stop it. He was so angry he almost didn't notice that something soft and ticklish brushed the back of his hand in his pocket. Almost.

"I can feel your anger, Bo. We're connected, you and I. Both abandoned by our mothers, both treated differently — hated because of things we cannot control, things others have done to us. Don't you think that's unfair, Bo? Don't you want to make people pay for how they have treated you?"

Bo felt Tam's warm hands squeezing his shoulders tight enough to hurt, but it felt as if it were from a distance. Like there were miles and miles between them, and Bo was all alone, listening to this woman voice the thoughts he had tried to keep locked deep, deep in the Darkest corners of his heart.

The truth was, he *was* angry.

So very angry.

Because Mads had lied to him.

Because his mother hadn't wanted him.

Because the villagers blamed him for things that he couldn't control.

Because nobody trusted him with the truth.

He was so angry. All that anger he tried to keep hidden deep inside was bursting into flames, trying to find a way out to destroy the world, to make it pay for how it had treated him.

And he wanted to explode.

But as he uncurled his fist and rubbed the soft, ticklish thing in his pocket, he realized it was Tam's feather: the blood bind. Tam, who had wandered the land looking to ease her guilt with revenge, had instead offered friendship to an enemy, to Bo. Instead of taking lives, she chose to save them.

That thought lodged itself in his head and wouldn't budge. It soothed his burning anger, and reminded him that he had friends and he had come this far with them by his side, protecting him, supporting him, loving him.

"Do you think the people of this land will celebrate you if

you release the Stars and free them of the Dark?" said Freja, and laughed bitterly. "They will hate you just the same, Bo. They will always hate us."

Bo shook his head. "Perhaps," he said. "But *I* won't hate *them*." He closed his hand around the feather. He knew what hate looked like, how it twisted you — he had seen it in the Innkeeper, Sister Agnethe, Galvin, the green-eyed soldier, the baker's cousin, and King Saros; he had felt that bitterness and rage turned against him too often. He didn't want to be like that. It was okay to be angry but it wasn't okay to take that anger out on other people; he didn't want to fight hate with hate.

"Doesn't mean I'll forget what they did and it doesn't excuse it," he said. "It means I won't give them power over me anymore. Because that's what hate does. It gets me all tangled up with people who don't even care about me — trying to figure out why they treat me bad, what I did wrong, how I can get my revenge on them. But their hate isn't my responsibility. I'll do what I can to put things right but I won't hate them; I won't punish them like for like. I'll fight back. I'll make a difference. I might even forgive them one day, if they earn it. But I won't let hate win."

Bo wasn't sure if he believed all he was saying, but he felt certain that if he said it enough he might. Hate was a twisty, sticky, knotted thing that burrowed deep inside you — it couldn't be released all at once but if you picked at those threads, unknotted them slowly, determinedly, then Bo was certain it could be untied.

"You can earn forgiveness too, Freja," he said. "If you give up this fight, if you let me release the Stars, and if you make amends for what you did."

The witch flexed her hands, eyes growing colder and Darker as she stared at Bo. Bo didn't look away either.

"I don't need forgiveness," she sneered. "I need revenge. Give me the keys."

Nix growled at the witch as Tam edged forward.

"If it is the keys you are after," said Tam, "then we are of no use to you. We do not have them."

"Is that so?" said Freja. "Then, might I ask, who does?"

"The Irin trader," said Tam. "Galvin. He stole them and ran away."

Freja tapped her nails against her thigh. "When people lie to me, Korahku, it makes me mad. And do you know what happens when I get mad?" Her icy stare ran the length of Tam up and down, and then she smiled. "Never mind. I'm sure I can think of ways to make one of you tell me the truth."

"No! Please!" Bo grabbed Tam's arm.

"It is fine, little one," said Tam, crouching ever so slightly, ready to pounce. "I fear no witch."

"But—"

Tam cried out as she was suddenly yanked through the air, as though Freja had thrown an invisible rope around her. Tam tried to dig her talons into the rocky walls, kicking up stones as she went, but still she was flung, up and down and all around. Finally, she was dumped on her knees before Freja.

"You may think the Korahku have eyes and ears all over this land," said Freja. "You may think the Scribe and her owls are all-seeing. But my reach is farther than them all. Think carefully before you lie to me again."

"*Tsk, tsk, tsk,*" said Tam, snapping her beak. "I have given your question further consideration and my answer is: We still do not have the keys."

Tam was hoisted to her feet by the invisible rope and lifted high. She dangled in the air, toes barely touching the ground.

"If you don't have the keys," said Freja to Tam, "then what use are you to me?"

Bo's mouth opened and closed but no words came out. His bottom lip trembled. What could they do?

"I thought so," said Freja, and flung her across the cave. Bo gasped as Tam crashed hard against the rocky wall. She slid to the ground and rolled onto her side with a cry of pain. And then silence.

Bo trembled, staring at Tam's limp form. It felt as though an icy claw had clamped around his heart, the nails digging in.

"Is she . . . ?"

"Simply knocked out," said Freja. "I will have more fun with her later. But for now, I have you two children to myself."

Nix barked, baring his teeth at the witch.

"You're not the only one with magic," said Selene, eyes hard.

"I am aware," said Freja, "though I am afraid your limited, fumbling powers are no match for me, child."

Freja raised both hands above her head and a roar of black lightning shot from her fingertips; a giant Shadow Creature formed like a menacing rain cloud above her.

The creature sprouted wings — one, two, three sets — and from its neck grew nine heads, each with a single eye, a long snout, and giant fangs. Spikes jutted up and down its spine and all along the end of its tail, needle-sharp.

The creature flew in a circle above Freja, breathing noxious black fire and roaring.

"By the Light," breathed Bo. He ducked as the Shadow Creature swooped toward them, black sparks shooting from its mouth. Selene threw her hands up, and out shot a wall of ice, shielding them from the pitch-black flames. The beast's tail swung, knocking Bo and Nix to the ground.

"Leave the boy," called Freja. "Kill the rest."

As the Shadow Creature circled for a second pass, its tail crashed against the cave wall, sending rocks flying. Selene shot ice arrows at the beast's chest. The creature reared back, a blast of black flame searing the cave wall behind them. Selene threw a shield up but the creature's fire bored into it. She fell to her knees, gritting her teeth, trying to hold the shield in place. The sweat poured from her.

"I can't hold it!" cried Selene. The shield was tearing, sparks spitting at them through the cracks. When it broke, Bo gathered rocks in his arms and began pelting them at the beast. With a wave of her hand, Freja laughed; each rock Bo threw turned into a white butterfly, then burned to ash in the Shadow Creature's terrible black fire.

The beast flew high, its tail swiping the sides of the cave; rocks tumbled, raining all over them. Bo heard Tam groan as she crawled to her knees, rubbing her head. He breathed a sigh of relief — at least Tam was conscious.

And then he had an idea.

The beast began another attack before Bo could tell Selene what to do. She threw up ropes of lightning that snapped around the beast's wings and legs and held it in place. But that didn't stop the creature from breathing swirling, shadow-black fire-bombs at them — *bam, bam, bam!* Nix grabbed Bo's trouser leg between his jaws and pulled him out of the way seconds before a firebomb crashed right where he'd been standing.

"Good boy," said Bo. He turned to Selene. "The roof!" he shouted. "Aim for the roof!"

Selene let go of the lightning ropes and the creature reared back. She threw balls of Light at the roof above the creature, catching on to Bo's plan. The balls exploded, sending rocks flying down, bashing into the creature and knocking it to the ground.

"Take that!" shouted Selene. She thrust more and more fireballs at the rocks behind the Shadow Creature, sending a mini avalanche tumbling all over the beast.

But Freja cast her own fireballs toward the rocky roof above Selene. She cackled loudly, throwing back her head, content to watch Selene run for her life as half the roof caved in, driving down rocks and dust. The witch was toying with them.

The Shadow Creature hurled itself at them again, its spiky tail knocking Bo off his feet. Nix charged at the tail and sank his teeth in, locking his jaw.

"No!" screamed Bo. "Nix, let go!"

The creature roared in pain, thrashing its tail side to side, whipping Nix through the air.

Selene sent firebombs crashing into the other side of the cave. Freja was knocked over by a falling boulder, screaming out in surprise and pain. Her form shimmered.

"No!" she cried. "I'm stronger than that now! I can hold on!"

She began to fade, turning into liquid silver before being sucked up into a ball of Light that blinked once, twice, three times and then was gone.

But the Shadow Creature was still alive.

Very much alive and out for blood.

And it had Nix.

"Quickly," shouted Tam, "get out of here!"

But Bo could not run away, not when Nix was in danger. Instead, he stood his ground. "Leave him alone!" he yelled. He picked up a rock, readying to throw it.

The beast beat its giant wings and took off, its tail crashing against the cave walls as it flew, dragging Nix higher and higher until suddenly, Nix was falling.

Falling, falling, falling like the ash and dust in the air, tumbling until he landed in a crumpled heap on the cold, hard ground.

"Nix!" Bo charged toward the fox, dodging falling rocks and the beast's thrashing tail. He didn't care; he only had eyes for his best friend.

He skidded to his knees beside the fox and shook him. "Wake up," he cried. "Wake up!" Bo gripped the fox's bloodstained fur in his fist and called his friend's name over and over.

But it was too late.

The little fox was gone.

THE TRUE HISTORIES OF ULV, VOL. I

DEATH

I t is a fact of life that everything dies.

All peoples have their way of dealing with death. The Nev'en mourn with silence, the Korahku wrap their dead in yasunlehdet leaves, burn their bodies, and spread their ashes in the clouds, and the Irin bury their loved ones under blossom trees. Even animals have traditions. The svane, a large, graceful bird from Lahesi, mate for life. Should one die, the other will sit by its partner's side and never rise again.

But these traditions do little to lessen the pain of a loved one's passing. While the Seven Great Kin have many differences, when faced with death we are all the same; we hurt just the same. And if there is one thing that we all share, it's the overwhelming desire to do anything — *anything* — to bring a loved one back.

CHAPTER TWENTY-SIX

THERE WERE NO WORDS.

Time stopped.

There was nothing but pain. It consumed every inch of Bo's being, like a strangled cry that filled him from the inside out, threatening to break him apart, to shatter him like glass.

Bo threw his arms over the still-warm body of his best friend and wept as the world fell apart around him.

"We have to go!" cried Selene.

Tam gripped Bo's arm and tried to haul him up, but Bo wouldn't budge.

"I won't leave him," he said, voice muffled by sobs. "I can't." He gripped Nix's fur tightly, blood staining his hands. He knew the cave was collapsing, that Freja could return any moment and the Shadow Creature was gathering itself for another attack, but he couldn't bring himself to care. He would stay here forever if he had to; he was not leaving Nix behind.

Tam pried Bo's hands from the tufts of deep orange fur, then knelt and gently lifted Nix from the ground, cradling him in her arms. "Come," she said quickly.

Though his limbs were weak and his heart heavy, Bo stumbled after Tam in a daze, dodging rocks and the Shadow Creature's thrashing tail, smashing the walls behind them.

As they ran through the tunnel opening, Selene turned back and threw her magic at the cave roof until the whole thing collapsed, locking the Shadow Creature inside.

Bo crumpled, scuffing his knees as he fell to the ground.

He *was* cursed. He was a curse to those who loved him.

He rubbed the heel of his palm against his chest; though the crystal pendant still burned faintly, he felt nothing. He was empty inside.

"Stand up," said Tam. "We have to keep going."

"What's the point?" Bo could not bring himself to even look at the tiny bundle of bloodstained fur in Tam's arms. He choked on a sob. "I lost my best friend and Mads only used me and my mother didn't want me and I won't be able to free the wolf and convince him to give us the Stars — I just know it."

There was a pause; silence hung heavy in the air around them.

"It is for nothing if we stop now," said Tam.

"It *is* for nothing!" shouted Bo, his words echoing off the rocky walls. "It's all for nothing!"

"Nothing?" said Selene, incredulous. "It isn't nothing to *me*.

I'm glad you came on this adventure and we met. You made me feel better about discovering my magic when everyone else made me feel like a curse. You were my first friend. And we're going to find the wolf's cage and we're going to release the Stars and we're going to rid this land of Darkness and Shadow Creatures and that evil, vengeful witch." The Nev'en smiled at Bo through her tears. "Don't tell me that's nothing."

"I'll never be able to defeat Freja. She's too powerful."

"Perhaps," said Tam. "But you will not know unless you try, and there is power in trying even when you know you might fail." She cradled Nix in the crook of one arm and held out the other for Bo to take. "You do not have to face this alone. From here on out, you will never be alone."

Bo blinked at the Korahku's outstretched hand, the hand of a creature who should've been his enemy but instead had been his protector, his friend. Tam had lost everything—her sister, her father, her flock—and yet she had still been willing to risk her life for a stranger. Selene, too. She didn't have to rescue them with her magic when Ranik attacked, and she didn't have to help Bo find the Scribe and figure out the riddles on the keys. But she helped him anyway. Maybe Tam was right. Bo had lost Nix, but he wasn't alone.

Part of Bo wondered why—why would they risk so much for him? He wasn't worth it. Look at everything he'd done wrong! But another part—the voice inside that had always been shouted down by the villagers and the nasty, hateful things they convinced him to believe about himself — reminded him of all the good he had done. Hadn't he proven that it didn't matter how many times he failed? He'd always tried again until he'd succeeded. He had chased after the keys, even when it seemed all was against him. He had solved riddles and fought monstrous creatures and faced up to his fears. He had made unlikely friends and learned it was pointless trying to earn the love of people who had none to give. He had been scared but he had also been brave, and his friends had been beside him the whole way, fighting for him, believing in him. It was time he started believing in himself.

Just like Nix always had.

He would not let the little fox down now. He would find the wolf and release the Stars — he would get that wish he so desperately needed, now more than ever.

So he took the Korahku's hand and stood.

∞

They trudged for miles and miles up narrow passages, still guided by the glowing keys in his pocket and the orb of Light Selene had cast to bob along in the air in front of them. Bo stole glances at Tam and the little fox in her arms, and each time, the sight knocked the air out of his lungs.

He gripped the crystal pendant around his neck. It had long since cooled but it offered Bo a strange sort of comfort.

• 327 •

When they reached a crossway they paused: left, right, or straight ahead? Each way looked identical. Each looked Dark and forbidding.

"What do the keys say?" asked Selene.

Bo pushed his hand into his pocket before suddenly he grew rigid. "Did you hear that?" He paused, waiting to hear the sound again, but there was nothing. What *had* he heard? A voice? A groan? He held his breath: Had Freja returned? Was she chasing after them? Was it another Shadow Creature?

There!

There it was again!

A song! Someone was singing a song!

A song Bo knew . . .

Without waiting to see whether his friends would follow, Bo took the left path, clambering over rubble, pushing off from the narrow walls, the Light orb dancing through the air ahead of him. He didn't need the keys anymore.

Selene and Tam called after him, the *thump, thump, thump* of their footsteps chasing him. But he did not pause. "Hurry!" he called. His heart raced. The voice was growing louder, loud enough for Bo to fully make out the words: *"Wolf so hungry, wolf so bold, don't hurt us, do as you're told . . ."*

There was only one person — one *creature* — who would be singing that song right now, deep in the tunnels of Lindorm Mountain.

Bo's footsteps echoed off the rocky walls, mingling with the husky singsong voice drifting down the passage.

"Little Star, little Star, the hungry wolf knows where you are. He'll chase you round, up and down, he'll never stop until you're found . . ."

Selene called Bo's name but he didn't turn around. He reached another crossway and paused to listen.

"One, two, three . . ." said the voice, louder now. Much louder.

Bo turned down the left path again, running full speed.

"The hungry wolf has fed, now all the Stars are dead . . ."

Bo's footsteps pounded, his breath laboring.

"The Dark will come, you'd better run, now all the Stars are dead."

Bo gripped the wall as he came to a sudden stop. The passageway had led them to a small cave, the orb hovering near the roof, casting soft white Light across the dank space. Water dripped down the walls and in the center was a cage of golden tree roots.

But all Bo could focus on was the wolf.

He was a haggard, broken thing, all bones and patchy red fur and hollow eyes. He was trapped inside the tree roots and tethered to the ground with silvery ropes that slithered and hissed.

Bo felt Selene and Tam come to a standstill behind him.

Selene's breath hitched in her throat. "Is that —"

The wolf looked up, a sly grin revealing his fangs. "Company," he said with a voice as sharp as the rib bones jutting from his skin. "How nice. Though I am never alone. Always such noise. Can you hear them?"

Bo took a tentative step forward. He squeezed his hands into fists to stop his arms from trembling. "I heard you singing. Is that what you mean?"

The wolf tried to shift forward, but the slithery ropes pulled tight and Bo winced at the sudden stench of burning fur and flesh. That was when he noticed the crisscross of burn scars covering the wolf's pelt.

"Never alone," said the wolf. "They sing to me. Such sad songs."

The wolf hunched, his milky white eyes meeting Bo's, and he could feel the wolf's pain, as though an invisible tether linked them.

"You're the wolf who ate the Stars," said Bo. He felt Tam press a hand to his shoulder and squeeze gently.

The wolf lifted his chin, a nod. "My name is Hagen. Mathias imprisoned me. To keep Freja from the Stars. So much power. Too much. It aches. It burns." The wolf pressed his nose between two tree roots and sniffed the air. "They haunt me. I can't quiet them. They writhe and scream in my belly all day and all night and it drives me mad. Can't you hear them?"

All Bo could hear was his own labored breath and the *zizz*ing crackle of the slithering ropes.

"Won't you set me free?" said the wolf. "Have waited so long."

"If I do, will you give us the Stars? We need them; the world is dying and there's Shadow Creatures and a witch and I need a wish and —"

"I do not want them," said Hagen. "Set me free of these chains and I will give them to you. You have a deal."

Bo could have cried in relief — he had done it, found the wolf and, soon, the Stars. It would be worth it. He could fix everything and get his wish.

Bo dug his hand into his pocket and gripped the three keys — they were almost too hot to handle now and were glowing so brightly Bo could see them through the thin material. He swallowed over the lump in his throat and stepped forward.

"Careful," whispered Tam. "How do you know you can trust him?"

Bo looked into the wolf's eyes. They were the same eyes as those of Ranik, the creature who had killed Mads and tried, over and over, to kill Bo. Would this wolf be the same?

Hagen tilted his head, gently nosing the tree roots that formed a cage around him. "When you set me free, we can release the Stars together before the witch can destroy them. We will end the curse."

"I do not like this," said Tam.

Bo turned to face her; it was still a shock to see Nix cradled in her arms. It knocked the breath out of him.

"I do not like it at all," continued Tam. "There is too much risk. I promised you safety and this is not it. We must find a way to set the Stars free without releasing the wolf."

"But —"

"What if you free him and he eats us?" said Selene, narrowing her eyes at Hagen. "He looks hungry."

Bo turned to look at the miserable, bone-thin wolf in the cage. How long had he been chained here for? It wasn't even his fault he had eaten the Stars; Freja had tricked him. Bo understood perfectly how it felt to make such a terrible error and to have so many people pay for it — he understood how it felt to have made such mistakes because of lies others told you. But Ranik had said he wanted to rule over Ulv with the power the Stars would give him. Was Hagen the same? Was this a trick? Did Bo want to save Nix so badly that he was ignoring an obvious lie?

And then Bo heard a sound.

It was quiet at first, barely a whisper.

The whisper danced in the air, weaving and twisting until it had slithered deep into his ears, and then it was screaming. It was the sound of a million Stars crying out, wailing at the pain of being hidden in a wolf's belly for hundreds and hundreds of years, the pain of being unable to do the one thing they were created to do — Light the world — and it was killing them. They were dying! The Stars were dying. He could *feel* it in their voices.

Bo covered his ears, scrunching up his face; he couldn't bear to hear any more. It hurt too much. "Stop it!" he cried. "I'll do it! I'll free you! Just stop! Please!"

Tam shook Bo by his shoulders. "What is wrong? What can you hear?"

The screaming Stars grew louder and louder until Bo feared he would shatter. He doubled over in pain, begging for it to stop.

And then it did.

There was silence save for Bo's heavy panting.

He looked up and into the eyes of the wolf.

And he understood.

He knew what he had to do.

Bo took tentative steps toward the wolf, despite Tam's calls for him to come back. "I trusted another enemy once," said Bo with a glance over his shoulder at Tam. "And I don't regret it for a second."

"Ah well," said Tam, and nodded. "Ah well."

Bo trembled as he approached the wolf, who waited with his head bowed, his eyes on Bo's every step. Bo pulled the three glowing keys out of his pocket and frowned at the cage of golden tree roots.

"There!" said Selene. She nodded at the base of the cage. "A keyhole!"

Bo bent down and sure enough there was a small gold key-hole. He inserted the first key into the lock and turned it.

Bo braced himself as the entire cave shook, rocks raining down around him as the tree roots slowly untangled and rose through the air. They were absorbed into the cave roof, exposing the wolf and the web of silvery ropes covering him.

Bo sucked in a shaky breath and stepped forward.

"The chains," said Hagen.

Now that Bo was closer he could see that the silvery chains shackling the wolf were snakes. They moved constantly, coiling around Hagen, holding him down. It appeared they were magic of some kind, and Bo knew from the burn scars covering the wolf that they were too hot to touch.

"I don't know how," said Bo, frowning. The snakes had little red eyes that scrutinized him as he sucked on his bottom lip in thought. Perhaps . . .

Bo took several steps to the right and began a slow loop around the wolf. There had to be a keyhole somewhere . . .

He found it on the other side, at the base of a tethered snake tail: a little silver lock. He crouched and carefully inserted the matching key, then turned it without touching the snakes. With a click, the snakes slithered into the ground, disappearing into nothing.

Bo stood quickly and backed away.

But the wolf did not move.

"The collar," said Selene.

There was indeed a collar around the wolf's neck that Bo had not noticed, hidden as it had been by the slithering mass of snake chains. It was thick and coppery and dug painfully into the wolf's throat.

Hagen watched Bo as he took a step forward. To free the collar, Bo would have to come face-to-face with the wolf, barely a wisp of air between them. He took another step. And another. The stench of burnt skin and fur was overwhelming; Bo could not take his eyes off the wolf's yellow-stained fangs, thick and curved and sharp.

"Careful," warned Tam.

"I'm okay," whispered Bo. His heart beat hard and fast against his rib cage. *Please don't eat me, please don't eat me, please don't eat me . . .*

He reached out a trembling hand, shivering as his fingertips brushed the wolf's fur, and gripped hold of the copper collar. He inserted the final key into the lock just beneath Hagen's chin.

Bo turned the key and the collar fell away, shattering as it hit the ground, vanishing in a haze of sparks.

Bo stumbled backwards as the wolf arched his spine. A breath caught in Bo's throat as Hagen turned to look him in the eye and smile. So much like Ranik.

"Free," he said, and stepped forward. "Free at last."

CHAPTER TWENTY-SEVEN

THE WOLF CONTINUED TO CREEP FORWARD, pawing the ground before each step with a cautious *pet, pet, pet*. He kept his shoulders hunched and his ears back. Bo stumbled until he hit the cave wall, fear squeezing like a claw around his stomach. Had he done the right thing?

Hagen shook out his mangy fur, wincing. The magic ropes had vanished but he remained cowered as though still chained; those crisscross scars would never let the wolf forget. He blinked slowly, running his tongue along his lips. He eyed Tam and Selene.

"Thank you for setting me free, Irin child. Tell your friends I mean no harm."

Tam and Selene scuttled out of the way as the wolf padded past them and into the passage. "Follow me," he said, and vanished around the corner.

Bo's mouth opened and closed a few times. Finally, he said, "I guess we just . . ."

"Follow the giant magical wolf with the Stars in his belly?" said Selene with a wry quirk of her lips. "Sure. Why not?"

"Simple," said Tam, and turned to do exactly that.

The wolf zigzagged upward through the mountain maze, never faltering at junctions; it seemed he knew the way. Perhaps the Stars in his belly were whispering directions. But where they were headed, Bo did not know.

"Not far," said the wolf. Bo could tell they were nearing the outside — they were walking steeply uphill, headlong into a swirly breeze, cold enough to make Bo shiver.

Bo checked over his shoulder for Tam and Selene, the Korahku still cradling Nix.

"Hurry," said the wolf, his breath labored. "We need to be as close to the heavens as possible before —"

All at once, a distant *thump-ta-thump* drifted up the passageway from behind them.

Bo froze.

"What's that?" said Selene, fear fracturing her voice.

"Hurry," snarled Hagen, breaking into a run.

Bo chased after the wolf, adrenaline sparking like fire in his veins. The *thump-ta-thump* haunted their every step; whatever was coming was big and fast and unrelenting.

When they finally breached the surface, they were high up Lindorm Mountain, where the wind howled and the pale Light was slipping beyond the edge of the fourth quadrant—soon it would be half-Light.

Bo gasped as he craned his neck; the Dark was gathering in writhing clouds above them. He could vaguely make out teeth and claws and talons thrashing in its depths. The Light was low in the sky, nearing the horizon.

"Don't look," warned the wolf, turning to climb the snow-tipped rocks higher up the mountain.

"Where are we going?" shouted Tam, hunching her shoulders against the cold, snowflakes gathering on Nix's fur.

"To the top," said Bo. He shielded his eyes against the falling snow and climbed after the wolf.

The wind and snow lashed at them, and all the while the Dark crept closer, pressing down upon them. The falling snow was so thick Bo had trouble seeing the wolf ahead of him.

Not far from the top of the mountain, the *thump-ta-thump, thump-ta-THUMP* grew louder than the wind and snow and Dark. Through the half-Light and swirling snow, Bo turned and saw Ranik charging toward them.

The wolf came to a skidding halt, teeth bared, hackles raised. "Caught you," he rasped. It was clear he had been travelling through the Light; his fur had all but burned away.

"Keep back, Ranik," warned Tam.

"Have hurt. You before," wheezed Ranik. "No match. For me." He growled, pawing at the ground, readying himself to attack. "I will. Have truth. Now. No more lies. Where are keys? Where is brother?"

Just then, the wind changed, parting the haze of snow so that Ranik caught a glimpse of Hagen farther up the path. His eyes grew wide. "Brother?"

Hagen turned and paced back toward them. He slipped between Bo, Tam, and Selene, bowing his head at Ranik. "Brother," he said.

There was nothing but heartbreaking reverence in Ranik's expression as he padded forward and gently nuzzled Hagen's snout. He sighed, his eyes squeezed shut. "Found you," he said.

Bo swallowed thickly as he watched the two wolves standing close — close enough to breathe the same air.

"You have Stars?" said Ranik. "We can. Rule Ulv. Now?"

Hagen slowly shook his head, nuzzling his brother's snout as though he couldn't bear to stop. "They are poison," he said. "The witch lied. Tricked us. Such power cannot be contained. I am already gone — only the Stars keep me lingering, but they are dying too. We must set them free before —"

"No," snarled Ranik; his body grew tense. "If free Stars. You die."

Hagen looked away from his brother. "I will die anyway."

Bo sucked in a breath. He grabbed hold of Tam's elbow to steady himself. Hagen was dying?

"Will not. Let you. Die." Ranik's hateful stare slid across to Bo. "Will stop you."

"Not your choice," growled Hagen, and turned his back on his brother. "Do not stand in my way, little brother."

Ranik drew back on his haunches, baring his fangs. "Will not. Let you. Die!" he roared, but Hagen kept walking.

Tam passed Nix into Selene's arms, then crouched into battle position, pushing Bo away. "Follow Hagen," she said with barely a glance over her shoulder. "Both of you."

But Bo was frozen to the spot, his heart trapped in his throat.

"Do what she says," said Selene. "Don't be a dileedoor on a swollygump."

Without warning, Ranik leapt at Tam. The Korahku kicked out with her talons; she struck the soft underside of the wolf's belly, drawing blood and a howl of pain.

"You cannot," roared Ranik, "take my brother. From me. Again!"

"Come on!" shouted Selene. She turned and ran up the mountain, Nix in her arms and Hagen in front.

With one last look over his shoulder to see Ranik charging Tam again, Bo followed Selene. He kept his head down. *Tam will be safe,* he told himself. *She has to be.*

At the top of the mountain, where there was a large, flat, snow-covered expanse, Selene lay Nix on the ground and together she and Bo approached Hagen.

"I can't kill you," Bo said to the wolf. Hagen climbed onto a large, flat rock on the very highest point of the mountain, shivering against the wind. He looked so small. "If that's what you're going to ask me to do, I won't do it." Bo shook his head. Though his teeth were chattering and his whole body shook, his words were as firm as stone.

Hagen sniffed the air, closing his eyes with a look of bliss. "Have missed the air," he said.

Bo could still hear the cries and thumps and rasps of the fight between Tam and Ranik nearby, but the look on Hagen's face made everything seem so still, so quiet, so peaceful.

"I won't hurt you," said Bo, a hiccupping sob cutting through his words, undoing all his attempts to appear strong.

"You won't," said Hagen, turning his blissful smile to Bo. "It is my time."

Bo locked eyes with the wolf and couldn't help but smile too — it was a small and sad smile but it was a smile nonetheless. He did not doubt the wolf's words for a second. But it didn't make it hurt any less.

Bo hugged his arms to his chest, shivering as the Dark crept closer. "What do we do?" he said.

"You give the Stars to me and I let you live," said a tinkling voice behind them, followed by a long, low cackle that set the hairs on the back of Bo's neck to standing.

Bo and Selene whirled around to see Freja gliding through

the snow toward them, her hair whipping in the wind like writhing snakes.

Selene moved to cast a spell but Freja was too quick; with a flick of her hands she sent a magical rope flying through the air, wrapping around Selene's wrists, pinning them in place.

"The Shadow Witch," growled Hagen.

"Hagen, my old friend," cooed Freja. There were no shimmering edges or rippling silver waves, no flickering in and out of view this time.

"You lied," snarled Hagen, hunching his shoulders and baring his teeth. "You said I would have power, that my brother and I would rule over Ulv while you ruled the heavens, but this is poison you have given me. You killed me!"

Freja laughed. "For a weak creature like you, of course it is poison. Star-magic *is* poison — the world will be much better without it." She held out her hand, long metal nails pointed at them. "So give the Stars to me. They must be destroyed once and for all."

"Never."

"Then I will take them for myself." Quick as lightning, Freja threw out her hands and shot more shimmering red ropes that snapped around Bo's waist, pulling tighter and tighter and tighter and . . . Bo couldn't breathe! It was like being wrapped in flames and suffocating all at once. He fell to the ground, teeth locked together; he couldn't speak, it hurt so much. Beside him,

Selene dropped too, howling in pain as more ropes tangled around her.

"You are corrupted, Freja," growled Hagen. "The Dark rules you. If the Moon could see you —"

"If she cared, then she should not have abandoned me!"

Through the haze of pain, Bo watched Freja spark with rage, bolts of lightning and licks of flame and a rolling wave of Darkness. The whole mountain shook.

"It's her fault," cried Freja. "I would still be in the heavens if it weren't for her. She loved you all more than me — she wanted your undying love and devotion and could not bear the idea of anyone else being worshiped. And now where is she? Where is she while this pathetic land turns to ashes?"

With a roar, Freja conjured four daggers of ice that shot through the air and pinned each of Hagen's paws to the ground. The wolf howled as suddenly — *zap, zap, zap!* — there were hordes of silvery magical snakes writhing all around him, chaining him where he stood.

"No! You can't do this to me again! You can't!"

"Stop it!" cried Bo. He wriggled to standing before two bolts of Light zapped into his chest and he was flung backwards and landed with a crash on the icy ground. Selene squirmed against the ropes, trying to free her hands enough to cast her own spell. But she was trapped. They were both trapped.

All Bo could do was grit his teeth and watch as Freja conjured a knife, small and solid silver and sharp. She gripped it tightly and glided toward Hagen.

"Remember whose fault this is, wolf," she sneered. "Remember who abandoned this world because she was selfish. You can call me witch, you can spit my name, but I know this was not my doing. I will rule this world as it should be ruled while the Moon hides in shame."

Freja raised her hands, readying to slam the knife into the wolf's side. But Selene finally managed to break free of her restraints and sent a bolt of lightning into Freja. The witch hurtled through the air; the knife flung from her hand as she crashed into the snow.

With a flick of Selene's wrist, the magical ropes fell from Bo. She cut them from herself and stood; the air fizzled and crackled around her.

Bo sucked down lungfuls of air as the pain subsided, but his body still trembled with aftershocks. He wobbled to his feet as Freja stood too, baring her teeth at Selene.

"We won't let you take the Stars, Freja," said Selene. "Magic is not supposed to be used for evil. It's good — *I'm* good — and we can stop you."

Freja threw back her head and cackled wildly. "You — a *child* — think you can stop *me?* Not even my sister, Elena, could stop me. I trapped her in a statue. And my brother, Mathias. Oh, he helped me at first but then he grew a conscience, hid the wolf from me and then imprisoned himself in that godforsaken Irin forest and tried to make amends by ridding the land of magic so I could never return."

Freja beat her chest again and again. "He betrayed me! He hid the Stars from me and locked me in that crystal. But I knew I would return. I knew all I had to do was bide my time until he made a mistake. And what a mistake! Trusting a child to maintain the spell! And what justice that Ranik should be the one to kill him!"

Bo couldn't breathe—no matter how heavily his chest heaved, he just couldn't get enough air. What did she mean? She was talking about Mads but she was calling him Mathias . . . It didn't make sense! If what she was saying was true, then . . . Mads *was* Mathias.

It was like a punch to Bo's gut. He doubled over, clutching his stomach as the truth hit him again and again. Mads was Mathias. Mathias the Gift-Giver.

Mads was a fallen Star.

Freja curled her hands into fists, drawing back her shoulders. "So you cannot stop me, *child*. My magic is stronger than yours." Freja raised her hands and suddenly there were whirlwinds of Darkness spiraling from each of her fingers. She threw the whirlwinds at Selene, who sprang out of the way, twisting to dodge the deadly spirals.

"No, it *isn't!*" Selene screeched, planting her feet. "The

strongest spells call for a child to cast them — every Ulvian knows that. But you might have forgotten because you're so self-absorbed." She pushed both hands forward — as though shoving the air. Out shot vines of golden Light that whipped around Freja's hair, her arms, her legs, tying her up. "Yes!" She turned to Bo. "Did you see that?"

"Get these off Hagen," said Bo, pointing to the snakes.

Selene thrust out her hands and a wave of heat radiated from them, melting the snakes and the ice daggers in the wolf's paws, setting him free. With a whimper, Hagen collapsed; Bo ran and fell to his knees beside the wolf. "What do I do? Tell me!"

"Get the knife," said Hagen, each word punctuated by a rasping breath. "Quick."

Bo looked to where the knife lay in the snow by Freja's feet. The witch had cut the golden vines loose with icicles shot from her hands, and now she was firing them at Selene. Selene flung up a wall of shimmery, silvery Light; the icicles bounced off the shield — *clink, clink, clink.*

Above them, the Dark clouds churned as the Light slipped ever closer to the horizon. There wasn't much time.

Bo ran for the knife at Freja's feet, Selene running with him, her shield protecting them both. He dived to the ground, fingertips brushing the edge of the knife before the breath was knocked out of him and he was lifted into the air. His shirt was ripped, Mads's crystal pendant spilling out from behind the fabric, swinging like a pendulum as he was flung side to side. He looked down and saw he was dangling above the edge of the mountain, close to a cliff with an abrupt drop.

Freja was laughing, wild and unhinged. She was using so much power that her form rippled, fading in and out.

She was still weak.

What had she said about the crystal? Mads had locked her inside. That was why it burned whenever she had shown herself to Bo. Because she was *still* attached to it. The release of magic was giving her the power to return, like a ghost, but she was *still* trapped inside the crystal pendant — she had never left. She needed the power of the Stars to set her free completely before she destroyed them. So that meant . . .

"Selene! The crystal!" Bo yelled. "Blast it!"

Freja snapped her head around, eyes locking on the crystal pendant swinging from Bo's neck. She reached out as if to make a grab for it.

Bo ripped the pendant from his neck and threw it high above them just as Selene pointed her hands in the air and shot a lightning bolt into the heart of the crystal.

Boom!

A piercing scream shattered the air and Bo fell, landing heavily as sparks of Light shot every which way, like a shower of fire beetles. He shielded his eyes and ears and curled into a ball as the piercing scream grew so loud he thought he would explode.

There was a deafening blast, rocks and snow flying through the air. When it subsided, Bo's ears rang and his vision shimmered as he sat up, wondering what on Ulv had happened.

He saw Selene groggily sitting up, but no Freja.

And then he saw the crystal, lying on the ground. The earth around it was blackened and it burned hot in his hands as he picked it up. It was intact, not a scratch to be found.

"Did it work? Is she gone? Is she —" A claw slashed at Bo's arm and he screamed in pain.

Suddenly, the Shadow Creatures were everywhere, slashing with their claws and forked tails. Selene shot orbs of Light into the sky to illuminate the Darkness, but the creatures still came for them. She blasted long golden swords into the writhing mass, then sent out a series of swirling balls of ice that spat shards of knife-sharp icicles. "Yes!" she cried as several of the creatures fell back, but then she screamed as one of them took her by surprise on the left, slicing a long gash down her arm. She threw a shield up. "There are so many!" she cried. "I'm not sure I can hold them off for long."

Suddenly, Tam was beside Bo, gripping his underarms and hauling him to standing. "Ranik is unconscious," she said, her robe shredded and cuts along her face and neck. She breathed heavily. "Selene and I will fight the creatures. You release the Stars."

Bo's head pounded and every inch of his body ached, but he slid the crystal pendant over his neck and ran toward Hagen.

He didn't have time to think.

He had to set the Stars free.

He had to be brave.

He needed that wish.

The wolf was motionless on the ground — Bo only had eyes for the poor creature as he ran. Was it too late? Were the Stars dead? Had Hagen already passed away? His heart ached at such a thought.

Bo was so swept up in pain and grief and a determination to reach the wolf's side that at first he did not notice the figure standing over the wolf.

Not until he was a handful of steps away did he see the man.

Galvin.

The Irin was looming over Hagen, Freja's magical knife in his hand, his mouth twisted into a gold-toothed smile. Bo skidded to a halt, gasping in surprise.

"The Stars are mine," said the Irin, raising the knife over his head. "You're too late."

CHAPTER TWENTY-EIGHT

WITH A GLEEFUL HOWL, Galvin stabbed the knife deep into the wolf's belly.

An explosion of Light burst from the wolf, throwing Bo and Galvin to the ground. With his head ringing, Bo looked up: a torrent of sparks fired into the air as thousands upon thousands of shimmering diamonds of Light poured from the wolf and into the sky.

It was magic.

Bo had seen magic before but nothing like this.

This was *pure* magic.

This was the Stars.

"They're getting away!" cried Galvin. He clambered to his feet and jumped, grasping at air, trying to capture the Stars in his flailing arms. But they were too fast, zooming through the air and into the Darkness above; Shadow Creatures were screeching as the Star-Light burned their flesh and turned them into smoking piles of ash.

Bo scrambled upright and ran; he needed a Star, just one. Just *one*. But as he ran, Galvin kicked out with a cry of "Mine! My Stars! Hands off!" and sent Bo flying, rolling until he stilled just short of the steep drop at the edge of the mountain. He looked down, far, far below into the dizzying depths. Bo gripped his pounding heart and scuttled backwards, away from certain death.

In a frenzy of flailing arms and cries of "Mine! All mine!" Galvin threw himself after a low-flying Star without looking where it was leading him.

Bo cried, "Watch out!" as Galvin barely skidded to a halt in time. The Irin's eyes bulged as he looked down and realized he was teetering on the edge of the cliff. He swung his arms wildly and arched his back as he wobbled and swayed on the ledge. "Oh dear! Oh no! I —"

With a cry, he tumbled over.

Bo flung himself to the edge and grasped hold of Galvin's arm just in time, leaving him dangling over the side of the mountain. The Irin swung from Bo's grip, crying, "Help me, you fool! Pull me up!"

"I'm trying!" Bo said between teeth clenched in pain. The Irin was heavy! "Crawl up."

But Galvin wasn't listening. "Aha!" he said as he spied a Star caught on a small ledge partway down the cliff, well out of reach. "There you are! Thought you could get away! Think how much

I could sell a *real* Star for if I can sell a *fake* one for a thousand Raha!"

"I can't pull you up on my own," said Bo. "You have to help."

But Galvin was too obsessed with the Stars to heed Bo's warning. Instead, he began to swing himself from side to side, his tongue poked between his teeth as he wiggled his fingertips. "Can't . . . quite . . . reach. Just . . . a . . . bit . . . more."

"Stop swinging!" cried Bo, Galvin slipping farther down in his grip each time he swung. And he was dragging Bo with him. "Just crawl up before I drop you."

But Galvin swung harder. "I can reach it," he said. "I can — argh!"

He slipped from Bo's grip and fell.

And fell.

And fell.

Bo couldn't watch. He drew back from the cliff edge and buried his face in the snow and sobbed.

No one deserved such a fate, thought Bo, not even Galvin.

Bo wasn't sure how long he sat like that, breathing hard and fast, hiccupping with sobs. It was all too much. Freja, Nix, Mads, the Stars — all gone, swept up into the heavens, taking their wishes with them — and Hagen . . .

"Hagen!" cried Bo, scrambling to his feet and running headlong for the wolf in the snow. The poor creature seemed so small, crumpled on the ground, all those scars that told of his years of imprisonment. Bo fell to his knees beside him, placing a hand in the creature's still-warm fur. He was breathing—thank the Light he was still breathing! "Hagen? Can you hear me?"

At the sound of Bo's voice, the wolf lifted his head, but Bo gently placed his hand on the creature's cheek and eased him down.

"Don't move. Save your energy. We'll get you help, I promise." Bo sat back, wiping his wet cheeks with his hand. Through tear-blurry eyes he watched blood seeping into the snow from the gash in the wolf's belly.

"Not much time," wheezed the wolf, a smile playing at the edges of his lips. His chest was heaving—small, sharp breaths that did not seem to gather enough air.

"We can fix you," said Bo. He ran his hand along the wolf's mottled fur, fingertips brushing every rib, every scar. "Selene's got magic. She'll fix you."

"Can't be fixed," said the wolf. Despite his agony he smiled at Bo. "But I am free now. We are *all* free. Look up."

Confused, Bo tilted his head back and gasped when he saw the night sky.

It was so bright!

Bo didn't have words to describe it. It was like nothing he had ever seen. All those little diamonds of Light—how did they manage to make the Dark seem so . . . beautiful? Bo couldn't imagine how he could ever have been afraid of the Dark before now. Because it was still Dark. But it was Light, too — it was both in a perfect, mesmerizing harmony.

Bo stared into the heavens and could not look away, not even when his neck began to ache. Tam came and stood by him.

"We did it," said Bo, and tightened his grip on Hagen's fur. He looked down at the wolf and smiled. "We freed the Stars." He was happy they had saved Ulv but his heart ached, his throat constricted. *If only the Stars weren't so far away; if only I had been able to catch one before they found their way home . . .*

"Galvin?" asked Tam.

Bo looked up at his friend and shook his head.

"Ah well," said Tam, reaching out to squeeze Bo's shoulder. "I am sure you did your best."

Bo knew he had but it still hurt. He lowered his gaze to the wolf; his chest was barely moving now.

"Hold on," whispered Bo. "Please hold on."

But Hagen's eyes fluttered to a close. "I am free," he said with a smile. "I am free."

Bo waited but the wolf did not open his eyes again.

He was gone.

Bo stroked the wolf's fur and murmured his goodbye and thanks. He heaved a shuddering breath and sat back on his heels. Tam let him sit in silence for a long time, shuffling away to give Bo space.

Eventually, Bo felt labored breath huffing against the back of his neck. He turned and saw Ranik. Bo couldn't help the frightened gasp that shot from his mouth but he was frozen to the spot, unsure what to do. He might have scrambled to his feet and made a run for it if it weren't for the wolf's eyes.

Ranik was bruised and bloodied but there was no more rage in his eyes. All that was left was sadness.

So much sadness.

"Brother come. With me now," he said.

He nudged Bo with his snout — Bo fell to the side, skidding out of the wolf's way. He watched as Ranik gently clamped his jaws around the scruff of Hagen's neck before dragging him through the snow. He was limping and burnt from the Light and his progress was painfully slow. Bo watched the wolves depart, chest aching. He didn't think he'd ever be able to scrub the stench of death from his skin.

Tam came to stand by Bo again, reaching out a hand.

"Brave child," she said as she helped Bo to his feet. The snow glowed white around them, glistening in the Star-Light. Bo looked up and the pain in his chest eased a little.

"Aren't Stars the best?" said Selene as she joined them. She waved her hands and created a bubble of warmth around them, then tilted her head to the sky. "They wink at you, don't they? Like it's all some kind of joke and they're laughing and they want you to laugh too. I like that."

Though Bo didn't feel much like laughing he knew what she

meant. He hoped one day soon he would be able to laugh along with the Stars.

"They are truly beautiful," said Tam. "They were worth fighting for."

Bo's chest contracted at the bittersweet sadness in her voice. He understood it — she had lost so much and yet had gained so much, too. They all had. He glanced at Nix, motionless in the snow.

"Did we really defeat Freja?" Selene asked. "For good?"

Tam brushed her finger over the crystal pendant hanging around Bo's neck. A shiver rippled up and down Bo's spine at the thought of the Shadow Witch trapped in something he was wearing. That she had been there all along. "I would guess that a direct hit of Selene's pure-hearted magic to the crystal sent Freja back to her prison," said Tam. "With the Stars restoring balance to magic, it should be for good this time."

Bo nodded, his fingertips hovering over the pendant as he eyed it carefully.

"That was very smart of you to work out, Bo," Tam said, lowering her gaze until she could catch Bo's eye. "You protected the land and its people. Ulv owes you a debt."

Bo blushed.

"It owes all three of us a debt," said Selene, folding her arms across her chest and raising her chin.

"Four," said Bo instinctively. "All *four* of us." Because

there *had* been four of them. Bo, Tam, Selene, and Nix. Bo felt a fresh wave of grief overtake him, bitter and painful and never-ending. His heart grew so heavy he could barely stay upright.

But then Tam held out her hand and in her palm was a little diamond of Light.

Bo sucked in a breath. It wasn't possible. It wasn't . . . "Where did—"

"This one didn't survive. I plucked it from the air as it was falling. And I have a feeling you need this more than anyone else." Tam pressed the Star into Bo's hand.

"But don't you want it?" Bo asked. He knew that both Tam and Selene had much they could wish for. But both of them shook their heads. Selene was fervent.

"It's yours," she said.

"Thank you," murmured Bo. He could not take his eyes off the Star—it felt pleasantly warm against his skin and he couldn't shake the feeling that when he listened very, very carefully he could hear it still singing.

Selene held her palm over Bo's, her long, narrow fingers splayed. Bo felt the Star pulse as a small blue flame began to ease out of the center of it.

"I read that scroll to you, remember?" she said. "Wish-catching is a dangerous art but luckily you know someone who can extract a wish without losing any fingers because she has magic. And because she's very smart and very talented and *very* brave."

Bo watched with awe as the little blue flame was dragged all the way out; the Star shivered and died and all that was left in Bo's palm was a blackened rock. He let it fall to the ground and accepted the ball of surprisingly cool blue fire that Selene dropped into his palm. For a long moment he stared at it — a wish! — with anticipation stomping through his insides like an angry troll. He felt sick and he felt terrified but he felt so much hope.

"Close your eyes and repeat your wish three times," said Selene. "That's what the scroll said."

"Make it a good one," said Tam.

Even though Bo had spent a long time thinking about the wishes he would make — all those things he had wanted: his mother, to have Mads back, to be accepted by the villagers, for his life to go back to the way it had been before — there was only one true wish in his heart. He didn't have to think twice.

Without even taking a breath, Bo looked over at the little crumpled fox, then scrunched his eyes closed and wished three times: *Bring him back to me, bring him back to me, bring him back to me!*

He gasped when the wish grew hot in his hand, a flash of heat that wasn't painful, just unexpected. The wish fizzled and sparked and then — *zap!* — it was gone and his palm was empty.

Selene laughed. "That was incredible!" she said. "Did you

see it, Tam? All those colors and the sparks and the sound and the . . ."

But Bo wasn't listening because he was waiting, watching Nix in the snow and waiting.

Nothing happened for a long time — too long.

Why wasn't it working?

The angry troll stomped within him, beating his fists against Bo's rib cage and wrapping his tree-trunk-thick arms around Bo's heart and squeezing.

Still, nothing happened.

Bo looked down at his empty palm.

Was he too late?

Had he done it wrong?

Had he ruined his only chance?

He squeezed his eyes shut again: *Bring him back to me, bring him back to me, bring him —*

And then Bo heard a small whimper.

A familiar whimper.

Hope burst like a wildfire in his chest as he opened his eyes. He could hardly breathe! Tam stepped aside so Bo could run to Nix. He fell to his knees beside the fox, unable to believe what he was seeing.

The little fox sat up — all his injuries healed except for the scar on his snout — and licked Bo's arms as Bo flung them around his best friend and held tight.

Nix was alive!

Bo's wish had come true.

Nix was *alive!*

"You're back," said Bo. "I thought I'd lost you."

Nix barked.

"Am not," said Bo. "I'm *not* crying — I've just got snow in my eyes." Nix barked again and Bo couldn't help laughing, breathless bursts of laughter that shook his whole body and made him feel more alive than he had ever felt.

"Don't leave me again," he whispered into the fox's fur, hugging him close. "Couldn't bear to be without you."

He held the fox until Tam told them they had to go. And even then, he held him longer still.

Eventually, Bo wiped his eyes with the backs of his hands and stood. Nix stood too, not a mark on him. He shook the snow from his fur and pressed close to Bo's calves.

"Me too," said Bo. "Me too."

Selene gave Nix a scratch behind the ear, and then Tam offered a little *pat, pat, pat* to the top of his head after the fox nipped at her heel and barked.

"*Tsk, tsk, tsk,*" said Tam. "Guess I am glad to see you again too."

Bo was so happy he thought he would burst.

Selene was staring up at the sky, a wistful frown wrinkling her forehead. Bo moved to stand beside her and looked up too.

"Stars mostly fall in the Valley of One Thousand Deaths," he said, bumping her shoulder lightly. "We can go there, if you like. We can wait for a Star to fall and you can make a wish. If there was someone you wanted to find . . ."

Selene's lips pressed together in a grimace. She turned to Bo and shook her head. "He doesn't deserve to know me," she said. "And I hope you know that any parent who leaves their child in a forest to be eaten by Shadow Creatures doesn't deserve to know you either."

Bo grinned. "I think you might be right," he said. "Besides, the Valley of One Thousand Deaths sounds like a *very* dangerous place and I've had enough adventures for a lifetime."

Tam chuckled. "No more adventures? Then perhaps you will want to find a forest where you can live in a hut and ask no more questions. Does that sound good?"

Bo fought the urge to stomp on Tam's foot. "That sounds *awful.* And just for that, I plan to ask you at least ten questions a day for the rest of your thousand years. How about that?"

Tam laughed, a rich, warming sound. "We may have to find a compromise, yes?"

"You can ask *me*, Bo," said Selene with a hand over her heart. "After all, I have read *the most* scrolls in the Great Nev'en Library."

"Or you could teach me to read for myself," mumbled Bo, lowering his eyes. His cheeks flushed in embarrassment.

But Selene clapped her hands, bobbing up and down on the spot. "Oh yes! I like that idea. I'm going to be the best teacher ever and put Sister Magrid to shame. Ha!"

Bo nodded. "Then let's go," he said, his voice hoarse, but he couldn't stop smiling. He didn't even care that he had no idea where they would go from here; he had his best friend back and two new friends by his side and that was all that mattered. Things would certainly be different now that the Stars were back and the Shadow Creatures defeated. Would the Moon return too? What would life be like now that there was so much magic in the land? So many questions and for once Bo didn't mind not knowing the answers: perhaps because he knew that he had the courage, the wits, and the friends to help him discover them.

"Do you think I could find someone to teach me how to use my magic properly?" asked Selene.

Tam nodded sagely. "With magic such as yours, you will be captain of the Queen's Guard in no time."

Selene jumped up and down. "Oh, I'd like that," she said. "I'd like that very much." Nix jumped too, barking and yapping. "And you can be my second-in-command, Nix. You're very brave after all." Selene and Tam began to walk away.

"Will they have a job for me?" asked Bo, hurrying to catch up to them, Nix on his heels.

"Perhaps they will have a job for all of us. There is much to do now that the Stars have returned," said Tam. "Let us see, shall we?"

As the four of them trekked down the mountain, Bo looked over his shoulder. He could have sworn he saw a constellation in the sky, a little pattern of Stars that shone brighter than any of the others.

It was in the shape of a wolf.

THE TRUE HISTORIES OF ULV, VOL. MMCI

THE RETURN OF THE STARS

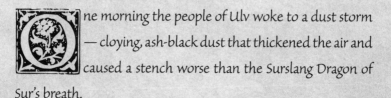

One morning the people of Ulv woke to a dust storm — cloying, ash-black dust that thickened the air and caused a stench worse than the Surslang Dragon of Sur's breath.

Not that they knew it at the time — not everyone can be all-seeing, you know — but it was the Shadow Creatures turned to ash by Star-Light and left to be tossed about by the wind.

Nevertheless, the people stayed indoors, fearful of what would happen if they breathed in the dust or let it touch them. They sat by their windows and watched it slowly float away.

And then night came. And oh my. Doors and windows were thrown open and people poured onto the streets, where they wept and danced and hugged and howled with glee because the

Stars! The Stars had returned and their Light kept the Dark at arm's length and the people felt safe again.

They celebrated all night long.

But as day came and the Stars faded from view, instead of laughter and crying and singing there were whispers: Where had the Stars come from? Where had they been all this time? Were the Shadow Creatures gone for good? How come the trees were returning to life? What had caused the flashing Lights and screams and howls on top of Lindorm Mountain two nights before?

And then came the stories, stories that traveled from village to village, never quite the same each time as they passed from one mouth to the next. *It was a troll! He kept the Stars hidden in his cave for centuries! The Stars were in the Forest of Tid all this time! No wonder we thought it was haunted! A giant ate the Stars and when he fought with a kroklops and was killed, they burst from his belly! The Korahku stole them — see? I told you they were evil! The Queen had them plucked from the night sky to top off her personal collection of wishes but they must have escaped!*

Until finally the people began to tell the story of a boy. The story of a boy who had been abandoned in a forest to die. He was an Irin child and he had three friends: a Korahku, a Nev'en, and a fox. It was the story of a boy and a mistake and three keys and a wolf and a witch and a wish.

It was a good story, best told huddled close to someone you love under the Star-Light. And it was told again and again and again until no one could be certain how true it was, but they liked to tell it nonetheless.

It gave them hope.

ACKNOWLEDGMENTS

This story has been a long, *long* time in the making. So I'm incredibly happy and relieved and proud to finally have it finished. And, of course, finishing it would not have been possible without a little help from my friends . . .

Big, big thanks to my agent, Katelyn Detweiler, and all at Jill Grinberg Literary Management, for championing this book and for not blinking an eye when this YA contemporary writer thrust an MG fantasy at you. A special thanks to Cheryl Pientka for being there at the start.

I cannot express how wonderful it has been to work with the gang at HMH Books for Young Readers. To have found a home for Bo's story with people who love it as much as I do has been truly special. Thank you to Nicole Sclama for being a brilliant editor — your enthusiasm for the story and the characters (especially the Scribe!) has made the process of publishing a book easier than it has any right to be. Thanks also to Cat Onder, Emilia Rhodes, Mary Claire Cruz, Mary Magrisso, Samantha Bertschmann, Margaret Rosewitz, and Anna Dobbin. Special thanks to Rawles Lumumba for your valued insight. And to Julia Iredale for your absolutely gorgeous cover illustration.

And of course thanks must go to the ever-lovely Michelle Madden and Lisa Reilly at Penguin Random House Australia. Thanks also to Tina Gumnior, Dot Tonkin, Marina Messiha, Amy Thomas, Deb Van Tol, Kristin Gill, and everyone else.

Thanks as always to my writers' group: Rosey Chang, Marie Davies, Cathy Hainstock, and Sarah Vincent. Your support and advice are second to none. Thanks to Eddie and Cath for the use of your beautiful home when I needed time and space to finish this thing.

An early draft of this book won mentoring time with the incomparable Kate Forsyth through the Australian Society of Authors mentorship awards. Thank you, Kate, for your astute advice and thanks also to the ASA for bringing the two of us together.

I would also like to thank the many students, teachers, and librarians I've spent time with over the last few years. It's such a privilege to spend time with young people to talk books and writing and life — thank you for welcoming me into your class-rooms and libraries. A special thank-you to the teachers and students of St. John Paul College in Coffs Harbour — this book was on submission when I was a writer-in-residence at your school, so a big thank-you for being a brilliant distraction and support while I tore my hair out with nerves.

I would be remiss if I didn't thank my local writing com-munity — the writers, the advocates, the booksellers, everyone.

Particular thanks go to Adele Walsh, Will Kostakis, Michael Earp, Writers Victoria, Melbourne City of Literature, Beck Hutcheson (your enthusiasm always makes me so happy), Jess Walton, and Nicola Santilli. And a big thank-you to Fiona Wood for introducing me to Cheryl. Thanks also to the community of readers and bloggers who champion books and reading — your enthusiasm for the characters and worlds we create keeps us going.

Last but not least, a big thank-you to my friends and family, especially to Mum, Dad, Peta Twisk, Alexis Drevikovsky, and, of course, Fenchurch.